Edited by Matthew Cash, Burdizzo Books

Published in Great Britain in 2018 by Matthew Cash, Burdizzo Books Walsall, UK

Today's Forecast

Our Tempest

Adam Millard

"The Tempest threatens before it comes; houses creak before they fall." - Seneca the Younger

It took less than an hour for the world to succumb to the Tempest; buildings, once standing tall and proud across the globe, were reduced to rubble in a matter of seconds. Monuments crumbled and fell as the winds topped out at 600mph. Entire countries shifted from left to right, or so it seemed to the people soaring through the air – the last of their breath sucked unceremoniously from their lungs by the gale – whose lives were already over. And they knew it, for how could anyone possibly survive such a thing?

There had been no warning, which is what made it worse (if that were possible). The first most people knew about it was when their feet left the ground. The governments knew – of course they did – but the average Joe, that unfortunate bastard on the street, well, he never stood a chance. And neither did his family

"There's an anomaly, Mr President." Those words had been uttered in the Oval Office almost an entire year before the Tempest struck.

Average Joe wasn't there to hear them, and Mr President simply didn't want to worry the poor fella, for what good would it do to tell him that something was coming for him, for his family, hurtling through space like a cosmic spinning-top?

No, no, no, there was no point telling the public to get to their bunkers on January 27th, 2029, "'Cos the day after that is gonna be a helluva windy one!" Most of them didn't have a bunker to get to.

Of course, other nations were aware of the approaching anomaly, now commonly referred to between world leaders as Caliban, but they too chose to remain silent. Several high-ranking officials – whose mouths were a little too loose for their superiors' liking—were executed by a specialist task force known as The Sycorax Project.

More and more of these loose-lipped officials washed up on riverbanks, and no one thought to question why.

Even when the British PM—an otherwise healthy middle-aged woman—was found dead upon the black-and-white chequerboard floor of 10 Downing Street's reception hall, no one took a step back and said, "Hmmm... how could a woman of so few years suffer a massive stroke without warning?"

Months flew by, and Average Joes across the world continued with their lives, oblivious. They took out loans, not knowing they would never have to pay them back; they took family holidays, soaking themselves in the sun and reading shitty paperback novels—not something they would have been doing if they had known Caliban was a-coming.

Those same people, just a few short months later, would be tossed around the streets like ragdolls, skewered on sharp metallic objects like kebabs, blown miles away from their families—the same families they had applied sun-cream to as little as one day prior.

Meanwhile, in mile-deep bunkers, those in the know sat drinking brandy, watching it all unfold on black-and-white screens, safe and warm with their families by their sides.

"It's awful!" said the US President's daughter. "All those people. Wiped out in a flash."

"At least it wasn't us," said one of the US President's more exasperating advisers. "Down here we're safe. We can exist here in perpetuity, if we must. We have the means to go on, the food to survive, the amenities to grow more food."

And wasn't that the truth? World leaders deserved to continue with their lives, for they were far more important than Average Joes.

Except, up there where the Tempest still blew three years later—albeit not as violently as it once did—Average Joes were coming out of the woodwork, dusting themselves off, and rebuilding.

This is the story of one such family...

Lukas returned to the cavern covered in dust and with a backpack filled with tinned food. Peach slices. Marrowfat beans. Chicken soup. Stewed steak. It was enough to keep them going for a few days, which meant it would be a few days before he'd have to venture out… *there* again.

As he descended deeper into the chasm the Wilsons had called home for the past three years, he imagined Lydia's face when she saw the haul, the way it would light up as if it were Christmas morning. It was only peaches and chicken soup, but even his eight-year-old daughter knew how fortunate they were to have such luxuries.

Up there, Lukas had seen just one other soul, an elderly blind lady whose twisted legs and awkward gait suggested she had suffered greatly in the Tempest. And yet there she had been, pushing a battered shopping trolley over rubble, filling it with whatever she could lay her hands on, no matter how unusable or weather-beaten it was.

That's what we're doing down here, Lukas thought as he reached the midway point between earth and home. *Just like the old lady with the cataract eyes and the rickety cart, we're doing whatever it takes to make it through another day.*

Over the past three years, Lukas had ventured out in search of provisions. At first, he'd worn so many clothes, so many protective coverings wrapped around his face, that he had barely been able to move or breathe. For months he had gone out like that, armed with only a golf club, which he'd discovered behind a shipping container the first time he'd left the cavern in search of food. Back then, he had quickly become accustomed to the myriad moans and groans emanating from beneath the rubble of felled buildings. The Tempest was strangely silent after its initial attack. It was, Lukas had thought at the time, like being a deaf man in a tornado.

And so those screams and cries and plaintive wails from below were not only audible but inexplicably amplified.

Lukas had wanted to help, to stop and begin shifting rocks and rubble so that he might dig someone—*anyone*—out from beneath, but the Tempest was so strong, it was all he could do to remain on his own two feet.

And besides, Amy—his wife of ten years—had told him that under no circumstances was he to go looking for trouble. *Just find us something to eat, and come home.* Which is what he had done, for it was one thing to go looking for trouble beneath the crumbled buildings up there, but it was quite another to incur the wrath of his childhood sweetheart.

Not much further to go now.

Lukas couldn't wait to tell his family the good news; that, while it was still awful up there, the Tempest grew weaker with every passing month

Soon, perhaps three months or so, he would be able to take his family out of the cavern, and they would rebuild, find somewhere topside to call home.

That was something to look forward to, at least, although he wondered what his wife and daughter would say when they emerged for the first time to see the chaos and debris of their former world. It worried him a little, but he would cross that bridge when they came to it.

"Honey, I'm home!" he called out comically into their main living quarters (a fifteen-foot square grotto interlinked with tinier caverns by small, damp tunnels) and awaited the shrill scream of happiness from Lydia as she rushed through the tunnels to get to him. When it came, his heart skipped a beat, for he hated being away for any longer than two days. This scavenging expedition had lasted four.

"Daddy! Daddy!" Lydia said as she came hurtling toward him across the cave, her long hair matted and dirty and trailing behind her like thin smoke. She threw her arms around him as he shrugged the backpack from his shoulders and leaned it against the cavern wall. "Oh, I missed you! I dreamed of you last night."

"Was it a nice dream?"

She shook her head, seemed reluctant to let go of his waist. "It was an awful dream, Daddy. You were eaten by marauders, just like Mommy talks about, and when they were done with you, you came back as a zombie."

Lukas sighed. He would have to have a little talk with Mommy later. "Well, I'm pleased to report that not only was I NOT cannibalised by marauders, I have also managed to avoid becoming a member of the living dead."

"Thank goodness!" Lydia said. "Because I would hate to have to put a bullet in your head."

Lukas was about to retort when, from out of the shadows, his wife appeared. Her eyes were glazed over with pure happiness, perhaps relief, and she paced across to be with her still-embracing family. She threw her arms around Lukas' neck and kissed him passionately.

"Do you have any idea how worried we were about you?" Amy asked when she pulled away a moment later. "You've been gone for four days, Lukas."

"Which is apparently about the same amount of time it takes for marauders to consume an entire human male," he said.

Amy looked sheepishly down at their daughter. "I told you not to mention it."

"I'm eight," Lydia said. "You should know by now that I can't hold my own water."

Lukas pulled them both into another tight embrace. "Oh, man, do I have some great news for you guys, but first I want to show you what I managed to find." He released them, snatched up his backpack and walked across to the huge semi-flat rock at the centre of the cavern, which they were utilising as a table. Amy and Lydia followed excitedly—Lydia more so than Amy. "Do you know that old store at the foot of the canyon? Used to be owned by the fat guy with the black gums?"

"I don't know *who* that is," Lydia said, grimacing, "but he sounds *charming*."

Amy ran a hand over Lydia's shoulder: *Let your Daddy finish what he's got to say, Honey-bunch.* Unzipping the backpack, Lukas smiled as he took out the first of the dented tins and placed it down on the rock. Even though its label was half-peeled off, Lydia rejoiced immediately.

"You found some!" she said, picking the custard up as if it were the holy grail. "Oh, Daddy, I love you! I mean, I loved you before, but this is, like, a whole *new* level of love."

"And," Lukas said, not quite finished, "I managed to find three cans of tinned peaches to go with it. They were just lying there in the middle of the store; I guess it takes more than an apocalypse to get some people to eat tinned peaches, huh?"

"You did well?" Amy asked, motioning to the backpack.

"*We* did well," Lukas corrected her. "I won't have to go up there for a while—"

"Did you see anyone?" The question always came from Lydia—never Amy—and she always looked hopeful, as if Lukas might reply with, *Yeah, the cast of Glee are all alive and well and selling bric-a-brac at the end of our old street!* He knew his daughter just wanted confirmation that things weren't always going to be like this, that there would be some sort of life beyond the cave system.

"I saw an old lady with a shopping cart," Lukas said, trying to keep his tone light (he wouldn't tell their daughter that the old lady was riddled with rickets, for fear it might take the shine off an otherwise reasonable tale). "I didn't have the heart to tell her that the nearest 7/11 blew out of business years ago."

As a joke, it was awful, but Lydia laughed, and that was enough for Lukas.

"Anything in that backpack other than dessert?" Amy said.

"You," Lukas told her as he reached for the backpack, "are going to love this."

The Wilsons sat upon their knees around the giant rock, a veritable feast set out in front of them. Over the past three years, Amy had perfected her campfire cookery, and they had all grown used to eating hodgepodge meals, but tonight they would dine in style.

"So, what's the great news?"

Lukas pushed a plastic forkful of stew into his mouth and swallowed it almost instantly; scavenging always made him hungry. It was quite easy to forget there were two young ladies waiting for him back in the cave when he was out there in the Tempest. Sometimes—although it always made him feel guilty as sin—he would find something edible and eat it instantly. It was silly really, for he knew he had to keep his own energy levels up (just to fight through the silent but deadly gale-force winds), but knowing his wife and daughter were equally as hungry, and reliant on him to bring home the bacon, or *anything* for that matter, it always left him with an overwhelming sense of remorse.

He put his plastic fork down on the rock and smiled. "How would you feel if I told you things are getting calmer up there?" He motioned to the dark, dripping cavern roof. "I mean, it's not like it *used* to be. Hell, I don't know if it ever *will* be. But it's nowhere near as bad as it was when that thing hit us."

"How bad is it?"

Lukas was not surprised by the apprehension on his wife's countenance.

It had taken them a long time to get this far, to make a life worth living; and it would take a massive decision for them to leave the cave now.

Lukas nodded slowly. "Remember that time we went to Scotland? You wanted to see Arthur's Seat in Edinburgh?"

Amy smiled. "I remember. You were pissy because I told you we couldn't go search for Nessie."

"Hey! She's there! Or, at least, she *was* back then." Lukas ate another forkful of stew before continuing. "Well, remember how windy it was when we set out that morning?"

"It was one of the worst winds I've ever seen," Amy said, lowering her own plastic fork. "Is it like that up there? Like Scotland?" She looked, Lukas thought, optimistic, which was a start.

"I mean, it's still a little bit worse than that, but I'm thinking if it keeps slowing down—and it has, even in the past few months—we might be able to get out of here."

Lydia, across from Lukas, became wide-eyed. "Really, Daddy? *All* of us?" she said, excitedly. Amy reached across and placed a hand on their daughter's arm. All at once, Lydia's joyful expression faltered.

"Don't get your hopes up, Lyd," Amy said. "It still sounds pretty bad up there."

"I think she *should* get her hopes up," Lukas interjected, for was this not what they had been waiting for all these years? A chance to return to the real world, a world they could make some sort of life in, instead of hiding out in the dark like some grotto-dwelling troll family?

Amy straightened up; Lukas could sense his wife's annoyance before she even spoke. "I just think," she said, "we ought to take our time with this, yeah? You said it yourself, it could be months before we get out of this hole in the ground. Years, even."

"But Daddy said it's not much windier than Scotland," Lydia said, a hunk of gravy-carrot slipping down her chin and plonking back into her bowl.

To Lydia, Amy said, "It's not just the wind, honey. There could be other things up there we don't want to face."

"Like zombies?" Lydia winked in Lukas' direction, and he couldn't help but smile back.

"Like people," Amy said, always the stoic one. "People who want what we have. People who will do anything they can to get it."

"Marauders," Lydia said, nodding slowly. "But Daddy can take care of them. He has a golf club—"

"And they have knives," Amy said. "And guns. And unless your father suddenly knows how to stop bullets, I think we're safer down here for the time being."

Well, that didn't take long, Lukas thought bitterly. *For four days I have fantasised about this moment, only for Amy to pull the cloud from underneath me in less than three forkfuls of stew.*

"We can't stay down here *forever,*" Lukas said. "We were fortunate to be down here when that godforsaken thing hit us," Lukas remembered it like it was yesterday.

The sudden roar of something overhead.

Dust and rocks falling from the heavens. At the time, he'd thought it was a landslide, and that they were about to be sealed into this series of cave systems for all eternity. But landslides do not persist for hours, days, months.

Lukas had managed to get his family to the cave exit, which fortunately was shielded on three sides from the torrent and with only a tiny aperture through which to crawl. He didn't have to stick his head outside to know that the world had gone to Hell in a handbasket.

"I'm not saying we're going to be down here forever," Amy said, in that casually dismissive tone she reserved for arguments such as these. "I just think we should think about things. Think about Lydia. It's going to be a mess up there when we get out—"

"Do you remember what my old bedroom looked like?" Lydia said through a devilish smile.

"And what about marauders, Lydia?" Amy said. "Did you have any of those in your bedroom? Waiting to rob you of your worldly possessions?"

"Come one, Amy," Lukas said. "You're not being fair. I haven't seen a marauder in days. Didn't you hear? Today there was just that solitary old blind woman—"

"And that was your downfall," said a new voice.

Lukas leapt to his feet, turned to face the entrance to the cavern. They *all* did.

Standing there, flanked by two of the biggest men Lukas had seen outside of professional wrestling, was the little old blind lady.

"Anything worth taking, boys?" she asked of the beast-men standing to her left and right.

One of them glanced toward Lydia, and then to Amy, his grin growing wider by the second.

"Oh, yeah," he said, drooling thick black chewing-tobacco onto the cavern floor. "There's *plenty* worth taking here."

Amy's scream set Lukas into motion; he rushed across the chamber at exactly the same time the two hefty men started toward his wife and daughter. The old blind lady remained in place, a creepy—almost beatific—smile upon her wrinkled face.

"Stay away from us!" Lukas heard Amy scream as he snatched up his golf club from the edge of the chamber. He turned to discover that one of the marauders—a huge bastard with almost no teeth left in his skull—bearing down on him.

I'm their main threat, Lukas thought. *Take me out of the game, and the rest is easy…*

Lukas would not allow *that* to happen. He swung the golf club through the air—whoosh—and connected sweetly with Toothless's jaw. Toothless grunted and spun, slammed into the chamber wall so hard that dust rained down from the cavern roof.

From the semi-darkness (the only light in the chamber came from a single candle on the rock table) Lydia screamed, "Put me down! Put me down!"

Heart in mouth, Lukas raced toward the light source.

And that was when he saw that the other marauder—Baldie—had snatched his daughter and was carrying her, kicking and screaming, across the chamber. Amy was unconscious on the cavern floor; the fucker must have hit her while Lukas took care of Toothless.

And still the rickety old hag smiled.

Lukas, running on pure adrenaline, barrelled toward Baldie, golf club poised, ready to strike.

"I wouldn't do that if I were you."

It was the old lady, raising her voice for the first time since her arrival in the chamber the Wilsons called home. Lukas almost didn't hear her; the racing hush-thump of blood in his ears was almost deafening.

But he *had* heard. And he *had* seen the large knife in Baldie's hand. And his heart *had* skipped a beat when Baldie turned and pressed it to his daughter's throat.

"Unless you want to see her blood splattered across these walls like a cave-painting," Baldie said, "I'd take a long, hard think about whether it's worth it." He nodded at the golf club Lukas wielded like a baseball bat.

"You don't have to do this!" Lukas said, his gaze switching from Baldie to the old lady, then back again. "Please, let my daughter go!" He hated the sound of his voice; that he should be pleading with these *demons* enraged him.

"Do you have any idea how much we could get for her up there?"

The old lady was calm, still smiling; Lukas didn't care if she was blind or not, he wanted to smash the grin right off her face.

"We gotta eat, you see, and your daughter would go a long way to making sure me and my boys are still around come Christmas."

It was so strange hearing that word. Christmas. Lukas didn't even know what season it was; surely Christmas was a thing of the past.

"Please. You can take *our* food." Lukas motioned to the open backpack sitting unzipped a few metres away on the chamber floor.

"Oh, we wouldn't want to do that, would we, Kyle?" the old lady said. "I'd hate to think you starved down here, alone. That wouldn't be very Christian of us, now, would it?"

She's a fucking lunatic! A raving madwoman!

"No, we'll just take your daughter," said the old lady.

"And that bitch," Kyle said, nodding in the direction of Amy, who was coming to beside the rock table.

"And we'll be on our way," finished the old lady. "Kyle, where's your brother? Tell him to grab the other one so we can get out of this goddamn hole."

Kyle squinted through the darkness, called out his brother's name. "Eli! Quit fucking around and get in here and pick this bitch up!"

Lukas took a deep breath. Eli wouldn't be picking anyone up, not in his current state. Lukas wasn't certain, but he thought he saw grey matter splatter the cavern wall when he hit Toothless. If that was the case, Eli—Toothless—was out of action.

Perhaps sensing that (call it a mother's intuition) the old lady sighed. "Kyle, I believe this man killed your brother. Killed *my* son. Are you going to let him get away with that?" There was something about the way she said it—with complete indifference, which led Lukas to believe she *wasn't* Eli's real mother.

But he was most definitely Kyle's real brother; Lukas saw it in Kyle's eyes as he drooled black chewing-tobacco juice all down Lydia's trembling back. To Lukas's right, Amy was trying to get to her knees, groggily moaning, seemingly unaware of the predicament they were all in.

"I'm gonna kill you!" Kyle roared. "I'm gonna fuck—"

But that was as far as he got, for Lydia—out of nowhere—twisted in his arms and Lukas didn't see what she did next, but Kyle howled like a wolf in a bear-trap and staggered back one step, two steps, three steps, four, until he slammed against the chamber wall.

Lukas rushed forward; this was his opportunity, and perhaps the only one he would be afforded. And when he reached Kyle, he saw, through the darkness, his daughter had clamped down hard on the sonofabitch's nose. Kyle was slashing and digging at Lydia's back with the huge knife, but Lydia still refused to let go.

"Lydia!" Lukas screamed, and she finally pulled her face from Kyle's to reveal a nose hanging on by a thread. Kyle's face was black with geysering blood and tobacco-juice. And Lukas didn't waste any time in fucking that face up even more. He brought the golf club down hard on the top of Kyle's head. There was an almighty *crack*—and Kyle's right eye popped right out of its socket—and both Kyle and Lydia were then heading toward the chamber floor.

Sideways they went, Lukas reaching for his daughter, whose back was ribboned with slashes from Kyle's knife. He managed to grab her arm and yank her away from the felled giant, just before he hit the deck.

That was when Lukas knew his daughter was crying. Sobbing uncontrollably. Red-hot tears streaming down her face, intermingling with the warm blood coating her lips and cheeks.

"Kyle!" the blind old lady screamed. "Kyle, speak to me!"

Lukas placed Lydia down and urged her to run to her mother, who was now on her feet, trying to comprehend all that had happened in the last five minutes. She looked toward Lukas, and Lukas pressed a finger to his lips: don't say a word. Amy nodded and crouched, scooping Lydia into a tight embrace.

Lukas turned his attention back to Kyle, who was not dead - not yet, anyway. He was grunting incoherently, trying to drag his bulk across the chamber floor toward the blind old lady, whose head turned this way and that as she tried to figure out what was going on.

"Kyle!" she screeched.

Kyle might have been about to reply when Lukas brought the club down hard on the back of his head. This time there was no *crack*; just a meaty *thud*, like steak being slammed onto a butcher's counter.

Another hit.

And a third.

After that, the only movement from Kyle was an involuntary twitch of the legs. Lukas was pretty sure the sonofabitch wasn't getting back up, was already on his way to whatever Hell awaited him in the afterlife.

Lukas took a deep breath and straightened up, the head of his driver dripping blood and bone and flesh all over the chamber floor. Under other circumstances, it would have sickened Lukas.

Through the gloom, Amy and Lydia were silently watching him, waiting to see what he would do next. He nodded once at Amy, and Amy turned Lydia around and pulled her tight to her chest. This wasn't for the eyes of little girls. Not even ones strong enough to bite a man's nose clean off.

Once he was satisfied his daughter would not see what came next, Lukas stealthily walked across the chamber, watching as the blind old lady's frantic search for answers reached its crescendo.

"Kyle! Kyle! If you've done anything to him, I swear to fuck..."

Lukas brought the golf club down—whoosh—one final time, splitting the old lady's head in half as if she were a desiccated old mummy.

She didn't require a second hit.

Outside, the Tempest continued to weaken. Silently it blustered; at night it grew strong again, as if it felt more comfortable causing destruction in the darkness. More and more people began creeping across the earth again. They came from everywhere, slowly at first. Men. Women. Children. Emaciated. Filthy. All of them exhausted. Confused.

All terrified of what awaited them.

Months later, a family would emerge from the series of caves and chambers and crevasses in which they had resided for almost four years, united and ready to face the world once again. They would prepare, they would hunt, they would kill, for they would have no choice.

They would survive.

They would fight.

They would go on.

Together.

Raindrops

Paul Hiscock

Is he awake?
Drip!

Neil woke with a jolt as a cold drop of water landed in the middle of his forehead. Automatically, he reached up and wiped it away.

As he slowly regained consciousness, he wondered where it had come from. His bleary eyes couldn't see anything out of place. The ceiling was the same dirty white as usual. The cobweb in the corner that he kept meaning to swipe away with a duster was still there, albeit slightly bigger than when he had last looked. Nothing seemed out of place.

Wondering if the water had come from outside, he rolled out of bed. Still woozy from having only just woken up, he staggered drunkenly across the room. Once he had made it to the window, he drew aside the heavy curtains. A sudden onrush of light assaulted his senses and he had to screw his eyes shut for a moment.

Slowly, he opened them again, blinking to help himself adjust. It was a beautiful sunny day, and for a moment, he couldn't remember why it had been so urgent to look outside. Then he remembered the drop of water. However, there wasn't a cloud in the sky and no sign that it had even rained in the night.

Neil shrugged. It must just have been the last fragment of a dream.

When will he be ready?
Drip!

It happened again as Neil was getting ready for work. He was standing at the breakfast bar, mindlessly eating his bowl of cornflakes while browsing through the news headlines on his phone when, once more, a single drop of water landed in the middle of his forehead.

Surely, it *couldn't* be a dream this time. He pressed the tip of his forefinger to his head and was relieved to find that it felt wet. The water wasn't a hallucination.

Just as before, he looked at the ceiling for some sort of explanation, but there was nothing obvious to see. Looking at the kitchen clock, he saw that he was in danger of missing his bus if he didn't leave soon.

He could just ignore the water. It was only two tiny drips after all. If they had fallen anywhere else, he probably wouldn't have even noticed them. However, what if there was a problem with the water tank or the pipes in the loft space above him? He could find his home flooded by the time he returned from work.

Reluctantly he opened the browser on his phone and started searching for emergency plumbers.

It's been a couple of hours.

Drip!

"Are you going to be up there much longer?" Neil called up the ladder to the plumber. "I've already had to take the morning off work. I really can't miss the afternoon as well."

He wiped away the latest drop of water in irritation and listened for a reply.

The banging on the pipes that had been going on for the last quarter of an hour stopped and there was a *thump* that sounded suspiciously like a box being knocked over. Neil hoped that it didn't contain anything breakable.

A few moments later, a pair of feet appeared at the top of the ladder and the plumber started to climb down. His trousers slipped as he descended, and Neil turned away to avoid having to stare directly at the man's exposed bum crack. When he reached the bottom, the plumber hiked up his trousers and turned to face Neil.

"Well, Mr Williams, you've got an old water tank up there. Not surprised it's causing you problems."

Neil sighed. "So, you've found the leak then?"

The plumber scratched behind his ear. "Not exactly. I mean, I could keep looking, but these things are tricky and once you get one leak..." He trailed off, leaving Neil to imagine the worst for himself.

"What am I meant to do then?"

"I'd recommend replacing the whole lot."

Neil groaned. "How much is that going to cost?"

"I'm not going to lie. It ain't going to be cheap. But then peace of mind never is. Of course, if you're willing to pay cash I can probably knock a little off for you."

Neil looked at his watch and considered what he should do. The amount of work being suggested was probably totally unnecessary. After all, this guy hadn't found anything. He could call another plumber to get a second opinion, but what would they say? Pretty much the same, he imagined. They weren't going to pass up the chance to make a quick buck. Meanwhile, Neil would just be wasting more of his valuable time. Easier to just agree to let this bloke handle it.

"Fine. How much are we looking at?"

The plumber smiled and, having retrieved a notebook from his pocket, started adding up a series of alarmingly large numbers.

We must be patient.
Drip!

In the end, it had taken another half an hour to get everything sorted out and Neil grew increasingly impatient.

Finally, he had almost pushed the plumber out of the house, all the while trying to extract some sort of assurance that the work would start first thing in the morning, not sometime before lunch.

It was just as Neil was locking the door that another drop landed on him. He looked up in surprise. That couldn't have been a leak now he was outside.

"You've got to be kidding me," he shouted at the sky.

The plumber, who was on his phone ostensibly ordering parts, looked over at him. "Sorry, were you talking to me?"

"No, no. Don't worry about it. Just one of those days. I guess I'd better go back for my umbrella."

"If you say so, mate," the plumber said, looking up in bewilderment at the wispy, white clouds in the sky.

By the time he looked back down, Neil was already inside the house, emerging a few seconds later with a large red and white golf umbrella. The plumber shook his head in bemusement, but he didn't really care about his client's eccentricities if he got paid.

He will give in soon.

Drip!

Despite the size of his umbrella, a raindrop still managed to land on Neil. No matter what he did, they just kept coming - homing in on his forehead like heat-seeking missiles designed to suck all the warmth out of him.

He pulled his unwieldy and seemingly ineffective protection lower. His arms ached from holding it above his head and he wondered if he should just put it down. He hadn't failed to notice the strange looks that he was getting from the people he passed in the street. When he had set off, he had been convinced that a storm was just about to break. But now he wasn't so sure.

"Mummy, why can't I have an umbrella?"

A little girl, around four or five-years-old, had stopped in the street and was pointing at him.

"You don't need an umbrella," her mother said looking down in exasperation. "We only take umbrellas out when it's raining."

She pulled at the girl's hand, but the stubborn child did not budge.

"But I want one. I *want* one," cried the girl.

Now the mother was staring at Neil too, angry at him for having triggered this meltdown. No doubt it was not the first or last that she would have to put up with today.

"Come on, Evelyn," she said. "We need to get back to the car. Mummy will be cross if we get another parking ticket."

"It's not fair!" The cry had escalated to a full-on wail and Neil considered joining in. It felt like it would be an appropriate reaction to the way his day was going. Instead, he just hurried past them, eager to be away from the tears and the mother's accusatory gaze.

It won't be much longer.
Drip!

"I'll be there soon. I promise."

Neil swiped away the latest drop of water. There was a bunch of teenagers on the bus messing about. Had one of them flicked something at him? Spat at him? He considered shouting at them, but you could never be too careful these days. Knowing his luck, they'd be members of some gang and all carrying knives.

He turned his attention back to his phone call. He'd missed what his boss had just said, but doubted it was that important. It had almost certainly been some pointless management jargon – Mr Harris specialised in such drivel. Just another of the trivial annoyances designed to wear down the workforce.

As his boss droned on, Neil rubbed at his forehead. There was a dull ache right in the middle that seemed to be getting worse. Would he have time to pick up some Ibuprofen before he reached the office? Trying to deliver his presentation with a full-blown migraine would be the last straw today.

He suddenly realised that Mr Harris was saying something significant at last.

"No, you don't have to get Naomi to deliver the presentation. I promise I'll be there in time."

Neil hoped he sounded more optimistic than he felt, given that the bus had slowed to a halt in the busy traffic and was showing no signs of moving any time soon.

However, there was no way he was going to let that bitch, Naomi, swoop in and steal the credit for all his work at the last minute. This project was the ticket to finally getting that promotion he'd been after for years and nobody was going to steal it from him.

"Yes, I'll see you shortly. No need to worry."

With those last hollow words of reassurance Neil ended the call just as the bus lurched into motion again. The sudden jolt jarred his back. Damn, he was aching all over like some old man. There was no choice. He'd have to pick up some painkillers. If he got off a stop early, there was a small supermarket that should have what he needed. It would mean a longer walk - or rather run - but he couldn't go into that meeting room feeling like this.

He rang the bell and made his way down the swaying stairs so that he could jump off as soon as the bus stopped.

That blank stare is disconcerting.
Drip!

Neil stopped short in front of the glass door of his office building and stared at his reflection. Was that a red mark on his head where the latest drop of rain had just landed?

You didn't hear much about acid rain these days. It had been a big deal when he had been a child, but he couldn't remember much about it apart from the name. Is that what this was? Acid raindrops falling on his head?

He squinted at the glass, but the image wasn't clear enough to properly examine himself. Besides, the longer he stayed outside, the more chance the acid rain would have to attack him. He pushed the door open and walked over to the security guard sitting behind his desk.

"Afternoon, Mr Williams."

"Afternoon, Mike."

"You're in late today."

"Don't I know it. Still, better late than never, eh?"

Mike didn't look convinced by this sentiment. He'd been sitting there since seven o'clock that morning and was frankly jealous of the young executives wafting in and out at all hours, whenever they felt like it.

"Look, Mike," continued Neil, "do you see anything on my head?"

Mike shook his head. "What am I meant to be looking for?"

"A red mark. Right here," Neil said, pointing at it.

"I'm not sure. I guess there might be something."

Maybe it had just been a trick of the light, but it certainly felt real. The drugs Neil had hastily swallowed as he ran down the road didn't seem to have touched the pain. If anything, it had increased.

He considered whether he should go to the bathroom and take a proper look, but the meeting was just about to start. He'd just have to hope that Mike was right and that, if there was a mark, it wasn't too obvious.

If any of the clients commented he could always claim to have converted to Hinduism. No doubt that would be considered politically incorrect, but at least the thought made him laugh. It was the first thing that had that today.

Should I pack some more ice?
Drip!

"Could somebody turn off the air-con?" asked Neil. "It's freezing in here. Besides, I think the system is leaking."

Mr Harris looked at him, puzzled.

"I can't say I'd noticed it, but if our guests don't mind..." He looked over at the group of Chinese businessmen on the opposite side of the conference table. They shrugged back at him, so Mr Harris sent an intern to have a fiddle with the thermostat.

"Can we continue?" he said to Neil.

"Of course. Just let me find my place." Neil stared at the presentation slide projected on the screen, but his mind was a complete blank. Had he even prepared this slide?

He looked over at Naomi. Was she smirking? Surely, she couldn't have been so petty as to mess about with his presentation to make him look bad?

No, he remembered now. This was a slide he'd added last week. Naomi had far subtler ways to stab him in the back.

He was just being paranoid, and he was certain the water was the main reason. The droplets seemed to be following him everywhere; like one of those cartoon strips where one unfortunate character has a personal storm cloud that follows them everywhere.

Neil looked up to see if there was indeed a black cloud hovering over his head. Then he remembered where he was and snapped his head back down, so fast that for a moment he saw stars.

"If you'll look at these projections," he said to the clients, hoping that nobody had noticed his latest lapse. However, out of the corner of his eye, he noticed Mr Harris looking concerned and Naomi smirking again.

Are you sure he's listening?
Drip!

"Earth to Neil. Are you listening?"

Neil sat bolt upright. Had he somehow fallen asleep at his desk? A drop of water trickled down into his eye. He hadn't even felt this one land. His forehead no longer throbbed with pain. Instead, it just felt numb.

"Look, mate, it can't have been *that* bad."

"You weren't there, Steve. I was a mess in there. Kept losing my place, forgetting basic details. I think old Harris felt sorry for me. I didn't think he was capable of any emotion as human as pity."

"Well, we all have off days. Give it a week and everyone will have forgotten all about it."

Steve didn't get it. He had no ambition. He was happy being one of the unidentified masses floating in the middle of the company. He just wanted a quiet life in a job where he didn't have to work too hard. If he was paid well enough to afford his sports channel subscription and go drinking on a Friday night, he was happy.

"Naomi won't let them forget," said Neil. "Didn't you see her? Darting into Harris's office the second we got out of the meeting. You can bet she was lobbying to take over my account and, if she gets that, how long is it until she gets the promotion too? Harris will probably be grateful. Promoting a woman will help him improve his diversity figures."

"You are being paranoid, mate," said Steve. "The world isn't conspiring against you."

"Could have fooled me. Even the rain is attacking me today."

Steve looked concerned. "You sure you're not working too hard? You wouldn't be the first high-flyer to burn out from stress."

"Unlike you? Whatever gets you in the end, it certainly won't be down to overwork."

"Hey, there's no need to get personal. I'm happy with my life and the way it is. I'm just saying, if you're not happy, maybe you should make some changes."

"Sorry. That was mean. I know you're being a good friend. I'm just having a bad day."

"It's alright, mate. We've all been there. You'll find a way to get back into Harris' good graces. Mark my words. Maybe stop scratching your head, though. It's sore enough already."

Neil dropped his hand. He hadn't even noticed what he'd been doing.

"You can see a mark?" he asked Steve.

"Sure, of course I can see a mark. You've been worrying away at it since you got back to your desk. It looks quite sore. What did you do to yourself?"

"I told you; it's the rain. It keeps landing on my head."

"Like in the song?" Steve started humming.

"Cut it out. That isn't funny." Neil wasn't in the mood for any more of his friend's jokes at his expense. He stood up and stomped off to the bathroom to look at the mark properly for himself.

"He's definitely losing it," Steve said to himself, then turned back to his important game of Solitaire.

Should we ask him something?

Drip!

"You don't mind me asking, do you? I mean, if something's happened in your personal life, I'd like to think you could talk to me. What is it? Problems with your girlfriend? You're not married, are you? Or your boyfriend? I suppose I shouldn't assume anything these days." Mr Harris laughed, but it was so obviously fake that even he realised it and stopped quickly.

Neil wondered what answer would get him out of here fastest. He was trying desperately not to touch his forehead and draw attention to the wound there, but another drop of water had just landed on him, and he was having to fight the instinct to wipe it away. The water rolled down his face and, for just a moment, it felt like he was crying.

Would a little white lie hurt? Amazingly Mr Harris seemed inclined to be sympathetic. What harm would there be in playing on that a little?

"You're very perceptive, sir." Neil wondered if that was laying it on too thick, but Mr Harris seemed to lap up the compliment. "My girlfriend broke up with me and I guess it's affected me more than I realised."

"I thought it was something like that. Instability at home is always bad for business."

Suddenly, Mr Harris seemed a lot less sympathetic, and Neil began to realise that he had miscalculated.

"I know times have changed," Mr Harris continued. "Young people don't want to settle down, but I was married before I was twenty and that was the making of me. Responsibility makes a man responsible."

Neil tried to interrupt, but his boss was working up a head of steam and there was no stopping him.

"Now, you're not quite there yet, but you will be. However, in the meantime, I think it's better if someone with more focus takes over the Xiàng account. Miss Knight is engaged; did you know that?"

Of course, Neil knew that. Naomi had made sure everyone had seen that massive rock on her finger.

"Please, Mr Harris, I just had one bad day. If you give me another chance…"

"The problem is, the clients just weren't impressed, and after all, the customer is always right. Now, don't look so dispirited. You'll get another opportunity soon enough. After all, I'm sure it won't be long before we find Miss Knight is leaving us to take care of a family. Use that time wisely and I'm sure the next opportunity for advancement will be yours."

Neil doubted it. If Naomi had children - and Heaven help the world if she produced any Devil spawn - she would almost certainly hire a nanny and be back at work within a couple of weeks. However, there was no separating the boss from his antiquated and misogynistic attitudes.

Mr Harris leant back in his chair, the universally recognised signal that he had decided that the meeting was over.

It's best to let him focus on the pain for now.

Drip!

The pain in Neil's shoulders was becoming unbearable. It was as though he'd done too many pull-ups at the gym - not that he'd been there since the customary moment of fitness madness back in January.

He trudged back to his desk and wondered if Steve wasn't the smarter man. All that effort and Neil wasn't any better off than if he hadn't bothered at all.

"How did it go?" asked Steve, looking up from another game of Solitaire. Then he saw the look on Neil's face. "That badly, eh? I really thought Harris would give you another shot."

"I reckon Naomi had this all planned from the beginning. Get me to do all the work and then swoop in at the last minute to reap the rewards."

Steve looked dubious. "I don't know. Seems like she was just lucky."

"I keep telling you, it's not paranoia if they're actually out to get you. She was probably conspiring with Harris from the beginning."

It wasn't even four-thirty yet, but Neil realised he couldn't face staying at the office any longer. He grabbed his coat, bag and the big golf umbrella.

"If anyone asks, tell them I've had to get home to deal with the plumbing emergency."

"Really? I can't remember the last time you bunked off early. Maybe I should come too; check the taps are working properly down at the Red Lion if you know what I mean."

"Another time, okay? I think I'm just going to head home and take some more painkillers."

"For your head? I didn't like to say, as you seemed a bit sensitive about it, but it's looking a lot worse. Maybe you should be seeing a doctor about it?"

"Worse?" Neil reached up and pressed his finger to the damp spot on his forehead. He wondered if he could feel an indentation there now? It wasn't deep, but then it hadn't been there at all before. He didn't dare look at it in the mirror. Instead he headed straight for the lift, without even stopping to say goodbye.

What do you think is going through his head?
Drip!

Neil was halfway home when a high-pitched shout broke the tranquillity of bus passengers carefully ignoring one other.

"Mummy, Mummy, that man is a zombie!"

"Don't be silly George," his mother said in a resigned tone. "There's no such thing as zombies. You've been playing too many violent games again."

"But, Mummy, zombies eat brains."

"I'm sure they do, darling."

"And then the people they eat become zombies."

"That's really not very nice is it, George. Can you talk about something more pleasant? Or maybe just sit quietly?"

"But, Mummy, a zombie has eaten that man's brains, so now he must be a zombie… and he'll want to eat us… and he'll probably want to eat me first because I'm clever… and then I'll be a zombie… and I can eat brains. What do brains taste like? I hope it's not peas, because I don't like peas. I hope they taste like sausages."

The woman turned to look at Neil, probably to apologise for her son's disturbing narrative, but gasped when she saw him. Neil stared back confused and a bit insulted. So, he had a small mark on his head; what was so terrible about that?

"I bet the zombies sucked his brains out with a straw," George seemed more curious than scared, "and drank them like a milkshake."

His mother pulled him close… before he could run over to investigate more closely.

"Maybe we'll go sit somewhere else," she said and dragged her protesting son towards the stairs.

Self-consciously, Neil reached up and felt the red spot again. It wasn't just an indentation now. Instead, there was a noticeable hole. He could put his little finger inside, almost up to the bottom of the nail.

He took his finger out, with some trepidation, and studied it. It was wet where water had accumulated in the wound, but there didn't seem to be any blood. Still this wasn't normal. He clearly needed medical attention.

This won't kill him, will it?

Drip!

The Accident and Emergency department was crowded when he arrived. He was starting to feel dizzy and would have liked to sit down. However, all the seats and most of the spaces by the wall where one could lean had already been taken. Neil felt guilty adding to the pressure on the already overcrowded hospital, but when he'd called the GP, he'd been told that the next free appointment was in a week.

He'd tried to explain about the hole, but they seemed determined to refer to it as a headache. So, he'd ended up here instead.

He went over to the reception desk. The woman behind it didn't look up, she just started asking him questions.

"Name?"

"Neil Williams."

"Address?"

Neil gave it to her, followed by his date of birth.

"And what is wrong?"

"Well, it's my head?"

"Did you hit it on something? Is it bleeding?"

"No, it's nothing like that. It just started hurting."

"Mr Williams, it's very busy. If you are wasting our time just because you have a headache..."

For the first time, she looked up at him. She was silent for a moment. Then she shouted at the top of her lungs. "I need a doctor in here! NOW!"

Everyone in the room looked around and doctors started appearing from every direction.

"How is he still standing?" one of them asked.

"Somebody get a gurney," another shouted by way of a response.

Neil tried to tell them it wasn't that bad, but before he knew what was happening, he found himself being lifted off the floor by a burly nurse.

Are the restraints tight enough?

Drip!

Neil had tried to struggle, but they had responded by strapping him down. As they tightened the restraints, he had screamed out at the pain in his already aching shoulders, but they seemed too fixated on his forehead to care.

They bombarded him with questions. When had he first noticed it? How painful was it on a scale of one to ten? Was it painful when they pressed here, or here, or here? The questions kept coming and Neil didn't feel like he had satisfactory answers to any of them. However, after three hours and a procession of doctors, they finally started to lose interest in him and the interrogation ended. Multiple specialists had come and gone, each declaring this to be somebody else's area of expertise. The way the hole kept filling up with water did keep them entertained for a while, but it wasn't blood and there wasn't anything to see on their scans, so the doctors were left feeling that there was nothing much they could do.

In the end, they booked him in for some more tests in a few days and sent him home with some industrial strength painkillers. It seemed like an anti-climax, but Neil was just thankful to be out of there.

I think we're getting through to him.

Drip!

Neil walked into his house and breathed a sigh of relief. Despite everything, he had made it through the day. He didn't even mind when the umpteenth drop of water fell on him. The plumber would be there in the morning and he would fix everything.

A small part of his mind told him that this thought was irrational, but he didn't really care. If it helped him sleep tonight, then he was happy to cling to the fiction.

Thanks to all the hours spent at the hospital it was already eleven o'clock. He saw the half-eaten bowl of cereal still sitting on the breakfast bar and realised that he'd also skipped lunch in his rush to get to work. Maybe that was why he felt so rotten.

He reached up to lift a can of beans down from the top shelf of the cupboard and his shoulder blossomed with pain again. No, dinner wasn't going to happen. It just wasn't worth the effort. He closed the cupboard again and went to get ready for bed.

In the bathroom, he peeled back the dressing that the doctors had affixed across his forehead. In the mirror, the hole looked deeper than ever. He thought that if he put his finger in now, he could probably reach right in and touch his brains, like the little boy had suggested. He quickly reapplied the dressing before morbid fascination compelled him to try.

Neil went through to the bedroom and lay down. It was a kind of relief to stop struggling. There was nothing he could do now except sleep.

Looking back on the day, none of it seemed real, and he wondered whether it had all been a long nightmare. Maybe he was about to wake up, back in his real life. That was probably the answer. Everything would look brighter when he woke up.

He closed his eyes.

He's coming around.

Drip!

Neil opened his eyes, but the bright light in the room dazzled him, forcing him to screw them shut again.

It's good to have you back with us Mr Williams.

Drip!

Neil could hear the people talking to either side of him, but even when he opened his eyes again, he found that he couldn't turn his head to see them.

Drip!

He tried to sit up, but his arms were fastened tightly above his head and his legs were similarly strapped down.

Drip!

All he could see was the device above his head. Water was collecting into a droplet at the bottom of a nozzle until it grew too heavy to hold on to and…

Drip!

Mr Williams, are you ready to talk to us?

Drip!

Neil remembered where he was and realised that he had been right - this was real life. He screamed.

Drip!

Excellent. Then we will begin.

Drip!

Red Frost

Lex H. Jones

Ronald Powell switched off the engine of his black 1941 Packard Clipper and rested the back of his head on the chair. The leather on the headrest was peeling slightly; a small flap catching his neck as he turned towards his companion in the passenger seat.

"Are you ready?" Ronald asked.

Larry Wilson didn't look ready for much of anything. He was sweating, despite the negative degree temperature outside, the ice on the floor, and the softly falling snow that marked the season. Larry removed his trilby and wiped his forehead, preventing more sweat dripping into his eyes. When he replaced the hat, Ronald leaned over and pulled the brim down lower, shadowing more of Larry's face.

"I think so." Larry shrugged, finally answering the question. "Remind me again why I have to go in? I'm the one with the bum leg. I'm the one who's going to get recognised if anyone's in there."

"Nobody's in that factory at this time of night, Larry. And yeah, you got a bum leg. So, what, you want to be the driver instead? Cause the way I remember it, you had to sell your car because you couldn't drive the damn thing anymore since you took that bullet."

"Yeah, I guess."

"That's right, you guess. In fact, you don't guess, you *know*. We *both* know this is right. They took your job, Larry. Three years you spent over there fighting the Nazis and the Japs. Took a bullet for your country, protecting your fellow man, and for what? To get fired from the factory you worked at when you got home just because you can't move around so well anymore? Bullshit!"

"They were kind of right, though, Ron. I mean, I couldn't..."

"Bullshit, Larry! They could have found you another job, one where you don't have to walk around. They owe you. The whole damn country owes you. Me too, whilst we're griping about it. I ain't got nothing wrong with me that the doctors can't fix. It's just a little head problem, that's all."

"It's called shellshock, Ron."

"Don't matter what it's called, Larry. It ain't justification for them taking my job. I gave them years before I went off to do my duty. Just like you did. And they stabbed us in the goddamn back. So, yeah, now we're taking what we're due."

"Wouldn't it make more sense to rob the Savings and Loan? Surely, they got to have more cash than the factory. I mean, there's *some* here, but..."

"More security at the Savings and Loan, Larry. We've been over this, more than once. They expect that place to get robbed. Only folk who know how much money is left at a factory are the folk who've been inside one; the ones who know when the bank runs are due to move the cash. Like you, who knows it's not for two days, meaning there's a nice fat safe in there, which you know the combination to."

"They're going to know it's me."

"Wrong. They might *think* it's you, but what evidence will they have? We're gonna invest that money, launder it good. Leave them nothing that resembles proof. Innocent until proven guilty, Larry. They might *think* they know what went down, but their case has got to be airtight. We're decorated vets, remember? You think any judge or jury in the country right now is going to take the side of some rich factory boss over ours? Not a chance in Hell. We'll get away clean and smooth."

"Alright. Just keep an eye on that door for when I come back out. I want to leave as soon as possible."

"Don't worry about that. The second your ass is back on that seat, my foot's hitting this pedal."

Larry took a deep breath, then opened the car door and immediately slipped on the frost-covered ground, bracing himself against the car.

"Get it together, you mook!" Ronald yelled.

Larry raised his hands in apology, then moved round to the back of the car to open the trunk. He took a grey burlap sack which he slung over his shoulder. After closing the trunk, he walked as quickly as he could towards the factory side-door. His limp was very pronounced. There was no real way he could hide it, but for short spurts like this, he was still surprisingly spry on his feet. It was long stints of standing and walking - such as his job moving boxes at the factory had required - when he really suffered. Still, despite the speed with which he was able to move for small periods at a time, he was taking it steady given the condition of the pavement. The frost had settled thickly overnight, and with the factory being closed over the weekend, nobody had thought it necessary to throw any salt down.

The night air seemed to be dropping in temperature with each minute. The key in his hand was so cold that Larry could feel it through his gloves. He shouldn't even still have the key, of course. As far as the foreman was concerned, he'd handed in his keys on his last day of working there. And he had, there was no deception in that. Except for the fact that Larry had got a spare key which everyone had evidently forgotten about. He'd been lent it when he lost his own; only to then find his key in the lining of his coat pocket. Nobody had ever thought to ask for the spare back, so Larry had never thought to offer. It was going to come in useful now, though. With his bum leg there wasn't much chance of Larry being able to force his way through the door with brute effort, and Ronald was too slight a man to be of much use in that regard. Being able to simply unlock the door made the whole operation that much easier.

Ronald watched as Larry slipped inside the deserted factory, and then glanced at his watch. It was an unnecessary action. They weren't on any set schedule and it wasn't as though a security guard was working the night shift and they needed to time their robbery to avoid his route. The factory didn't even have one, not right now anyway. The last one had been let go under similar circumstances to Larry, and they'd yet to hire a new one. There was nobody here to avoid, and the factory was too far out from the main roads to chance any passers-by catching them in the act. Still, Ronald naturally felt a sense of urgency that kept drawing his attention back to the ticking watch.

After he'd sat for ten minutes or so, he saw Larry exit the door, lock it, then limp back towards the car. He was dragging the grey burlap sack at his side, but it was now full and evidently rather heavy. That fact made Ronald smile as he watched Larry struggle with the bag on the icy ground.

"Didn't hear any alarms or anything. Good work, pal," Ronald called, glancing in the rear-view mirror to watch Larry bundling the sack into the trunk of the car.

"I'm not stupid." Larry reminded him, limping back around to join Ronald in the car.

"Well that went nice and smoothly," Ronald beamed, punching his friend in the shoulder.

"Your turn now. Get us home safe; don't drive too fast or nothing. We don't want to give any traffic cops a reason to pull us over."

"I'm not driving too fast on this ice anyway." Ronald pointed out, turning the engine over and driving away from the factory.

"You didn't get snow chains?"

"No, Mr Sensible, I did not. How much did you get in that sack, anyway?"

"Everything that was in the safe. Which is more than I'd have earned from working there for another decade at least."

"Nice work. We take that money to a good bank - or several of them, in fact - and say we won it at a casino... morally dubious, but perfectly legal. Then we put it in a decent investment account and boom! We're set for life!"

"You make it sound so simple," said Larry, rubbing the back of his neck.

"Don't start getting the guilt now, Larry. It's done, and we're going to live a nice easy life from now on; modest but easy. We're not fleecing people; we haven't gone around doing repeated robberies to live like kings or nothing. We just done enough so we don't need to worry about keeping a roof over our heads or food on the table. It's fine, alright?"

"Yeah, okay," Larry sighed, sinking back into his chair.

Ronald nodded; satisfied the matter was dealt with and switched the radio on.

The car was now filled with the gentle warmth of Frank Sinatra singing 'Night and Day'.

The road ahead was empty.

The only thing cutting through the darkness were the headlights on Ronald's car.

The ground sparkled slightly in the reflection of the light, the frost giving sheen to the black asphalt below the tyres. Snow started to fall softly, the flakes settling on the windscreen.

"That's gonna get deep fast with this cold," Ronald remarked, switching on the windshield wipers and putting his foot down. The car went over the brow of a small hill, clearing the apex with such speed that the tyres left the road for a second. When they found it again, the build-up of ice meant they couldn't regain the traction quickly enough, sending the car into a skid.

"Shit!" Ronald yelled, frantically turning the wheel against the skidding motion to try and regain control of the vehicle.

The car went over the side of the road and head-first into the frozen body of water that lay beyond it, the covering of ice splitting open to welcome it.

"Shit! Shit! Shit!" Ronald repeated as he unbuckled himself and quickly opened the door before water poured into the car and made the act impossible.

"Ron!" Larry grabbed Ronald's wrist, a look of sheer panic on his face. "I can't move my leg! It's gone numb! I'm stuck!"

"Okay, err..." Ronald stepped back from the car, a dark idea spreading through him as he watched the icy water pouring into the car.

"You have to get me out!"

"Yeah... yeah... of course. Just let me come around to your side, okay?" Ronald assured him, getting out of the slowly-sinking car and wading round to the back.

Larry looked over his shoulder as Ronald walked round to the back of the car. "Come on Ronald... come on..."

He watched as Ronald opened the trunk of the car, which still protruded from the water as the front slowly sank. Ronald removed the grey burlap sack, then closed the trunk... and gave the car a push.

"Ronald!" Larry screamed, frantically trying to move his leg to exit the car, but the task growing more difficult every moment with the rising water.

Ronald took a few steps back, watching Larry frantically bang against the passenger window before the front of the car was completely submerged. Frank Sinatra could just be heard singing as the back of the car disappeared beneath the water.

'There's an oh, such a hungry burning inside of me. And its torment won't be through.'

He watched the lake for a few minutes to be completely sure that Larry was done for. If he felt any pangs of conscience about this sudden and dark change of plan, his body language didn't betray it. In fact, he started whistling to himself as he stared at the frozen lake, swinging the sack over his shoulder and buttoning up his long black coat. Then he walked down the road, continuing his journey home.

ONE YEAR LATER...

Ronald hummed to himself as he folded clothes and placed them in his brown leather suitcase that lay open on his bed. He was never quite sure how much to pack, but his focus now was on the warmer items in his closet. He'd decided to take a few days to enjoy the cabin he'd bought out in the country. The money he'd helped to steal from the factory had served him well. With a sensible investment portfolio, he'd turned it into enough to live comfortably on for the rest of his life. And with not having to split the take in two, he'd had enough left over to buy himself the cabin. His plan was to spend a week there in winter. He'd do some reading, enjoy the log fire, and perhaps do some hunting.

With his thickest scarf packed into the suitcase, Ronald closed the top and pushed down firmly. A glint of something caught his eye to the right-side of his peripheral vision as he closed the latch. It was a patch of frost in the corner of his bedroom window, and yet the frost had a reddish tint running through it.

"Goddamn factories pumping their crap into the air," Ronald grumbled aloud.

Returning to his suitcase, he lifted it by the handle and went to leave the room. The door-handle was cold to touch, enough that he snatched his hand away for fear of frostbite. This, in turn, reminded him to grab his leather gloves, which he'd left on the nightstand. Walking back around the bed, he once again came close to the window. The red frost had spread, covering several panes of glass now. The view of the garden through the frosted window was distorted and crimson, giving the bare trees and frozen ground a look that wouldn't look out of place in Dante's epic poem. Ronald shuddered, forced himself to ignore the bizarre weather phenomenon, then grabbed his gloves and left the room.

Locking up the house, Ronald noticed that the red frost had also spread to the downstairs windows. He promised himself he would write a letter to the city council about it, as proof of what the local factories must be doing to the air. He'd read all about the smog clouds that used to beset London in its heavy manufacturing days, and the post-war boom in America's industries must now be surely at risk of doing the same.

Taking care not to slip, Ronald walked down the path to his waiting car.

His suitcase fit easily in the trunk and left ample room for his long coat, but Ronald opted to leave this on, given how poorly the car's heater usually performed.

Settling into the driver's seat, it took three attempts to turn the engine over as it battled against the cold, but finally it burst into life and away he went.

Ronald shivered, turning the heater up as far as it would go and then taking a moment to tune in the radio. Bing Crosby's voice filled the car, causing Ronald to roll his eyes.

He'd never been too fond of Crosby, always preferring Sinatra. He'd had many an argument with Larry over who was the better crooner. Ronald eventually agreed that Crosby was better at the cosy Christmas stuff, but Sinatra was the guy you'd go to for a romantic evening.

Recalling the debate, Ronald cast his mind back over the past year. Men with morals might have lost more sleep over the whole thing than Ronald had, but he had a clean way of smoothing over any gaps in his conscience. The icy water had killed Larry - not him. The car was sinking anyway; he just made it quicker and lessened Larry's torment. No way was he getting out with that bum leg of his. Ronald would have died trying. Better one of them survived. This logic was all it had taken for Ronald to sleep like a baby afterwards.

In the weeks that followed, the police investigation had fallen flat. Larry hadn't even been a suspect given his injury and the inability to drive a getaway car.

His friendship with Ronald wasn't well known, so it wasn't even as though the police had come knocking at his door. Sure, they'd served together in the war, but so had lots of people.

That was a very long list to run down, and frankly, as Ronald himself had suggested, the police didn't want to be seen hassling war vets.

Not unless they had an airtight case against one.

So, it was that the theft remained unsolved, Larry's corpse remained stuck in that car at the bottom of the lake to be eaten by fishes, and Ronald bought himself a nice new car: a black Packard Clipper. Same as his old one, but a slightly newer model.

Newer car or not, the heating system hadn't improved at all. He'd been on the road for half an hour and Ronald could still see his breath leaving his cracked lips. His shoulders ached from the tension with which he'd held himself against the cold, unable to relax into the drive in the way he naturally would if it were warmer. A red glint shone in his wing mirror, catching his eye. Ronald glanced at it to see that the corner of the mirror had started to freeze over with the same red frost he'd seen at home. It was as though the crimson frost was following him, but he instantly dismissed this with a shake of the head and an exhalation of air via the nose.

The radio crackled and hissed, suddenly louder than it had before. Ronald frowned and cursed, but before he could reach for the knob to adjust it, the radio had retuned itself. It was the bumpy road, it must be. Whatever song had been playing before, the transmission became clear again halfway through Frank Sinatra singing 'Night and Day.'

'In the roarin' traffic's boom,
In the silence of my lonely room,
I think of you day and night,'

A deep chill travelled the length of Ronald's spine, so severe that, combined with his firm grip on the steering wheel, it made the car swerve for a moment. He brought the car back under control in time to see the red frost spreading rapidly over the windshield. His vision of the road was getting worse every second, the windshield wipers doing nothing but sliding over the frost.

"Sonnova bitch!" Ronald groaned, pulling the car over on the side of the road.

Opening the passenger door, he took the plastic ice-scraper from the glove compartment and set to work removing the red frost. It came away easily enough, but he was sure that he could see it reforming slowly. He was about halfway through the task, reaching over the screen to do as much as he could before walking around the other side, when Ronald noticed exactly where it was that he'd been forced to pull over. To the left of his car was the same lake in which he'd lost his previous car. The one in which Larry had been stuck in the passenger seat and sank to his death. He wasn't on the same road now; he was passing by the lake from a different route on his journey out of time. But it was the same body of water nonetheless. In fact, as Ronald stared out across the water he convinced himself that directly opposite him, on the other side of the lake, was the spot where the car had gone into the lake from the road. If Larry somehow got out of that car and walked straight forward… *limped* straight forwards… he would exit the icy water at the exact spot where Ronald now stood.

"For God's sake, Powell," Ronald chastised, continuing to work away at the windshield.

Still, feeling a little silly or not for his lapse of rational thought, Ronald allowed his gaze to constantly flick over to the water at his side to make sure the surface of it wasn't broken by anything rising from beneath.

Once he was satisfied that the windshield was as clear as it was going to be - the red frost already starting to gather again in the corners of the glass - he quickly got back in the car and went on with the drive to his cabin. He didn't once look back at the lake in his rear-view mirror for fear of what he might see.

Ronald lost control of the vehicle about a mile away from the cabin.

The road had become so thick with ice that it was like driving on glass. The car's tyres couldn't find any purchase, Ronald having neglected once again to purchase snow tyres for the winter season, and he was constantly battling with the steering wheel to stay on the road. It was a fight that he eventually lost, as the car skidded off the road entirely and ploughed into a ditch. The drivers' door was pressed against a mound of frozen earth, forcing Ronald to climb over the passenger seat to escape the car. Climbing out of the ditch, he opened the trunk of the car and took his suitcase.

Taking a step back from the ditch, Ronald surveyed the damage both to himself and the car.

There was nothing he could do for the former, although it appeared basically alright. He'd just need a tow-truck with a strong winch to come by in the morning and fetch it out.

As for himself, his head ached from where he'd struck it on the steering wheel, but when he touched his fingertips against it, they didn't come back with any blood.

He felt a little woozy, but beyond that, he seemed to have escaped without injury.

Glancing down the road, squinting into the darkness, Ronald could just about make out his cabin up ahead.

It wasn't far, although his pace was slowed somewhat by the care he was forced to take on the icy road and frosted ground alongside it. Both the ice and frost glistened red, he noticed, but he was out in the country now, far from the factories and their noxious fumes. Ronald assured himself it was just a result of hitting his head, perhaps a mild concussion. He'd be warm and resting soon enough.

As he walked, he noticed the silence all about him, broken only by the sound of his leather shoes crunching the frozen grass beneath them.

He focused on this sound, each footfall taking him closer to the warmth and comfort of the cabin.

He had a bottle of whisky in the liquor cabinet there, he remembered. That would be most welcome tonight. He'd get there, have a drink, sit by the fire and rest, then in the morning, he'd call for a tow truck to get the car. It didn't matter if the front was banged up; he had the money to fix it after all. A satisfied smile spread across his lips as he reminded himself of this fact, and that was when he heard it.

A second set of footsteps crunching the frozen grass, echoing his own.

At first, that's what Ronald thought it was. An echo in the empty night.

He took a few deliberately loud steps and then stopped, waiting for the echo.

His own footfalls were indeed followed by the sound of another, but they weren't his own.

The pace wasn't the same, for one thing.

They were staggered; a broken pace. Ronald froze, his blood chilled now by far more than the icy temperature of the night air.

He spun around, expecting to see something limping towards him on the road.

There was nothing. Nobody else as far as he could see.

It's possible they were further back down the road, of course, but if they were close enough that he could hear their footsteps then he'd surely be able to see them as well. Ronald made another, cautious footstep, quieter than before, as though he daren't tempt the echo. Still he paused and waited for a response. There wasn't one. He breathed a sigh of relief and walked more briskly the remaining distance to the cabin.

Ronald double-checked that he locked the door after he entered the cabin, feeling edgy and paranoid given the night's events. It wasn't a logical fear, not really.

Yet it was there all the same, chilling his bones even more than the cold had.

A cold which seemed to be equally present inside the cabin as it was without. Wasting no time to correct this, Ronald put down his suitcase and immediately went over to the fireplace. There was wood freshly chopped for his arrival, a convenient little service that could be paid for from the groundskeeper. Ronald tossed a few logs on and lit the fire with a match. He stared and watched the fire start to take hold, then removed his gloves and warmed his hands in front of the small flames.

Satisfied the fire would soon warm the room, Ronald stood up and breathed a sigh of relief. It seemed safer somehow with the fire's warmth. The cold had seemed threatening. As this thought occurred to him, a glint caught his eye once more, this time coming from the cabin window. It was the red frost, already spreading across the glass. As Ronald got closer, he could see the crimson chill spreading over the window panes in the manner of spilt water slowly spreading across a tabletop.

"Chemicals. The god-damned state department needs to get on this," he said aloud, as though the suggestion of logic might banish the fear of the frost. It wasn't working.

The fireplace no longer seemed like enough, so Ronald went into the kitchen and bedrooms and lit both of the gas-powered heaters. He also took the opportunity to triple-check every window was closed and locked, and that the door to the cabin remained so as well. This didn't bring Ronald any comfort, though, as the ice had spread to the windows upstairs as well. It now seemed like it covered the entirety of the outside of the house.

Ronald returned to the living room, still wearing his long coat as he stood in front of the fireplace, shivering. He could see his breath before his face.

The cold was seeping through the walls.

Poorly insulated cabin, he told himself. It had to be.

He cursed the silence, feeling like every creak of the expanding floorboards, every pop and crackle of the fire, was now an affront to his nervous state. That silence was broken by the sudden music emanating from the wireless radio that rested atop the mantelpiece. It hadn't been turned on - nor had Ronald touched it - yet still music started to come from it.

'Night and day, under the hide of me,
There's an oh, such a hungry yearnin' burnin' inside of me,
And its torment won't be through,'

Frank Sinatra's voice was distorted, the effect somehow stripping it of its usual warmth and replacing it with malice. Ronald grabbed the radio and went to turn the dial back to 'off'. Except, he couldn't because it was already turned off. Panic and confusion rose in him, causing him to throw the radio down onto the hardwood floor, smashing it with his foot.

Again, again, again he stamped on it; until it was just shards and broken parts. Sinatra's voice stopped, but the atmosphere of the cabin was none the warmer for it.

Ronald ran into the kitchen, opened one of the cupboards and took out a wooden box. From it he took as many thick candles as he could carry, then quickly ran around the cabin, standing them up and lighting them. Heat and light, that's what the place needed, he thought. He lit every candle he could find, yet the oppressive cold of the cabin remained unchanged. There was no draft, but the air was filled with a constant chill that made it impossible to get comfortable. His body shook. He contemplated leaving, but that meant going back out where the red frost was. No car. Nowhere to go. All that cold, open dark. No, inside the cabin was safer, he assured himself. Exactly what he was trying to procure safety against was a thought that he hadn't allowed himself to fully form. Madness lies that way, he knew.

The brand-new hunting rifle he'd purchased had been safely locked away in its display cabinet. Ronald removed it now and loaded it for the first time. He'd planned to hunt some deer or turkeys, but now the rifle was loaded for protection.

With the rifle firmly gripped, Ronald went and sat on the floor by the fire, as close to it as he could. He kept his eye fixed on the door and the windows, watching for any sign of… he didn't even know what. The red frost was thick on the windows, so thick he could barely see out of them now. He could see enough, though. If anybody… *anything*… moved by that window and approached the door, then he'd see it.

For the first time since this evening had begun, Ronald focused on what was happening, thinking about the night instead of just reacting to it as each event came up.

The car windshield froze, so he scraped it off.

His car crashed, so he got out and walked to the cabin.

The cabin was cold, so he lit the fire, the gas heaters and all the candles. He felt unsafe, so he loaded a weapon and kept it close. All reactions to the current situation, just like a soldier. You couldn't un-train that. But now it was precisely his time as a soldier that Ronald focussed on. Was this a new symptom of his shellshock? The past year he'd been free of episodes. Was this a long overdue episode, turning up with a vengeance to shatter his mind?

"I'm not crazy. I'm not," he said aloud.

The crackle of the fire at his side went silent, replaced with a dry cracking noise. Slowly, despairingly he turned to look at it. The fire itself had frozen. The flames held solid in red ice, still present and glowing beneath it like an illuminated glass sculpture. Ronald could see his reflection in it.

"No. No, that's not possible."

Ronald flipped the rifle in his hands and reached towards the frozen flames with the butt of the gun. He tapped it, cautiously at first. It was solid. He struck it harder now, intending to free the flames so they might once again bring him some warmth. The ice cracked a little, so he struck again. On the third blow the flame shattered, sending shards of red ice violently outwards. Some struck Ronald in the eyes, causing him to fall back in pain.

His vision was blurry now, his eyes searing. He could make out the larger shapes of the cabin, but nothing more clearly than that.

As the ice struck him, he'd dropped the rifle, and upon realising that, his thoughts instantly turned to retrieving it. The fact he couldn't see clear to aim it didn't deter his desperation to once again hold the rifle. The fire was gone. The rifle was his best chance at staying safe.

Ronald looked this way and that, painfully squinting his eyes to try and clear them. He got to his feet, then slipped and fell face-first back to the wooden floor. It felt colder now as he lay against it. Even with his blurred vision, he could see that the floor of the cabin was now covered with red frost. It wasn't stopping there, though. It had started to spread across the walls too, reaching up towards the ceiling.

Spotting the rifle laying on the ground to his right, Ronald started to drag himself along the floor to reach it. His ribs hurt where he'd fallen. He daren't risk standing again. Ronald was close to the rifle, within grabbing distance of it, when he found that his hand was now stuck to the floor. So cold was the ice that his skin had frozen against it. Worse still, as he turned to see that this had happened, the side of his face became similarly stuck. Ronald lifted his cheek away with all his strength, screaming as the skin was torn from it and left behind on the floor. The agony caused him to fall back down, stuck against the red frost and sobbing in terror.

The cabin door swung open with such force that the top hinge broke away and was left hanging down at an awkward angle. A shape stood in the doorway. Shabby. Rotten. Covered in red frost. Even with his blurred vision, Ronald was in no doubt about who it was. He screamed, unable to move himself from the floor as the frozen undead thing began to walk towards him with a very pronounced limp.

Ice Rage

Dave Jeffery

New Moscow, 2220 AD

"For fucksake, keep the light steady, Misha."

"I'm trying, Petrov," said the lady with the lamp. It was fuelled by kerosene and the flame sputtered in the chill breeze. If it had not been for the woollen folds of the scarf wrapped about her face, Misha's mouth would have frozen shut in three minutes. Her big gloves made handling the lamp cumbersome; the iced metal working against her like some greased snake.

"Try harder, woman," the big man said from beneath the hood of a Snowcat. "Unless you want us frozen."

"We've come out too far," Misha said. Not even her scarf could disguise the fear in her voice. "We've almost used up our markers."

The markers - red flags - were punched into the snow at quarter mile intervals. A gauge as to how far they'd ventured from their hazardous haven.

Their guide back home.

Home was now all that remained of the Presnensky District. Once, it had been known as the International Business Centre and located on the western embankment of River Moskva.

Then came The White Wall: the countdown to everlasting winter.

At first, it came in great, thunderous clouds rolling across the skies. Soon, it was one huge, never-ending cloud; a Black Mass for mankind, shunning the sun and liquidating the light. Then the snow: blizzards that lasted for months, locking people in their homes with snow drifts as big as the houses they occupied.

Continents became meaningless boundaries, blurred by blizzards. And when the snow stopped falling, and the temperatures climbed to a life-sustaining forty below, the survivors began to migrate from the places that had sustained them through the bleak whiteness.

Survivors like Misha and Petrov Chemitsky, once husband and wife with their own small security business. Now, they were nothing more than ghosts on a whitewashed landscape.

All that remained above ground were the buildings with the height to outlast The White Wall.

Seven floors of the Federation Tower could be seen above ground. Eighty-seven floors could not. Misha and her husband lived in an apartment they had made on the second floor above ground. Ground zero, that was. They were lucky: their windows still had glass and a heater. And furs. They were all that remained of the animals. Dogs and cats made good pets but far better eating. These days, the only fresh meat Misha and Petrov acquired came from rats. Those little bastards really could survive anything.

Good news for the handful of occupants of Federation Tower, of course. It meant they didn't have to use The Store *that* often. It was meant to be a last resort, but on occasion, when the rats got wary and human reaction got slow, they had to use The Store. It was a matter of survival: eating those that hadn't made it. Sure, they'd say a prayer whilst mourning the past and cursing the present. But they would still cook and carve, still salt the remains for another day and lie that this would be the *last fucking time.*

There had been so many "last times" lately.

They sent out recons so that another day of eating kin was staved off for a while. Therefore, the recons and their on-going survival were enmeshed. They also gave purpose. Hunger was one issue - maintaining sanity came clinging to its shirt tails.

"Enough, dammit! Just hold that light steady," Petrov griped.

"It'll be dark soon," Misha said.

"It's *always* dark," Petrov said absently. Overhead, the muted sky illustrated his point.

"You know what I mean," Misha sighed. "I promised Sonja that I would bring her back something nice for our *little miracle*."

More than a miracle: hope eternal for humans. Misha's sister was in her third trimester. And her pending baby had shown nature had done what science could not. It had found a way... despite all that had happened. Humanity was adapting. Evolving. Those who survived had found resolve. It was strong and warming to their frigid hearts; a beacon of what might be.

Still, nature wasn't choosy as to how it made its way through the world.

"I should be with her," Misha said ruefully.

"She's not alone," Petrov said from beneath the hood. "Dmitri is with her.

"Is that supposed to put me at rest?"

Dmitri the Drunk, they all called him. Not to his face, of course. Sonja's husband was a bad drunk, the kind that wanted to fight the world, but settled instead for lashing out at those dear to him. Petrov held him in check, but only just.

"It is more reason to keep the light still. Cold comes with the night."

Minus twenty, now. But in three hours the wind would power in from the southeast, driving temperatures down to minus eighty-nine. Antarctic weather had now gone global. And they were caught out in it.

"Ah!"

"What is it, Petrov?"

"Found it," he said nodding his head. "What a dumb bastard I am!"

"You've found it, but can you fix it?"

He straightened and turned to her, his huge frame exaggerated by the multiple layers of clothing. He pawed at his goggles and the eyes behind the smeared glass were bright with delight.

"I am Petrov Chemitsky," he laughed. "Of course, I can fix it!"

"Of course, you can, my love." Misha smiled beneath the mask, the material rough against her lips. As her husband set to work, she looked to the blanched horizon, and as bleak as it was, her spirit lifted a little at the thought of Sonja and the new baby.

Then she saw something: a fleeting flicker only a few hundred metres out; lights that had been both bright and brief yet dulled by her goggles. Twin lights - reflecting her lamp.

Eyes?

But that was impossible, right? Of course not. That that was why they were out here, wasn't it? Misha cursed her hopelessness. She *had* seen the lights and understood what they perhaps represented: life in the wilderness.

She made to step up to Petrov and make known her discovery, but something else caught her attention. Not twin, flickering lights and the promise of life. This was a big sound made small by her headgear. A sound that brought with it only dread and turned her heart to ice.

A growl.

She turned her head, the movement slow, as though she really didn't want to see the thing that had now powered up the growl to a savage snarl.

"Jesus Mary, Mother of God," Petrov said, his knees almost buckling as muscles jittered in shock. He gave his wife advice that she would never fulfil.

"Misha, *run!*"

But she didn't, couldn't.

Something big lunged through the snow, matted yellow-white fur blotting her vision. Then she saw the teeth - the *fangs* - in a mouth yanked wide open and bearing down on her.

Jaws circumvented her skull, clamping shut until the wind was joined by the sound of a pistol-shot crack and the whistling hiss of a punctured cranium.

And the scream: short, but no less potent.

Crimson mingled with white and yellowed fur; the gout of blood that managed to escape the vice turning Misha's head to mulch was fierce, arcing in the air like some macabre abstract work of art before freezing and shattering on the ice where it glinted like abandoned rubies.

The great beast lifted the petite, mangled woman into the air, its paws grabbing and slashing at her clothing to get to the meat beneath. It was frenzied now, like many living things living under the shadow of The White Wall, this creature was driven by a gnawing hunger. The meagre months were now forgotten as it gorged, flesh and material coming away from Misha's body in ragged, indistinguishable strips, the spreading pool of blood turning to crimson slurry as it met the ice.

Petrov watched, frozen, immobile in horror and grief, the snow drifting about his boots. *Poor Misha,* he thought.

But it was a moment of grief, self-preservation kicking in like a generator and urging the beast to stay focused on his partner whilst he got his fucking act together and reached for the gun.

It was in the Snowcat, wedged between the seat and the gear shift. An AK47, wrapped in a thermal sheath and semi-lubricated to protect the tempered steel from the extreme cold.

But something still held him. Fear? Yes, part of it was the shuddering terror turning his muscles to jelly with such efficiency he'd pissed his pants. No, it was something else.

Fascination?

Yes, that was it. Fascination that the thing now chowing down on Misha looked initially like a polar bear. Now, up close and personal, this was no Shako. This was–

Different.

It was shaped as a man, but it bore no features as such. Even hunched over its prey, the beast was huge. Its long fur, rippling in the growing breeze, hid a mountain of muscle.

The thought was there before he could stop it.

Yeti.

A thing of stories, yet did he not recall something from just before the coming of The White Wall? A flicker-flash of a news item in the Moscow Times came to him. He'd read it over breakfast whilst sipping strong coffee from his favourite FC Spartak mug. The item spoke of wildlife migrating from the Himalayas; snow leopards, wolves and Tibetan bears, all on the move - fleeing - as though the predators themselves were now in fear of their lives. The article was accompanied by a shaky camera shot of what looked like an upright bear, shaggy arms reaching out towards a wolf. The wolf was running towards the camera, eyes wild with fear. The cameraman said it was not a bear who chased the wolf, but something else; some creature he had *never seen before.* However, the quality of the shot was unconvincing and the shape too distant to make out clearly. Petrov had downed his coffee and concluded the photographer had taken more than thermal clothing to keep him warm.

Petrov didn't think that now. He had the misfortune to look at the thing in the photograph up close and personal, without a shaky camera and cheap newsprint to blur the effect. He could see why wolves would run from this thing. He gawped, as a myth made real - in a time when the world had gone mad - spilt the blood of its kill in front of him.

Petrov yanked his eyes away from the terrible scene, attempting to calculate the odds of escape before his brain was chewed from his skull by the great beast.

Forcing his feet to slither on the carpet of fresh snowfall, he edged toward the Snowcat.

Crunch.

His feet in the snow.

Crunch.

The beast's teeth on Misha's pelvis.

Near the cab now, gloved hands reaching behind him for the door handle, groping, reaching out for sanctuary in the form of Perspex and steel. Fabric-fat fingers found the door handle, yanked on it and dragged it open. Then he risked turning; clambering into the cab and returning with the assault rifle and a belly full of anger, primed and ready to reap retribution for his beloved Misha.

He dropped low, the beast that had robbed him of his wife in his sights. He fired once, the report thin against the wind, the trajectory of the bullet-marked as a line of fine mist, crystallising in the air. It caught the animal in the temple, blowing open its skull.

It collapsed, landing on top of the mangled remains of Petrov's wife. Petrov took a few steps towards the carnage, but they lacked conviction. He began to walk backwards, his heart as heavy as his footfalls, afraid to take his eyes away from the scene before him. He reached behind for the Snowcat. Instead of the vehicle, his arm found searing pain.

Petrov tried to draw his arm back, to protect it - nurse it - from the agony now consuming him but saw only bloody sludge pumping from what was left. The arm was gone below the elbow, the flesh ragged. The rifle slithered from the weakened grip of his remaining hand.

He spun, the stump flailing pathetically, and saw the thing that had snuck up on him: another Yeti, this one bigger, its high forehead and squat nose glistening, bejewelled with his blood. Its nostrils flared, its demeanour that of feral rage.

The beast lunged, the severed arm still clenched in its jaws. It reached out, paws coming together in one huge clap,

Petrov's head between them. His skull changed shape, both eyes launching from their sockets with a sickening, sucking sound. The beast fell upon him, tearing into him, and was joined by several others who took their spoils from both carcasses, now unrecognizable on the ice.

Lying in the snow, several meters away, Petrov's unblinking eyes watched their owner's brutal demise.

The beast who had slaughtered Petrov moved from the pack feeding on his remains. It bounded to the fallen creature and stooped to lift it from the bloody ice, cradling the limp, furry body as it let loose a huge, wanton cry of anguish.

The troop watched intently as the Yeti chief placed his fallen mate onto the ground and began to scoop snow over her. They sidled over, their presence a bid to support him in his grief. Soon, his mate was a mound of snow and ice, the beast sitting with it for a while, his head bowed, his breath emerging as great snorting sighs.

A small female edged toward him. In her hand she still held a femur yanked from Misha's remains. It was clogged with chunks of meat and cloth. She held it up to him and gave a series of small barks, at which the big beast stooped and took several delicate sniffs.

His brain processed the scent, turned it into a reasoning that was primal and powerful. It gave a nod of its head, understanding and accord fused in an instant. The female bowed and took the femur to her breast, cradling it as she would an infant.

The chieftain's anguish came with unfettered images.

They were memories of when the clan had migrated from Eastern Asia.

Many perished from famine and exhaustion, and those who fell were consumed to support the others, to perpetuate their species. But the eating was not without sorrow. These creatures knew pain and suffering as well as they knew rage, accepting all without recourse.

The Yeti chief identified something on the breeze; an incessant, alien sound that pulled its keen eyes towards the strange shape in which their newfound prey had travelled. It moved towards the Snowcat, its head tilted in concentration, growling with irritation until the source of the crackling hiss presented itself thirty meters from the vehicle.

The marker flag, its pennant dragged horizontal, shivered in the rampant breeze. The Yeti barked to its troop, the others coming to him as he made for the marker.

It saw the second marker - a quarter of a mile away - before reaching the first. In its primitive brain, the strange vibrating sticks were equated with the fresh new food source, a food source that was succulent and tender.

But it also represented something else.

They moved out as one, snapping and snarling, their pace matched only by their lust.

"They should be back by now."

Pleger was old before his time. He worried a lot. About everything. He was no different before The White Wall, but back then, his fears were the product of the kind of neurosis that came with wealth; a man who had made a fortune in the property boom of 2014 and retired at the age of forty-five to a penthouse suite in Federation Tower that he'd bought outright.

Tax-deductible, of course.

These days property didn't boom. It groaned under the weight of impacted ice.

Pleger adjusted his spectacles, their bent, wire frames held together with duct tape and hope. A far cry from Ray Bans and Bentleys with tinted windows.

"You're making me dizzy, Pleger," the man sitting on a big sofa said as he watched. "Sit down, dammit."

Pleger stopped pacing but remained upright, his expression drawn, his skin wan. "Dizzy? That will be the hooch," Pledger said continuing his stroll across the room. "I only hope that they're both alright. It's not a night to be out."

"Petrov is strong," Dmitri said, his pointed finger wavering as though it couldn't be sure where it needed to settle. "Before the White Wall he was a Spetsnaz Commando. He saw action, too. Afghanistan, no less. He eats fear for breakfast and shits it out at midday."

"Yes, yes, we know the stories," Pleger sighed.

That was all Dmitri had left, stories of his friend and his exploits. It was prestige by proxy, the means of the inspirational. Dmitri may have had stature, but his body had been wrecked by homemade hooch. His hip flask spent more time at his lips these days. No-one dared ask what it was he was drinking. All people knew was that he drank lots of it.

"Perhaps sending him with his woman was not the best of ideas?" Pleger breathed.

This time, Dmitri's brow furrowed with anger and he sat forward. It was as shaky a manoeuvre as the pointing finger.

"Misha is stronger than a Western weasel like you," he said, his words as thick as his black and grey beard. "A woman of the Motherland would no sooner shirk her responsibility to her kin as you would to your redundant bank accounts."

"I do not doubt Misha's resolve. Nor her commitment to her family."

But I doubt you, my pickled, pathetic friend, he thought. *I doubt that you have ever been of use to anyone, much less your long-suffering wife. What positive aspects she sees in you is a whimsy that she will probably take to her grave.*

Sonja was a sedate and gentle creature. Even in pregnancy she appeared delicate. Pledger thought of her in the next room, the baby in her belly mere hours from a life of cold and a father who valued little more than the next swig of hooch. It was to be a pitiful existence, but Pleger knew that Sonja would make up for what little Dmitri had to offer.

The flask was disappearing into Dmitri's beard again. The man swallowed, Adam's apple pumping the vile liquor down his throat. He was rewarded with a series of shoulder shivering coughs, culminating in a loud fart.

That stuff is going to kill you faster than The White Wall, Pleger thought.

Such was his hope.

Food may have motivated them, yet so did their rage. It was deep in their psyche, an incessant penetrating fury that drove them onwards, across the desolate landscape, their inner-fire shielding them from the terrible cold.

The Yeti chief paused at the next marker; his huge, snorting breaths billowed like venting steam. His clan waited patiently behind him; twelve hulking, growling shapes, hell-bent on following their leader to the end of the Earth.

The chief raised his muzzle, nostrils flaring as he caught the familiar scent on the wind. His stomach churned with fury. The loss of his mate was the flickering fuse on a keg of powder. For those responsible, time was running out. He bolted west, his troop following moments later. The small female kept pace with him, seeing an opportunity to assert herself as the chief's new mate. He would recognize in her speed and strength. She still held onto the femur, cradling it. Her discovery had brought her to the chieftain's attention and now she was keen to impress.

They saw the lights of the way station within half an hour of finding the first marker. The troop pulled up and scanned ahead, watching the actions of their leader as he crouched and sniffed the air, his eyes penetrating the darkness with ease; espying the shapes in the windows, silhouetted by shimmering lamps.

After a few moments, he grunted, and three males came to him. The chief nodded once, and his scouts edged forward, moving into the best position by which to mount their assault.

Ahead, one figure sparked up a cigarette, oblivious to the violence that was about to emerge from the blizzard.

Sonja snuggled down into her mattress, disturbing the bugs and ticks which shared the heavy furs heaped upon her. The room was yellow-grey, the kerosene lamps flittering like long lost fireflies, the heat muted, but beneath the furs, it equated to a small inferno.

She stroked her swollen belly, her emotions an indeterminate mix of fear and hope. Life as she had known it was in ruins; her career in marketing long gone, like most of her family who had perished in the trek from Minsk to New Moscow. Only Misha remained, giving her strength whenever The White Wall threatened to topple and crush her spirit.

But the child nudging against her ribs and pressing on her bladder was also a symbol that anything was possible. She had Misha. She had Dmitri.

Dmitri the Drunk.

Sonja pushed the hurtful term away from her. Partly because she still yearned for the memory of the man she once knew; the man before the drinking, before his penchant for lashing out when the memories came thick and fast and the hooch ran too quickly in his blood.

Not so impulsive now, though. She liked to think that the pregnancy had put paid to that. It was her shield. From behind it, free from abuse, she was able to remember the man behind the iron flask; the proud man who had watched his two young sisters and mother turned to pulp by a roof so laden with snow it folded like cardboard under a heavy boot. The drink dulled the image, she understood that, and from this understanding the love seeped through the darkness. But it was the kind of love that left a stain rather than a mark these days. Now there was the baby, a little miracle that would know warmth those on Earth had long forgotten.

She was in the process of changing position to ease the discomfort in her lower back when her waters ran free and the first stab of pain began.

Through clenched teeth, Sonja yelled for her sister.

"See anything?" Danil Eltsin said.

At just shy of twenty, the youngster sounded nervous, but he knew that anxiety was as much a part of being alive as breathing.

"I see *snow*. Surprised?" Alexi Putin, his companion said. He was older - in his thirties - but like so many others, his loss could be measured in lifetimes.

Danil's smile was a crooked thing, as though he had borrowed it and was merely trying it on for size.

"So why have *that* ready?"

"That" was the assault rifle Alexi had rested on the sill, its muzzle nudging against the frosted glass with a series of tiny squeaks.

"What are you planning to shoot? Snowflakes?"

"You never know what might come out of the night," Alexi cautioned. "But I'm hoping that it will be Petrov and Misha. Soon."

"And I'm hoping that you don't shoot them!" Danil beamed.

"Like I would do such a thing," Alexi said, turning to look at the youth over his shoulder. " That's a fate worse than The White Wall."

They both laughed, but it was made hollow by the sparse interior. The lamps cast threatening shadows around the apartment walls: the remnants of the last of the International Business Centre towers. Once, they had been opulent, but most of the furniture had become firewood back in the early days of The White Wall. Indeed, there were blackened areas scattered about the building where fires had sought to give warmth to people long gone. Gone, but not quite forgotten.

When Petrov's group had first happened upon these buildings, only Pleger lived in them. The rest of the tenants had left to find other survivors. Instead, they found only the endless blizzard and perished in the snow. Over a period of weeks, Pleger had repatriated some of them back into the Way Station; inside The Store, the frozen apartment three walls away from where Danil now stood.

He tried not to think about it, but his stomach still grumbled. He dragged his mind back to Pleger to stave off a wave of guilt. Danil and the others had found the businessman half-crazed with loneliness and eager to embrace them. Over time, Pleger's amity had turned to tight-lipped tolerance; not helped by Dmitri's antics, of course.

"Do you think Petrov and Misha are-"

"Hush, now!" Alexi said. "I think I hear something."

"It's just the wind," Danil said after a few moments.

"It didn't sound like the wind," Alexi muttered. He could have sworn he'd heard something. Not a howl but a...

Growl?

Yes, a low rumbling sound, like a throat thick with phlegm.

Your imagination is loose, like a child in a playground, you fool, Alexi chided.

That was when something very real punched through the window, smothering him with glass, biting wind and razor-edged claws. The fingers around Alexi's throat tightened, the vice closing, his mouth pulled oval in a silent scream. Bones popped. Blood flowed - from his nose, his ears, and his eyes.

Then the head was airborne, popping from the body like a cork from one of the many bottles of Champagne unleashed in this room in more auspicious times. It struck the ceiling, punching into the tiles and, for a few seconds, hung there like some macabre chandelier, buried to brow in plaster. But gravity reclaimed it and yanked it back to the dulled wooden flooring with a thud. It came to a stop at Danil's feet.

Danil didn't see any of this; he was staring in terror at the thing climbing through the shattered window, a thing that was a mixture of fur and swirling snow.

He bolted for the apartment door, stumbling over Alexi's head. Danil went sprawling, and Alexi bounced off into the shadows, taking his silent scream and blinking eyes with him.

The Yeti came to Danil, crossing ground with ease. By the time the youth had flipped himself onto his back, the mountainous shape was standing over him.

He was screaming before the claws sank into his abdomen, the talons puncturing soft tissue and delicate organs; four taut, wriggling worms working their way into him until they found his spine, hooked around the corrugated structure and snapped it at the lumbar region.

By the time the beast ripped the column from his gaping gut, Danil may not have been screaming, but he *was* still alive. Paralyzed. Petrified. The youth was nothing more than a spectator to his own demise as other creatures forced their way into the room and, one by one helped themselves to him.

"Some alcohol is not meant for burning," Dmitri said, taking another snort of hooch. Again, the coughs followed.

"So, you think? Why do you use that stuff?"

"You nag like a woman," Dmitri said, wiping his mouth with the back of a gloved hand.

"The truth tastes worse than the gut-rot you're supping, I suspect," Pleger said.

"The truth?" Dmitri snapped. "What would you know of it?"

"Your wife needs a man, not a drunk who hides in a stupor."

"We all hide behind something," Dmitri said, his voice harsh. "You used to hide behind money. Now, you have no other value than keeping fleas off me." He chuckled.

"I gave you all shelter when you had nothing," Pleger reminded him. "I gave *you* a chance to live. To have a child."

"You gave us nothing that we could not have taken."

Pleger knew this to be true. The group had come to him armed and capable. But unlike Dmitri, Petrov was a noble man, one with honour and strength of character. He even understood the need for The Store. After a while, at least.

Dmitri, on the other hand, brought only Sonja. Dear, sweet Sonja, with her gentleness and wit; a sharp contrast to her brutish spouse.

"Sometimes we don't know what we have until it is lost to us," Pleger said.

"Shit house philosophy," Dmitri sneered. "We both know what you hold dear to your heart, these days."

"I don't know what you mean." Pleger could feel his face flush, his cheeks at least welcoming the heat even if his heart did not.

"You value time with my Sonja," said Dmitri. His bottom lip appeared to have stopped working, the hooch blurring his words. "I see the way you look at her, Pleger. I've seen the way you leer at *my* woman."

"You notice my actions more than you notice hers," Pleger said sharply, confident that Dmitri was too drunk to stand. "Difficult to see through the curtain of self-pity you've pulled around yourself."

"Shut your mouth, weasel." Though tethered by the hooch, Dmitri's words still came as savage entities. Spittle created white strings in his beard. He made to stand, but his legs would not allow it. Instead, he leaned forward.

"Sonja would no sooner lie with you than a stray mongrel."

"Then that shows how little you know her," Pleger said. It was a moment of madness; a little lie, designed to repel the hurt back onto the thug on the sofa.

It was just one night. Sonja had cried herself to sleep, huddled up to Pleger after Dmitri had swapped physical blows for harsh words, leaving his wife sobbing with despair. Pleger was there just to hold her and give comfort, stroking her hair and filling her ear with comforting words. It was always to be an exquisite, private memory, but now it was out in the open, having to take its chances just like the rest of them.

"Bastard!" Dmitri yelled.

Just as Pleger had underestimated the power of his half-truth, so it was with the effect of the hooch and its ability to stay the big man's ability to react. Dmitri was off the sofa and upon him in seconds, the older man reeling as several heavy blows landed about his face and shoulders.

He fell onto his back, a short cry escaping lips that had begun to swell. Gazing up at Dmitri, Pleger could see the way the shambolic figure swayed, thinking it was a miracle Dmitri did not fall. But it was a fleeting thought, ripped away by the hatred in his attacker's eyes.

A terrible shriek filled the air, but it did not belong to Pleger.

"*Sonja!*" Pleger cried. "*Dmitri!* Your wife needs you!"

"That may well be," Dmitri said flatly. "But some things cannot be disturbed." Reaching into the folds of his overcoat, Dmitri brought out a pistol and took aim at Pleger's chest.

"Don't be a fool," Pleger said, fear bubbling through him. He hadn't known the stupid fuck possessed a gun. "Dmitri, don't be hasty. We can make this right."

"I intend to," Dmitri grinned.

"For Christ's sake, will someone help me?" Sonja screamed, her hands clutching her belly.

The mattress was saturated with yellowed liquor, the contractions now vicious spasms. In the lull between knife-slicing agony and pulsing discomfort, Sonja was afraid. She couldn't do this alone. She needed Misha. She needed *anybody.*

"Will someone please come?"

She could hear nothing but the howling wind bombarding the windows. *Men,* she thought sourly. *They're never interested once the grunting is over.*

Another contraction came. Just before the pain took her breath away, she heard a crash followed by shouting from the next apartment.

"Dmitri?"

But not even the pain from her contractions could hide the next sound.

A single gunshot.

Federation Tower rose from the ice like a monolith. The Yeti clan made for it, blood on their tongues and the nagging scent in their splayed nostrils.

They had covered the two hundred meters separating the Way Station and the tower in a minute, their chief and his surrogate mate leading the way. The clan was confident now; undeterred by any potential dangers from their newfound prey.

Yes, the chief was more than aware that these creatures could fight. But their strength lay in their fire-sticks, and once deprived of them, the creatures who had robbed him of his mate were puny things, a food source and nothing more.

Over the gale came a shrill cry; its urgency galvanized the chieftain. He knew the cry and its location.

Another sound reached him. A dull popping noise that should have instilled fear, yet only served to induce further rage: a gunshot muted by concrete and glass.

His brown eyes settled upon a window on the second floor and he made for it. Several metres before reaching the tower's ground floor, the great beast launched toward the source of the dull cries: the room beyond. The female followed.

The rest of his clan stood motionless, waiting for instruction, white shadows in the swirling snow.

They knew their place in such things.

Through vision blurred with pain, Sonja saw Dmitri's lumbering form enter the room and reached out to him.

"Oh, my Dmitri," she winced. "The baby is coming. I need you-"

"You need to answer a question," Dmitri growled drunkenly. "Did you fuck the businessman?"

The question was lost to her. What he was saying did not make sense.

"Where is Misha?" she groaned. "Are they not back?"

"Did you fuck the businessman?" This time Dmitri's voice was loud. It was her husband of old, the man with a hardened heart and harder fists.

"Help me, husband!" she cried. "The pain is-"

Dmitri saw nothing of Sonja's agony. The world was receding. He was consumed with his own grief, his perceived sense of loss.

"Your lover is now fodder," he muttered. "Meat for The Store. I think I shall keep him for my own belly."

The gun came up just as the window exploded and the room filled with a buzz-saw snarl.

The Yeti chieftain bowled into him, the pistol shot loud in the small room. The beast hefted Dmitri into the air by his throat, smashing him against the wall, shattering his face with a single blow from its huge fist.

Dmitri the Drunk's body slid down the wall, leaving a vertical crimson smear in its wake.

The wind gusted into the room, the snow pattering against the meagre furnishings. Yet there was stillness in the air.

The Yeti female stood over Sonja with a puzzled expression. The chieftain went to her, looked down at the still form lying before them. He reached down a large paw, tentatively touching a torn and bloody patch in Sonja's left breast; a patch where Dmitri's discharged bullet had accidentally struck her, killing her outright. It may have been fate's caress - Sonja's husband had always meant to take her life from the moment Pleger inferred their probable tryst.

The female Yeti moved past her chief. She sniffed the femur in her furry fist and then did the same with Sonja's exposed, bloated belly.

The chief watched her intently as she placed an ear to Sonja's abdomen. She pulled upright and extended a wicked looking talon, which she dragged through the dead woman's skin, terminating just above the sacrum.

As the muscle and fat parted, and the blood began to flow, the female reached in and pulled the baby free, the umbilicus spooling like thick, electrical cable. She severed the cord with two bites, offering the child to her leader.

As the baby gave its first sound to the world, the chief took it and wrapped it in his fur, the body heat immediate and reassuring - to both Yeti and human child.

The Yeti chief felt whole again.

Petrov had not only killed its mate, he had also killed the unborn child in her belly. It was this scent of new life that had been strong in the creature's nostrils. Misha's femur had reeked of it, a beacon guiding the beast toward a simple hope.

Indeed, now that the human child was snuggled up against him, the chief gleaned comfort that all was well. Balance was restored.

The female gave out a small bark and the chief stood, watching her pensively. After a moment, he pulled the crying child from him and handed its tiny, shivering body to her. The female opened a flap of skin in her abdomen; the pouch designed for their own kind, but for now, kinship was as blurred as the blizzard blighted landscape. The baby was tucked inside, safe from the chilled winds that would try to claim it.

The chief went to the window and called his clan to him. They would make a home here in this place. It offered shelter from the hostile world outside, and within these walls, they would build a life. With his new mate and child following, the chieftain left the room to the clan now climbing through the window. They would soon get to know the faceless human on the floor.

But for the chief, the time for eating had passed. Now it was a time for family.

Life was not just about food, after all.

Richard Of Cork

Phil Sloman

My old man once told me a story about the rain. He used to be a farmer. Dairy farm. It wasn't a big farm. Herd of maybe fifty beasts, but it was enough to make a living once you added in the European subsidies and a bit of cash in hand stuff here and there.

Anyway, the rain…

He told me that he had this bloke come out one day to fix his tractor. Had to do it on the farm as the bugger wouldn't start and there was no way my father was going to pay to have it towed all the way to the garage. This bloke; let's call him Seamus. This bloke looks at the sky, which was practically apocalyptic from the way my Da told the story and suggests he should come back another day when the weather's a bit better.

"Nonsense", says my Da. "You've got a good couple of hours before that lot hits us."

Seamus did not look convinced.

"Tell you what," says my Da, "I'll double your pay if you get a drop of rain on you before you're done. But you'll have to work as fast as you had planned. No slacking off to cheat me."

Seamus's ears prick up at this.

"And," continued Da, "if you remain dry, how's about you throw in the labour for free?"

Now Seamus has a ponder, then looks back up at the sky. By this point, he is convinced that the heavens are going to open and the whole of the area will be submerged in a flood well before he's even opened his toolbox.

"Deal," he says shaking my Da's hand, thinking this will be the easiest money he's ever made. "But as soon as that sky starts leaking, I'm off home to come back and finish another day. On double pay."

"Deal it is," says my Da, and one hell of a cocksure smile springs up across his face.

Now, Seamus should have taken note of that because Da was a miserable old bastard who hardly ever smiled. In fact, the only time he ever smiled was when money was involved. And especially when he was confident he was going to save himself a penny or two.

So, Seamus begins bashing and crashing away at that old heap of a tractor, accompanied by the requisite amount of swearing you would expect from a bloke in the motor vehicular profession faced with an engine mainly held together with spit, string and prayers. And every so often he would look up to the sky, waiting for the merest hint of moisture to escape those clouds.

It was only when the last spark plug had been refitted and the engine turned, accompanied by a pollution-filled spurt of black smoke firing from the stack, and only when they had both agreed that the tractor was in fact fixed and that Seamus was as dry as the sands of the Sahara, it was only then when the sky gave way.

"You're a crafty bastard, Donal McGuire," said Seamus as the rain matted his thick brown hair to his grubby, grease-streaked forehead. "I don't know how you did that, but when I find out there'll be hell to pay."

And my old Da just stood there laughing as he waved poor Seamus off, tapping the side of his nose in the way of those who want to keep a secret yet want to brag about their own superiority.

"Do you want to know the trick of it, son?" That was what he asked me when he told me the story. Of course, I did.

I was twelve-years-old and in awe of my old man. I wanted to know how he did the magic.

So, he bent down until his mouth was level with my ear and whispered the following words to me.

"BBC Weather Report."

And that was about the last time I remember my father smiling… seeing as he was dead within the week.

You can smell the approaching change when the rains are due. The air develops a deep earthy scent, like moss and peat bogs all rolled into one. You can almost taste the imminent downpour; drink up the purity of the deluge before it hits.

I bloody love the rains.

They cleanse both body and soul. Washing away the detritus from the streets and the fields alike until everything is refreshed. They are God's way of bringing in the new - all the way back to Noah and his Ark.

It's the rainbows that scare the crap out of me.

My father was found at the bottom of a valley when he died, underneath a rock outcropping. The grass was still wet and the earth muddy with puddles. The sun was poking through the dirty rolls of cloud, with a shard of light picking out the tattered remains of his corpse. It was Old Man Ned what found him, and he was loathing to tell of what he found that day without the courage of at least three pints of ale in him and the promise of a fourth on its way. Ned had been out walking his dogs, as was his wont, three big old wolfhounds with shaggy grey coats and long gangly legs. If you believe what they say about dogs and their resemblance to their owners, then it was never truer than for Ned and those pets of his. Although they were more like family to him than beasts.

Ned said it was my Da's face which haunted him the most from that day.

He said it wasn't natural for a mouth to gape quite so wide, nor for a neck to be set at such an angle as it was.

The police were called in, as you would expect, and they proceeded to then invite the coroner along to pay a visit. Suspicion had fallen to Seamus at first.

He'd been mouthing off to anyone and everyone who would listen about how my Da had tricked him out of an honest day's work and how he was going to have his revenge. But he had a solid alibi. Working on the local chief inspector's car at the time of death, so there was no better proof of innocence than that. In the end it was settled as death by natural causes. A slip from that rocky outcrop which towered over him. An unfortunate accident, yet an accident all the same.

What the police won't tell you - but Ned will - is about the footprints.

He told me about them at the wake.

A few whiskies, the worse for wear, it was something he should never have mentioned to a young lad like me. And he knew that because I saw him glance up at Ma as he spoke while our neighbour, Tommy Dawson, comforted her a little *too* enthusiastically.

"All around the body, Richard lad," Old Ned said to me, sketching out the scene with a sweep of his arm, "all around the body were these little footprints in the mud. No bigger than your hand, lad. No bigger than that. And here's the thing, lad. Here's the thing. There was no path they had taken to get there. Not like a rabbit where you can see the route from the warren where the grass is laid flat and the earth bare. No, this was more like that of a crow or a raven where the markings on the ground start from nowhere and vanish as quickly. Pay heed to me, lad, these were dark forces which killed your Da and make no mistake about it."

Now I dreamt long and hard about those footprints that evening. My young mind conjured up images of what could have made them and where they had come from. The juvenile mind is a fertile place and when a seed is planted it will grow unabated right up until the truth of the matter is resolved. And it was that seed which led me out the next morning to crawl around on my hands and knees beneath the outcropping where my father supposedly fell to his untimely demise.

I was there for at least an hour, pawing over every blade of grass and each exposed expanse of dirt, looking for the teeny tiny footprints Old Man Ned had sworn he'd seen. For most of that time, I wept as the dirt got under my fingernails and the grass-stained the knees of my jeans. Futile isn't a word I knew back then, but it is the most apt and appropriate word to use now. Futile. Absolutely futile. All the ground had been trampled by the police and Ned's dogs and every other person or creature who had passed by since the day of the tragedy. I clawed at the turf, pulling vast clumps of it from the ground, slinging sod after sod over my shoulder in a vain attempt to wrench the promised footprints from the very earth itself. If anyone had seen me then, they would have thought me mad as a box of frogs and put their arm around my shoulders and led me away. Fortune favours the mad sometimes, though.

Without the drunken insanity of Old Man Ned and my own obsession, I would never have found the buckle which I have in front of me today.

I've fought fifteen Leprechauns to date in the hunt for my father's killer. Fifteen of the little bastards. I cannot walk past a packet of Lucky Charms without feeling a build-up of rage and adrenalin coursing through my veins.

Now everyone has this impression of Leprechauns being cheeky, ginger-haired, green-suited, mischievous tykes whose only desire is to protect their treasure hoards from the likes of you and I. "Stay away from me gold", "Begorrah." And all that other racist crap. People believe this about Leprechauns in much the same way everyone thinks Santa is a jolly, old fella. He's not. Trust me. Leprechauns are vicious little mercenaries eager to dish out a bit of punishment and retribution for a fee.

I met my first Leprechaun the day after my eighteenth birthday.

I killed my first one shortly after.

There had been a handsome celebration the night of my birthday, down at the local. I didn't have to put my hand in my pocket once. If you asked me how much I had to drink, I would tell you a number, but hand on heart, I have no idea. I lost track somewhere after five or six pints - and probably had the same again. When I woke up the next morning, my head felt like it had been hit by the hind legs of a donkey and then trampled on some more once I'd made acquaintance with the ground.

I was lying in a field somewhere to the West of my old Da's farm, except now it was Ma's and, by default, Tommy's, having taken his comforting at the wake a stage or three further.

It was the rain what woke me up. I think if there hadn't been that passing shower, then I could have happily lain there for another day and a half without moving. Even then, it took me a full hour before I was in any fit state to do anything. So, I lay there getting wetter and wetter, but not really caring too much as is often the way when you are young.

And that's when it happened.

The most miraculous thing I'd ever seen to that point, with me lying on my arse in the rain and muck, stinking of stale booze. That was when the rainbow appeared.

Now, the rational among you will listen to what I must tell you next and you will say bollocks and call me out with all kinds of fucking scientific reasons as to why that's not possible. Well, to you, I say go fuck yourself. I grew up in the land of the faerie folk and giants; a land where magic runs through the soil and the rocks and the trees. You want to challenge me with your science, then go for it, but don't be surprised if you're nursing a shiner the next morning and calling for your mother. Just remember this, anything's possible if you believe in it hard enough.

Now ask yourself this; have you ever seen a rainbow close? I mean, proper close. So close you could reach out and touch it. Watch as those colours skittered across your fingertips, sending a tickle of electricity along the length of your arm.

I have.

That morning was the first time for me. Steam rose up where the multi-coloured light kissed the ground, the air smelling of fresh cut grass and candy floss on a warm summer's day, entwined with promises of love, life and laughter.

Here's the thing, though. Promises are made to be broken.

I don't think he saw me at first, but I saw him. A twisted withered creature skulking from the rainbow's confines, sniffing the air as it emerged into daylight, its skin grey and membranous. Its skull was birdlike, rather than the ginger-haired head of fiction, narrow and elongated to a point. Dirty strands of spider's web passed for hair, plastered across the ash-coloured scalp, so as to be almost indistinguishable. Its chest was thin, the ribcage accentuated, the body of a cadaver, yet there was a raw power exuding from the creature. The only clothing it wore was a pair of tattered black trousers held up by a stout leather belt and gold buckle. I suspect it would have passed me by had the wind been blowing in another direction.

"Gold," he croaked. "I smell gold."

His nostrils twitched, his face angling towards the sky. Small, subtle shifts of his head, from left to right, homed in on the scent he had caught. It was only when he turned to fully face me that I realised he had no eyes.

Even so, he was on me before I knew it, crossing the ground between us at an alarming speed. Fingernails sharp as daggers raked at my clothing, shredding the fabric, drawing blood from my arms, my stomach and my thighs. And then he stopped.

"Where did you get it? Where? Where?"

Poison ran through his words, years of anger and hatred boiling over. I didn't know why he didn't kill me there and then at the time, assuming it was simply morbid curiosity which saved my life. I realised differently soon after.

"Where?"

"Ned," I stuttered. "Old Man Ned. He gave it to me."

And I couldn't say any different for that was the truth. Or near enough. It was Ned who had made me go scrabbling around in the earth all those years before, hunting for clues. It was Ned who had filled my mind full of hope and intrigue. And it was Ned's name which sprang to mind now as the Leprechaun straddled me with that piece of gold buckle hanging from a chain around my neck, exposed to the sun and the sky.

"You can have it. It's yours..." And then a thought occurred to me. "But I want answers in return."

"Answers?" The creature cocked its head to one side. "And who's to say that I shall give you any answers. Why shouldn't I just take this and your head whilst I am at it?"

"Because..."

And I stopped as a moment of clarity hit me.

"You *can't* do it, can you? You can't kill me. Or hurt me. Or do anything else for that matter. Not now you know what I have."

If it had lips, then I swear they would have curled back in a sneer at that point.

"Feck off."

"So, it's true," I said.

"I said, feck off. Filthy, human scum."

"Hah!" I jumped up, pitching the Leprechaun into the dirt. It flipped up onto its feet, claws drawn, ready to pounce. Except it didn't pounce. It stood still, considering me, wondering what to do with the pale mound of meat provoking it.

"What is it you think you know, human?"

"Well, for one thing, I think you can't touch me now that I have this." I held up the buckle to emphasise my point. "I think this protects me from you."

"Is that right?"

"Yes," I continued, "and I also think it means that I can hurt you."

There was a twitch to its eye, a half-seen quiver of confirmation.

"Perhaps that's true and perhaps it's not. But then again, perhaps there are ways around the old laws if you know how to bend them just so."

I ignored his warning, a surge of adrenaline flowing through me, pushing the pain from my brain, but not the stupidity and bravado. "I command you to tell me what happened to my father!"

There was a caw from the creature which I took to be laughter.

"And why would I do that?"

I held the gold up, letting it swing on its chain, glinting as it caught the sun.

A hiss this time.

"And who would your father be?"

"Donal McGuire. He died near here over five years ago. This was on the ground where they found him."

"Was it now? Interesting."

If I knew what I know about Leprechauns nowadays, then I would have realised he was simply stalling me, waiting for his cards to come into play. I was right that he couldn't hurt me. Not directly. Not now that he knew I had the buckle. You see, knowledge is a powerful thing. Knowledge and belief. If a Leprechaun believes there is nothing to stop them from killing a human, then they'll be able to kill them, even if there is protection on the body. It is only when they know they are compelled to obey you that they must stop. It's the same with Vampires and crosses, but that's another story entirely.

"I'll tell you what happened if you promise to let me go."

The younger me was an idiot. A man prone to agree to stupid things like that. I know better now.

"Good," said the Leprechaun as the yes passed my lips. "Very good indeed."

Behind me, the sky was darkening.

"Your father was killed on a contract."

My face creased, showing I had no idea what he meant.

"It's like this," he continued. "You humans have your petty squabbles. Things where you want revenge on someone. Either over women or money or perceived slights." The last word hissed from his mouth. "Humans come to us for solutions to your problems. Final solutions. Solutions which won't come back to haunt them. Solutions which give them complete credibility when the finger of suspicion is pointed their way. Solutions we provide for a fee."

If I had turned around at that point, I might have saved myself some hurt. Instead I focused on one thing.

Seamus! The thought and its confirmation were in my head as one, but I needed to hear it from the creature's mouth.

"Was it Seamus? Was it?"

"Oh, I would tell you, but our bargain is done. I told you what happened to your father. He died, boy. He died, so someone could have what they wanted."

"I command you to..."

But I couldn't get my words out. Claws, beaks and feathers tangled in my hair and the torn clothing I wore as I was blindsided from above. A present from my newfound friend. The last sight I had of the Leprechaun was of its body retreating into the streaks of coloured light as a murder of crows battered into me.

There are ways around the old laws if you know how to bend them.

I returned home bloodied and battered that day, yet wiser to a degree.

Over the coming years, I learnt lots about the myth of the Leprechaun and the reality. For instance, you can't kill one by forcing a four-leafed clover down its throat or by attacking it with iron unless you've made it into a sword, and even then, steel is better.

Neither can you wish them out of existence or command them to commit suicide when you have them under your power. No. None of those ways. And you know who came up with those notions. That's right. The bloody Leprechauns. The first one I tried to stuff a four-leafed clover down its throat was more in danger of choking to death from laughter than anything else.

The one thing the myths and legends have right is the rainbows. The trick is in knowing where they'll appear.

Now, the simpleton will blithely chase off into the middle distance when they see that beautiful arc crowning the sky in a bid to get to its point of origin before it fades away. And that is why most folk have never found the end of a rainbow. Idiots. Now, the knack comes from glancing out the side of your eye and following that. You'll look like a gormless fool as you gallop along like a cross between a crab and a championship mare, but it's worth it. And after a few attempts, you get quite adept until you can move through the surrounding bracken and foliage without tripping and stumbling in your efforts.

But you also must follow your nose. You must sniff out that smell of candy floss and cut grass I told you about. Only then do you have a chance at finding it. If you're too late, all you'll find is a flattened ring of grass. However, if you time it just right, then you'd better be prepared for all Hell to break loose. That is if you don't have something to even up the odds.

I got lucky with that first Leprechaun - if walking home with your clothes in ribbons and having lost a half pint of blood is considered lucky. Most will either kill you on the spot or vanish before you get a chance to catch them. For me, it often became the latter.

The one thing I'd learnt from my first encounter was to have the buckle on display for the world to see.

Or the Leprechaun at least. Be bold about it. Be proud. Just don't forget to do it, otherwise your throat will be slit before you know it.

Now, where you get that specific type of gold artefact from, that's your problem.

Even so, it still took me about ten attempts before I finally was able to sneak up on one of the little tykes. This was a good six months or so after my first encounter.

It had been a miserable shit of a day. One of those where you can feel the damp running through your bones and everything smells of soil and moss. Ma and Tommy were off down the local pub where they spent most of their time and most of our cash. Still, it gave me a chance to wait out the storm. See, like my old Da, I'd become a bit of a regular listener to the old BBC Weather Service and I knew that if I sat patient for an hour or so that there sun was going to come out and put its old hat on once again. And that's when I would go out to play.

The rainbow was in full bloom when I came across the creature. My luck this time was that it was hungry. The broken, bloodied body of a leveret was hanging from its mouth as it crunched and slurped at the carcass. Dark smears ran across the Leprechaun's chest where it had wiped its claws clean before adjusting its grip to tear out another lump of flesh. If it weren't for that, I fancy I would not have captured this one. Or not that day at any rate.

"Hey!" I shouted. The creature's mistake was to look in my direction. I held the buckle out ahead of me like a priest presenting a crucifix. "Hey!" I shouted again. "Stay where you are!"

The Leprechaun hissed and threw the remains of its lunch in my direction. Blood and guts splattered the front of my clothing, and a small fleck of flesh clung to my cheek. I ignored it all.

"And what do we have here?" There was a snarl to its words. "A main course, perhaps?"

"I've come to find out the truth." I was a pretentious little shit at times.

"Is that so? And just what truth would that be? I have many truths I can tell you… for a price."

"I want to know who killed my father."

The Leprechaun halted in its response, taking a moment before speaking.

"Oh, so it's you. We've heard all about you. My friend always wondered how you fared with his crows. I guess we know the answer to that now, though."

"Shut up!"

The Leprechaun's face split into what could only be taken for a smile, bowing as it did so. As I've said before, I could be an idiot at times.

"Oh fuck," I said. "You can speak."

"Speak or shut up. I wish you'd make up your mind. Now, remind me what you want to know so that I can be on my way. I have business to take care of and none of it involves you. For now."

"I just need to know the truth. I need to hear it from your lips. I need you to tell me it was Seamus who ordered the killing of my father."

The grin was all I needed from the creature. A sly smirk. And the words I wanted to hear.

And Seamus was dead and buried that evening on his way back from the pub. No one any the wiser with his body still resting at the bottom of that bog to this day.

It should have ended there, but it didn't.

So, here's the rub, officer, though I think you've guessed most of it already. But do make sure you get everything in your wee notebook. Every detail. I'd hate for you to have the wrong impression of me.

You see, I had it wrong from the off. It was never Seamus.

Sure, that Leprechaun said it was Seamus what put in the order. I heard it from its very mouth. *Seamus did it. Seamus was the one what asked for your Da to be killed.* I was still young and stupid even with all I *thought* I had learned. If you tell one of the wee folk to tell you something, they'll sure as Hell tell you it.

Tell me it was Seamus who ordered the killing of my father.

Idiot.

I might as well have asked it to tell me my name was Tracy and that I had eighteen toes on each foot for it would have rightly done so. Should have bought myself a parrot and saved myself the hardship. And poor Seamus at that. He is the one thing I regret in all this business, beyond the death of my father. If I'd used my brain instead of my heart, then he'd still be out there fixing motors and complaining about getting duped every now and again.

Anyway, I told you I fought fifteen Leprechauns to date. Well, it took me that many before I finally had the truth of the matter. And some of them didn't make it back over that multi-coloured bridge. It's true a few of them felt the strength of my grip around their scrawny grey throats and maybe I got a bit carried away. It's almost too easy when they can't fight back, but revenge has a way of making you slightly less than human; a way of skewing your moral compass to make the unpalatable that little bit easier. Especially when it's backed up with the right sort of justification. You see, I wasn't ever certain I would find the Leprechaun which did for me Da. The one who had the crows peck out his eyes. No, you're right, that bit was never mentioned in the police report. At least not the ones that I have seen. That's why we had to have a closed casket for him. No one could have lived with looking at that face mutilated as it was. So, I took a bit of my anger and aggression out on them once I knew what I was doing. And if a few didn't make it back, then so be it. But you get a taste for it, officer. A real taste.

The one who told me about Seamus was the first.

You see, he came back to gloat. To lord it over me that I had innocent blood on my hands. How it was never Seamus what ordered the killing. Smug little git. I told you they were vicious little mercenaries. Well, they're also vindictive, too. Seems this one had a particularly nasty streak and decided to have some fun with me at poor Seamus' expense. After all, he'd told me there was a price, but I'd not listened. Well, it didn't get to do that to anyone else again.

After that, I went on a bit of a rampage.

Every time it rained, I would be out there waiting for the sun to show.

I even tried to force my own rainbows with a big old halogen torch and a hosepipe, but it never had the same effect.

Even so, there were enough rainbows for me to build up a pile of corpses over time. If you still don't believe me, then you'll find them resting with poor old Seamus. Somehow it seemed appropriate like.

It was the last little bugger I got hold of which showed me the right of it. He recognised the buckle from the off as I held it in front of me.

"That's mine," it says. "Give it to me."

"No," I said.

"I will give you everything you've ever wanted and more."

"Is that right?" I said, having heard those words - or ones like them - over a dozen times before.

And then this one did something different to the others. He looks at me hard - a bit like you're looking at me now, except I can tell he's doing something. I can almost feel him rummaging around inside my skull, looking for a thread to tug on and then he says two words.

"Tommy Dawson."

You understand now, don't you, officer? Those little bits of the jigsaw falling into place? Except I didn't kill Tommy. Not like you think I did. Yes, that's his body lying cold on the ground. But it wasn't my hand what did it. No, I made a bargain with my newfound friend. You see, Tommy has become family over the years, no more so than when he put that ring on Ma's finger. How was I to know he'd cleared the path himself to his own happiness and mother's bed? That Leprechaun? Oh no, he's long dead. He couldn't carry on living now that I knew it was him what carried out the deed, even if he was under orders as it were. No, I choked the life out of that little shit, make no doubt about it. No, I got one of the other miscreants to do my dirty work this time. And I made sure he took the eyes just to even things up.

So, you can lock me up now, officer. I don't care anymore. And I deserve if for poor Seamus at least. You see, I just wanted justice and that's what I found, which is worth more to me than any pot of gold you could imagine. The one thing I would ask is to give me back that there buckle. The one hanging from the chain. You see, I think I've built up a following of the wee folk who would like something nasty to happen to me and that's the only thing which will protect me.

No?

Really?

Well, I have one request which you must grant then. Put me in a cell underground. Lock me up where I cannot see the light of day again. Or the rain. And if a rainbow shows itself as the showers stop and the sun comes clear then whatever you do, don't go hunting for the end of it because once they find you, they'll find me, and that will be the end of…oh fuck, what's that behind you? Don't you see it? Crouching. Scratching itself. No, don't turn around. Don't look at it. Don't–

The Beast Rain

Nathan Robinson

Before the Alsatian dropped from the sky and exploded on the kerbside outside the Colosseum Café, the signing of his divorce papers had been at the forefront of Bruce Whitelaw's mind.

He'd stepped out from Bainbridge & Bainbridge, occupied with perhaps treating himself to a new car now that his half of the settlement had finally come to fruition, when the black and tan German Shepherd dropped down head first and impacted hard with the tarmac in front of him, folding in on itself like a contracting accordion. There was a sickening *thump* which sent a shiver of sweat down his spine, trickling into the hairy crack of his buttocks.

The dog bounced upon impact, its belly split open mid-air and its innards spewed out; an arching wet curve of entrails. The second *thump* was followed by a splattering sound.

The Colosseum Café was only two storeys, the first floor presumably a flat or storage space for the Café below. Could the dog have jumped from a balcony or an open window from up there? The severity of the impact indicated that the Alsatian must have fallen from higher than this building. The Colosseum Café didn't have such heights.

With eyes squinting, Bruce Whitelaw looked up, searching the skies for a helicopter, an aeroplane or even a hot air balloon which could provide some clue as to where the dog had originated from.

The sky was free from any kind of aircraft and all he could see were dark clouds pulsating slowly above him.

And dots.

Hundreds of dots.

Another heavy *thump* from behind him intersected with the brittle smash of glass. Bruce spun around to see what else had been thrown from the sky, turning in time to jump back and dodge another canine body. It was one of those small, cute ones, a lapdog that was more annoying than endearing. Bruce didn't get the chance to identify the breed as it exploded and practically turned inside out almost as soon as he first saw it.

Bruce instinctively hopped to the left, tripping over the kerb like a drunkard as a cat meowed past at the speed of sound, just inches from his right shoulder. The white Persian didn't explode as he'd witnessed the first two dogs do, but rather liquefied on impact; as if someone had thrown a bucket of blood at its feet. The panicked "meow" of the plummeting cat was cut short with the sound of flesh being rearranged into a jigsaw puzzle of furred gore. The feline's innards ejaculated from its fur in an exploding hot red puddle that spattered in every direction. The cat's white hair was blood-soaked almost instantly. Following his unsteady stumble down the kerb edge, Bruce recoiled from the sudden mess, tripped and fell backwards, the advancing wash of gore splattering his trousers.

"What in God's fuck is going on?" Bruce shrieked out loud but to no-one. He looked past the chunks of bloody Persian and down the street. It was a Wednesday afternoon. Just a few other people were milling about in this quieter part of town. Bruce looked to them for connection, for affirmation that it was all in his own head and that somehow, he was dreaming. The other pedestrians had also stopped in their tracks in horror as another Alsatian crashed down and exploded in front of them. Bruce wasn't going mad. Not even close.

A suited businessman stood a few lampposts further along. In the madness that had erupted around him, Bruce clung to some reality by recognising his suit as one that he too owned; it was from Next and was hanging in his wardrobe at home, his safe, sane home. Business Suit clutched a Sainsbury's sandwich packet in his hand. Bruce watched him as the mess of the dead cat soaked into his trousers. He stood frozen to the spot, mouth gaping at the sight of the smashed Alsatian. The man also looked up to the sky as Bruce had, searching for an aeroplane, perhaps with some madman throwing out these unfortunate animals, sans parachute. He caught Bruce's eye and they shared a '*whattheactualfuck*' look.

The man's smile faltered before disappearing in a black blur as, what looked like a Rottweiler hurtled down from the sky directly above where the man stood, folding over and around him, both man and dog colliding together in an eruption of fur, bone, flesh and 65% polyester suit. The Rottweiler passed through the gentleman, both bodies splitting apart, their blood curdling into one ungodly soup that cascaded far and wide. The suited corpse crumpled. His sandwich rolled and settled into the emerging man/dog blood puddle.

Then it started raining kittens.

After scores of punctured squeaks, the mewling from the falling kittens ended with wet 'pops' as they met the hard, unforgiving ground. Bruce watched in disbelief as black, white, ginger and tortoiseshell bodies bounced off roofs and car bonnets onto the pavement, causing an array of twitching fur bundles, devoid of all trace of any former cuteness.

As the storm of fur intensified, dogs of various shapes and sizes fell along with all manner of felines from the turbulent skies above. Amongst the shower of cats and dogs, other small furry creatures joined the freakish downpour; rats, hamsters, rabbits and anything else cute and furry, all adding to the quickly thickening carpet of the deceased and dying.

Something heavy scraped past his shoulder and landed on his splayed hand. He recoiled, jarring his back in the process as he jerked and rolled away. This woke him. The situation was unreal - nightmarish - yet it was happening all around him.

Bruce sank a fingernail into the back of his thumb, digging deep into the flesh until it threatened to break the skin and hurt the bone beneath. This failed to rouse him from any nightmare. The madness continued. Pets and wild animals carried on their strange descent from the skies above, piling up and filling the streets with corpse after corpse.

A fox.

A deer.

A damned badger!

Fish now fell, writhing in the spilt guts, gulping in the warm blood in their last desperate attempts to live a little longer.

It was too much. This was *real*. This was *happening*. And if he didn't move soon, he'd be injured by falling animal debris.

Bruce crawled forward. His hand hurt. He examined it. Blood was seeping out from a deep scratch. The bodies kept falling. A scream pierced the air from further down the street, shrill and female. The scream - or any more cries for help from the woman - were not heard again. Deathly silence, apart from the thumping & squelching as the carcasses continued to fall.

Bruce got to his feet, tried to run, tripped and lost balance before staggering to regain it and hopping over the broken antlers of a deer, snaring his trousers.

The jagged tip of the antler tore through the fabric and into his calf beneath.

Bruce shrieked and crashed down, hands grasping at the new pain as his shoulders stiffened, anticipating the impact.

He rolled through the gore and the broken bones of the freshly deceased animals, pricking his back as he slid through the viscera which had started to pool and mingle into one giant puddle of copper that spanned the entire street.

Bruce grasped his leg in an effort to stem his own bleeding. The threat of infection blazed at the forefront of his mind as his animal blood-soaked trousers encompassed the fresh wound.

He seethed as the shrieking, squealing, baying bodies continued raining down around him, fresh fur soaking up blood as soon as they impacted with the deepening gore.

A heavy-laden sow exploded in the middle of the road; a gut bomb that sent football-sized chunks in every direction, followed by an enormous cloud of blood that bloomed upwards before settling, leaving a crimson mist in the air.

Something red, pink, raw and still half alive skidded past Bruce Whitelaw's leg. It had four squat legs and resembled a hairless dog.

Not a dog.

Not a puppy.

It was a piglet.

Aborted abruptly by the collision with earth, it mewled and grunted pathetically as it wriggled around on the ground. Its spine was broken so badly that it looked like it had been folded over backwards.

Bruce gagged, then vomited, bringing up the omelette, beans and coffee he'd had for breakfast, further soiling his trousers.

Half disgusted, half in fear, he kicked at the squirming piglet and continued lashing out with his feet, pushing himself backwards under a bus stop.

Bodies of animals continued to crack down in an ever sickening, further thickening pile of suffering and death. Bruce pulled himself up onto the grotty bench, taking a much-needed deep breath.

Death was everywhere. He couldn't process what he was seeing. Fur and flesh were becoming one. Unidentifiable legs and heads jutted up from the swamp of gore. No one else was around to witness it. Everyone else that he had seen on the street earlier had either fled or succumbed to a falling beast.

It had to be localised. This surely couldn't be a worldwide phenomenon. He needed to escape to safety from this onslaught.

Further along the street, the roof of Cork & Son Hardware exploded as something big crashed into the tiles, sending shrapnel raining down onto the street below.

Larger objects accumulated in the mass above, preparing to fall.

His eyes itched. Bruce wiped at the blood that had started to pool and dry at the corners of his eyes. It wasn't his, but he needed clarity in what he was seeing.

An elephant! He wasn't sure whether it was African or Asian, but he supposed that was irrelevant when it was falling at terminal velocity.

The great, grey beast hit the front of a shop, instantly splitting in two as it sheared through the brickwork and top window of the upstairs flat. Blood fell in a waterfall, sloshing down onto the concrete path below. The back legs of the elephant broke away, falling and crashing onto a parked car already swamped with dead animals, blood squirting up from the joined stumps.

The falling animals were increasing in size and weight. He could just about handle goldfish and pet mice. Small things that would bounce off him if he pulled his jacket up over his head. He needed to move before something moved him.

He pulled his arms from his jacket and pulled it over his head as a kind of impromptu umbrella; as you would in any other heavy storm.

It wouldn't protect him from larger animals, of course, but it would shield him from those smaller than a dog.

Anything bigger and he could only hope it killed him outright and quickly.

From beneath the bus shelter, he ran. Down the street as the cast of 'Animals of Farthing Wood' splattered on the pavement. He made it to an alley between two buildings and sprinted down it in a comedic, slippery skid. Bodies of every type had started to pile up in the gutters. Beyond the alley, he could see the carpark.

He sprinted and jumped over the fallen until he could see his car. The windscreen had been smashed by a still-twitching sheep, the bonnet badly dented. Splashes of blood decorated the bodywork and a wing mirror hung limply by the wires. Aside from these minor destructions, the car looked fine.

Bruce fished for his keys as he ran towards it and clicked the fob. Without any cause for concern, he grabbed the sheep by the wool and yanked it from the bonnet and onto the tarmac.

As he threw open his car door, a shadow loomed above, darkening the sky further. He glanced up and immediately quivered at the sight of the silhouette.

His bowels opened, fouling both the front and back of his leopard-print boxer shorts. Survival instinct took over and he leapt into his car, squelching down into the hot freshness of his own fetid mess.

His final thought wasn't of what sports car he'd buy or of the women he could now date being a free agent with a nice wedge of money in the bank. He thought back to a fact he'd known since school. Something that had stayed with him his entire life. A trivial fact that had been of no use to him whatsoever throughout his thirty-five years, but now decided to flash into his mind.

A blue whale is the largest animal on planet Earth.

The Light That Bleeds From The World

Paul M. Feeney

One day late in December, snow began to fall across the entire world and didn't stop.

At first, it was delightful, if a little unusual, the promise of a rare white Christmas to come everywhere. Children played in it and built snowmen while the schools closed. Adults grumbled but were secretly delighted not to have to traipse into work. It brought people and families together as they were forced to spend more time with each other than they had in a while. The first few days were picturesque and magical. But as it wore on, with no signs of ending, the charm began to fade. Panic started seeping in as shops ran low on supplies. Roads became impassable even to the ploughs that were working night and day. Whole communities were cut off from each other and left to fend weakly for themselves.

They didn't last long.

The ongoing snowfall brought cities to a standstill, burying towns and villages beneath its smothering, muted embrace, and led to the deaths of millions upon millions in the first few months.

And it did not stop.

Oceans rose to drown islands and coastlines. Power stations supplying energy began to fail, and steadily and surely, all the lights went off in the world. The existence mankind had built was soon lost under a soft, thick layer of suffocating white.

And still it did...not...stop.

Eventually, the remnants of civilisation were left to eke out a bare existence in this new landscape, scattered and few. The once magnificent and seemingly limitless cultures of man were gone, left behind. As decades and centuries passed, more and more knowledge would be lost to each generation until only a few thousand souls were left scattered on the now frozen planet. The golden age of man's supremacy was little more than a barely-remembered fairy tale.

Finally, the snowfall slowed, though it never fully ended, and warmth never came back to the world. It seemed that the planet was slowly dying, as though it had become untethered from its orbit and was drifting gently away from the solar system.

As the light of the sun slowly dimmed, as the cold pushed ever further into the core of the planet, a darkness began to creep into every corner of the world. As the shadows grew, so too came something else. An ancient presence, hateful and long-dormant until now.

And hungry. So very, very hungry.

Moving with as much stealth as she could manage, Tamera slipped out of her bed, wrapping a sheet around her shoulders like a cloak, padding softly over to the fire.

It had burned low in the night, allowing the cold to encroach into the cabin instead of holding it at bay against the walls. Built by the labours of herself and her husband, Jerad, their home was a simple roundhouse with the fire at the centre. Constructed from wood culled from trees surrounding them - tall, hardy specimens whose roots and lower trunks lay hidden beneath compacted snow - it was a serviceable abode, if not especially comfortable. But these days, comfort was a luxury lost to the past. And where else could they live? Towns and villages were gone, no doubt crumbled to rubble beneath the snows, and cities were inhospitable, only their tallest buildings rising above the uniform, white covering. Those remnants from a dim and distant past were treacherous places, death-traps of sharp metal, broken glass, and floors which were apt to collapse without warning.

She glanced over at the cot where Edele slept, her daughter's little face turned towards the wall, the rest of her bundled up in blankets.

From behind a tangle of damply-matted blonde hair there issued soft snorts and wheezes, the laboured breathing of her seven-year-old child. Tamera chewed on her lip as her insides twisted with a deeply familiar anxiety. She held her breath as Edele twitched in her sleep, seemingly on the brink of waking, then let it out in shaky silence when the girl remained in slumber. Hopefully, the child would sleep for a while longer. Whether or not it was helping her immune system fight her sickness, it allowed her some measure of rest.

At least, Tamera *hoped* so.

Returning her attention to the fire, she gently placed a log from the small heap sitting beside the fireplace onto the dully glowing embers. Sparks jumped and popped as the wood caught. Tamera watched a thick curl of dark smoke as it wound its way up to the ceiling, ballooning there in a small cloud before forcing its way out of the little smoke-hole. She rubbed her hands together and splayed them towards the fire, then pulled the duvet tighter around herself.

The few bits of wood left on the pile reminded her she needed to venture outside to get more from the bigger store at the side of the house. It was a task she did not relish, but one she had to undertake. But for now, at least, she could spend a few minutes warming herself.

Her eyes dried and stung as she stared into the depths of the growing fire, but she didn't look away. Not for the first time did she wonder how long Jerad was going to be, and whether he'd be successful in securing any medicine for their daughter.

Again, silently, unsteadily, Tamera sighed and waited for her body to heat up.

Using the doorframe, Tamera kicked clumps of snow from her oversized boots before coming back into the house, shouldering the front door open then elbowing it closed, shutting out the inhospitable landscape.

Using both hands to carry the big tin bucket full of chopped wood, she lurched over to the fireplace and dropped it with a relieved sigh. She stood up straight, stretching her lower back, and wiped sweat and hair away from her forehead. Despite the freezing temperatures outside the house, her exertions with the axe had warmed her considerably.

In her cot, Edele twisted and turned, making small mewling sounds that wrapped a tight fist around Tamera's heart but didn't wake.

After gazing at her child for a few moments more, Tamera smoothed her skirts beneath her and dropped to her knees to pile the newly chopped wood beside the fire.

The hearth was blazing now, but it was a constant chore to keep kindled. It had to be fed regularly and could never be allowed to burn too low, much less go out. It was their only source of heat and light, aside from a few candles scattered in various places around the house. Though they still had nights and days, daylight was watery, grey and weak, and the house had no windows to allow much in anyway. It was the same in every household left in the world. Or, at least, Tamera assumed this to be the case; she'd only ever seen the houses she'd grown up in, those of her parents and close family. But it was a tenet instilled in every child from the moment they could understand; fire was essential, fire was life.

Once the bucket was empty, she returned it to its place beside the front door and went to wash her hands in the large basin kept in the kitchen area.

Even though Tamera had never known anything different, she knew their life was harsh.

When she'd been a girl herself, she had dreamed about the ancient world of their ancestors before the snows came.

Her own mother had told her tales, fragments of a lost existence, too fantastical to be real; stories of hot and cold running water on demand, of food in abundance, of fantastical machines which people rode in and flew, of the 'scrapers' which had been homes and workplaces and more. And in those days, the snows had been relegated to remote parts of the planet - mountains and the poles - or was tamed by 'seasons', and for the most part, the world had enjoyed bright, life-giving sunshine, like their own little fire only infinitely larger and more beautiful.

Tamera knew it couldn't have been real, knew these myths must have been made up by long-ago storytellers, exaggerated and distorted as they were handed down from parent to child over hundreds of years. Yet still, her dreams had taken her to these fantastical places, given colourful and magnified life by her imagination. Dreams she would wake from suffering a deep sense of loss and melancholy.

The sound of Edele mumbling in low tones brought Tamera back from her reverie. She got up and went to the girl's side, gently sitting on the edge of the small bed.

Moving with care - as though reaching out to a small, skittish wild animal - Tamera placed her hand on her daughter's forehead, feeling around the side of her neck.

Edele's skin was damp and seemed to burn with an intense heat; as though her own fire blazed within the folds of her flesh. Tamera took her hand away and held it to the base of her own neck in an unconscious gesture of worry and self-comfort, teeth worrying at her lower lip, face pinched in a frown.

Edele had been like this for nearly a week now, and neither of her parents knew what had caused it, nor even what it truly was beyond some intense and tenacious fever.

Despite - or perhaps, in some strange way, *because* of - the harsh environment the last scraps of humanity toiled in, illness seemed to have been left behind with everything else.

No colds, flu, cancers, or dementia; no other serious diseases or maladies. People were born, grew old, then passed away. That wasn't to say no one ever experienced injury or the occasional very mild illness, but if one were careful, they could live a relatively pain-free life. Perhaps it was the hardiness of the perpetual winter; perhaps it toughened people's constitutions and immune systems. Perhaps it was the relative isolation they lived in. Tamera had been part of a tiny community of only six souls until Jerad arrived and they eventually left to start their own family. Or perhaps there was some other explanation. Whatever it was, Tamera certainly could not recall ever seeing anyone suffer in this way, though there were - again - stories passed down from a few generations ago, for it would seem these illnesses had not *long* disappeared from the world and still merited mention.

She placed her hand again on her daughter, gently stroking the girl's skin and whispering wordless sounds in hopes of calming her. And Edele *did* seem to respond, her movements becoming less frantic, slowing into a more restful state. Yet her mumbling did not cease. In fact, it began to take on an odd coherent word. Tamera brushed hair away from Edele's forehead, tried to smooth that wrinkled brow.

"Shhh, my sweet, shhh. It's okay. Everything's okay." The words were spoken without conviction, an empty salve to comfort parent as much as child.

And it was doubtful Edele could hear anyway. Beneath closed eyelids, her eyes darted from side to side. Her mouth moved as rapid whispers escaped from her throat. Slowly, those whispers coalesced into words.

"... no... no... *please*, no... leave us... alone... leave Mama alone... where is Papa... why is... who are you... who *are* you...?"

Tamera's chest ached at the fear she heard in those words, the note of loneliness. What nightmares must her daughter be trapped in to say such things?

Leaning over the frail child, desperate to take her in her arms but afraid of disturbing what rest she might, even now, be getting, Tamera spoke softly and, she hoped, with confidence. "Hush, Edele. Hush, my love. Papa has gone to get something to make you better and he'll be back soon.

There is nothing to fret over. You'll be well soon enough." Again, she felt as though she were saying only what she had to and was trying to convince herself more than her daughter.

And then the girl's eyes opened, staring directly into Tamera's. The brilliant green of the child's eyes so familiar yet in their depths, Tamera detected something which chilled her insides, though she could not put words to what it might be.

"Mama?"

Nearly crying at the clear tone, Tamera replied, "Yes, little one; I'm here."

"Mama, who are they?"

Tamera's brow creased in confusion. Was Edele still lost in delirium? "Who are *who*, my child?"

Finally, the girl's eyes ceased their unblinking hold on Tamera's and looked around the house in confusion, though the panicked fear seemed to have left her. "The shadows, Mama. Who are the shadow-people? I saw them walking through the forest. They said we had to go with them. Is Papa with them? I couldn't see him."

Though she knew the girl was only talking of things she'd seen in dreams - what else *could* it be? - Tamera felt a chill ripple up and down her back. Edele seemed so calm, so sincere, so *lucid*; nothing like the feverish speech she'd been afflicted with the last few days.

Trying to sound light-hearted, Tamera said, "It's nothing, love. It's only the dregs of your nightmares, visions brought on by the illness. Nothing to worry about. Nothing at all."

"No, Mama, it wasn't a dream. They said they're coming and they'll be here soon and we're to go with them. Did Papa send them? Or will they take us to him?" This last was said with such hope it nearly broke Tamera's heart.

Her stomach cramped, and she swallowed back tears of frustration and weariness. She wished she had an answer for Edele, and again she wished Jerad would hurry back. It appeared darkness had crept into the room; perhaps the fire had grown low again, but Tamera had not strength or will to attend it.

She sat on the edge of the bed for a while, staring at her daughter and wondering why the girl's words filled her with such a heavy dread.

The next morning, Tamera ventured out again, this time to collect snow. In lieu of a working plumbing system, their practice was to boil this snow to rid it of impurities, then put the water in one of a handful of large barrels to cool. This supplied them water for both ablutions and cooking. It was a chore they would usually be on top of, but because of Edele's condition and the subsequent absence of Jerad, it had slipped Tamera's mind. As had so much more, even though her husband had only been gone a few days. She'd always thought herself eminently capable, resilient to whatever life might throw at her, but these last few days, she'd felt herself on the verge of coming apart. It was as though she were a badly stitched doll and her seams were fraying.

Tamera clumped through the snow, heading towards the very edge of what she thought of as the woods.

Though they lived deep within what was, essentially, a massive forest - trees and hardy plant-life having reclaimed much of the world in the thousands of years since the fall of man - their efforts in building the cabin had created a small clearing, in the centre of which lay their home.

Close to the house and between the ragged stumps of felled trees, the snow had been trampled and dirtied by them over the years. It was out towards the edge of the clearing where the trees still grew wild and close together, that the snows remained largely untouched and clean. And it was from here they took their supplies.

As Tamera bent to her task, she hummed tunelessly to herself. For the first time since Edele had gotten ill, Tamera was almost able to forget the worries and fears which had plagued her. Almost. They still niggled at the back of her mind, pinching and pecking at the edges of her thoughts. But for the most part, she was able to let go, even if only for a few blessed minutes.

Just as the bucket was nearly full, Tamera paused in her work and looked up, keeping still.

Around her, the forest was almost completely silent, though there was the ever-present background hush of snow shifting in the lightest of breezes; a sound so low and eternal as to be almost inaudible, fading from awareness. Added to that was now the hum of Tamera's pulse, a thin rumble of blood through her ears.

But she thought she'd heard something else. Another sound, one which had pricked her instincts because it had sounded...stealthy? Deliberate?

Instead of holding her breath, she tried to control it, taking shallow sips of cold air. She knelt like that for over a minute, waiting to hear if the noise would repeat. It didn't, though her nerves kept twitching.

At first, she thought it might be Jerad, returning at long last, and her heart momentarily leapt.

But then she chided herself; if it had been him, he wouldn't be making furtive noises or going quiet just as she paused to listen. Perhaps it was an animal of some kind, though they were few and far between these days.

Only the hardiest of specimens were able to survive in these conditions, many evolving and adapting to their unchanging environment. But again, it was unlikely a creature would cease its movements simply because she'd become aware of it.

No... there was something out there, or else her imagination had taken flight on panicked wings. That latter scared her more than anything; though she'd had an active imagination as a child, as an adult Tamera wasn't prone to silly fantasies and didn't frighten easy. The thought that her mind might be cracking beneath the stress of all she was going through was terrifying.

It was the one thing almost guaranteed to lead to disaster in their wild surroundings.

Tamera squinted through the gloom of daylight. It was always thus; ever since she could remember, the divide between night and day had been a thin one. She'd never seen the sun, for it lay hidden behind a permanent covering of iron-dark cloud and had to rely on the old tales to tell her it existed at all. Something clearly did, for the days were marked with a watery, grey light, which was only marginally brighter than the night hours; themselves illuminated after a fashion by the weakly glowing snow. In these two states, shadows and phantoms were apt to caper and flit, abetted by a traitorous mind. It was one reason Tamera preferred to stay indoors as much as possible; it wasn't unknown for the near uniform grey/white - broken only by trees and sporadic other foliage - to drive a person delirious. But she didn't think she was quite there yet.

Nothing seemed to be moving out here. Even further out, where the shadows were darkest and deepest between tightly packed trees, she could discern no movement. But still she couldn't shake the sense she was not alone. Tension coiled slowly within her, a sensation she could almost hear, like the tightening of rope or the creak of twisting branches.

In the end, it was Edele's screams slicing through the chill air which snapped her attention back to reality. Heart thumping painfully, she jumped to her feet - still holding the bucket - and ran as fast as she could back to the cabin, dreading what she might find.

It had just been another nightmare.

Tamera held Edele tight to her chest, feeling the girl's unnatural heat through both sets of clothing; a fierce incandescence stoked by the fever. She rocked her daughter back and forth on the small bed, muttering words in hopes of comforting the child. It didn't seem to have any effect.

Edele was awake, though she barely seemed to know where she was. She babbled, speaking the same words over and over. This terrified Tamera more than anything. The illness she could - just about - deal with. The dipping in and out of sleep. The fever. But seeing her child - her little girl - seemingly bring the horrors of her nightmares into the waking world was almost too much to bear.

She'd come racing - as fast as possible given the snow and her bulky footwear - wide-eyed and shaking with fear at what she might find, only to see Edele sitting up in her cot, staring at nothing and screaming.

Pausing for a moment to catch her breath and make sense of what was happening, she'd been acutely aware of her heart pounding almost painfully inside her chest, as though muscle had somehow been replaced with stone.

She'd rushed over to her daughter, hoping to calm and reassure. In her distress, the sensation of being watched outside had faded, that nebulous suspicion torn to shreds by the far sharper need to protect her child.

That was until the words began to emerge from Edele's shrieking.

"No… no… *no*… they're coming! They're *coming*! Closer! They're so close now. They're nearly here and they want to take us all! They want to take us with them, and they're cold! So cold..."

Swallowing back tears of frustration and panicked alarm, Tamera felt a chill ripple up her back. No longer could she simply dismiss Edele's statements as mere nightmare, having experienced *something* herself outside only minutes previous. Yet what it all meant, she could not say. She still harboured the terrifying possibility her mind was breaking under the strain of dealing with a sick child alone, perhaps taking on some of her child's dream imagery in twisted sympathy.

Edele's voice dropped to a fearful whisper. "They keep saying they want to take us away. I thought it might be to a nice place, and Papa might be there waiting for us. But it's not. They showed me. It's dark and cold, colder even than outside. And there are so many of them. So many shadow-people. And they're hungry. Oh, Mama, they're so hungry."

At this, the girl's body went limp and she ceased her cries.

Tamera pulled her way, held her by the shoulders. "Edele? Edele!" Tamera gave her a gentle shake, but Edele didn't respond. Her eyes had tipped up to show only white beneath half-closed lids. If it weren't for the girl's rasping breaths, Tamera might have feared her daughter was—

But she refused to even countenance such a thought.

Instead, she gently lowered Edele to the bed, pulling the sheets around the unconscious girl's emaciated form. She smoothed Edele's damp hair away from her face and forehead.

And sat staring at nothing in silence, no more words of false comfort to give.

The darker shroud of night slipped over the world. Tamera kept vigil by Edele's bedside, pulling an old, wooden chair next to the cot. With nothing to occupy her mind or hands (they had no books - such things being a long-lost luxury - she did not knit and had no patience or talent for any kind of artistry) her fingers twisted and pulled at each other while thoughts chased themselves around and around her mind in dizzying circles until they fragmented only to start again. It was exhausting.

She had lit all the candles in the house and put as much wood on the fire as she could without smothering it, yet still it seemed too dark and chilly inside their home. Perhaps it had always been this way and she was only now noticing. Or perhaps the icy atmosphere originated within herself, and the creeping darkness represented her state of mind. It was yet another weight added to her recently acquired worry that her sanity might be cracking.

Despite this - and against expectation - she found herself fighting sleep as the night wore on. Without clocks, they relied on subtle changes through the day to mark the passage of time, their bodies in tune with these rhythms. So even though Tamera could not see any change in light outside, she was aware of it in every cell of her body.

Exhaustion kept up its assault until she could resist no longer. Her head dipped, jerked up, dipped again, jerked, before dropping one last time as though pulled by leaden weights, her eyes closing as her chin came to rest on her collarbone.

Her body slumped in the chair and she drifted into darkness.

And woke in a confused panic, heart racing and nostrils flaring as she pulled in rapid, shallow breaths.

For a moment, Tamera had no idea where she was, caught in the grip of that mindless juncture between waking and sleeping, her brain not quite adjusted to the rude change of states.

She placed her hands on the arms of the chair, half-lifting herself up. Slowly, her senses returned. She looked to Edele, but the child appeared to be sleeping peacefully; certainly, the girl's only movements were the steady rise and fall of her chest. It hadn't been Edele that had woken her. No, it was something else, something outside the house. She was sure of it. Her nerves jangled, her senses strained. She could almost taste the 'wrongness' in the air; the atmosphere had definitely changed, become charged with the threat of danger. She just didn't know where from.

Tamera pushed herself fully out of the chair and approached the front door slowly. The only sounds were the low roar of the fire and the phlegmy breathing of Edele. Tamera heard nothing else yet was convinced someone - or *something* - was outside the house. For the briefest moments, her hopes flared, thinking Jerad had returned, and her sleep-confused mind addled her instincts; but the brief optimism quickly died like a guttering flame in a gale. Jerad wasn't coming back. She knew that now.

She crept ever closer to the door, coming within a few feet of it before she thought to arm herself. What had she even been intending? To fling wide the door and confront whatever was out there? But what could she use? The axe was outside, as distant to her as if it lay on the other side of the world. She looked around the house, trying to ignore the panic bubbling up inside.

What, what, what?

And then she almost slapped her head in realisation. The metal poker for the fire. She quickly went and picked it up. It felt reassuringly solid in her grip.

Carrying her makeshift weapon aloft, Tamera made her way back to the front door. And paused. Now that action was required of her, she hesitated. ear and a powerful desire *not* to know held her back. It took a monumental effort to crack the door open enough to see out, all the while expecting it to be smashed wide from the other side.

She peered out. Even though it was night, and shadows covered the world, there remained the faint illumination from the snow. In the past, Tamera had found it eerily beautiful. Now, it seemed to warn her of danger. Anything could be hiding out there. The images from Edele's nightmares rose up in Tamera's mind, unclear visions of thin, dark creatures. It made her shiver, set her skin to crawling, sent tremors down her arms. She shook her head to try and cast these treacherous thoughts from her skull. And that was when she caught movement outside.

She stopped and stared, unconsciously shifting the poker to her left hand and placing her right on the partially open door.

Out there, past the first few trees, where the shadows were deepest, something seemed to be moving; a darker shadow, shifting and wavering. Tamera wasn't even sure it was real, wondered if her eyesight was playing tricks, and then it came again, and it wasn't just one movement, it was many. Slowly, almost as though they had been waiting for her to bear witness, lank figures stepped forward, leaving the deeper shadows and coming into sharper definition. Though she still couldn't discern any solid detail, she now knew they were real. Without realising, she held her breath. More and more they came, in twos and threes until there were dozens of this shadow-people (her mind naming them as Edele had done), standing just within the boundary of the outer edge of trees. It was too far to make out facial features, but Tamera knew they were all looking at the house; looking at her.

And she knew without question, they wanted in.

Where it was warm.

Where there was life.

They regarded each other across the gap for over a minute, and then a knot popped in the fire and it broke Tamera from the trance she'd been slipping into. Terror sparked through her and she slammed the door shut. She turned and ran the few short steps to Edele's bed and gently roused her daughter.

"Mama? What's *happening,* Mama?" The child's words were slurred with grogginess.

Pulling Edele closer, moving over to the fire, Tamera kept hold of the poker. Some instinct in her told her to keep close to heat. With her right hand she stroked Edele's back.

"Shhh, baby, shhh. It's okay, it's okay. We'll be fine, we'll be just fine."

Edele clung to her, though the girl's grip was weak from illness and lack of rest. "I don't understand, Mama. What's wrong? What are those sounds?"

Tamera heard the note of rising panic in the girl's voice, a timbre which her own hysteria responded to. She didn't know what her daughter could hear, but she was unaware of anything save the pop and crackle of the fire. And her own thudding heartbeat. As much for her own benefit as for Edele's, she replied, "It's nothing, my love, nothing at all. Just the wind, the snow, the trees creaking. Just sit here with me for a bit, and we'll be fine." Except Tamera didn't believe a word of it.

She pulled her daughter tight into her own body, aware of the girl's emaciated frame, of the sharpness of her bones through thin skin. And the heat, the constant, raging fire of her fever. She wanted to weep, for her sick child, for her absent husband, for the awful, harsh world they'd been born into.

And because of the terrifying things which were outside.

Edele's tired protestations faded away as Tamera kept up her attempts to comfort, knowing no other course of action to take. So, she knelt with her back in front of the fire, holding on to her little girl, hoping the shadows would simply go away.

But they didn't.

A soft rustling started up outside, seeming to come from all around. Tamera likened it to the sound of numerous voices whispering, dry and hoarse; or the noise her boots made when pushing through deep snow, but many times multiplied. It was the wind trying to speak, the trees shaking their branches. And it did not stop.

Then came the scratching, the clawing, the footsteps tracking lightly over the roof. Again, they came from all sides, an almost delicate testing of the solidity of the cabin, as though their owners merely wanted to come in and get warm.

Let us in, please. We just want to meet you...

Tamera thought she could almost hear words in their whispering voices - and she was sure the undulating susurration *was* voices, the multitudinous voices of the shadow-people - and though it did not change from a whisper, it seemed to rise subtly in volume until she couldn't hear the fire or her own, harsh breathing. Or the sob which escaped from her mouth. She was only aware Edele was speaking, low and unintelligible because the girl's mouth was moving where it pressed against Tamera's shoulder. But in her terror, she could only hug the child closer.

As the whispering increased in volume, so too did the scratchings and tapping, until it seemed scores of creatures were rushing all over the exterior of the house. She thought of ants, one of the few insects which still managed to cling to an existence in the deep cold; only in her mind they were far larger than the tiny beasts she used to watch crawl across the pristine snow. Her imagination created a vision of hundreds of human-sized black shapes, gossamer and smoke, rushing all over the house, covering it in shadow.

This thought sparked some awareness in her panicking mind; in her fright, she hadn't picked up on it, but now she was aware the light was dimming inside the cabin. Her head whipped back and forth in agitated dread, as she witnessed first one, then another, then all the candles gutter as if in a wind before going out. And it wasn't only that; her home was filling with a chill, an iciness she felt on her bare skin. When she breathed out, shaky and nervous, it plumed before her face in delicate tendrils.

Tamera looked over her shoulder.

Despite the number of logs she had put on the fire, despite that it should be burning as bright as it ever had, the flames were dimming. She didn't know how this could be, how a blaze could simply begin fading away. But it was; she was witnessing it happen.

As it grew darker, plunging the cabin into deep shadow with only the faintest circle of cold light emanating from the fire (and that slowly shrinking, closing around them), so too did the temperature continue to drop; the icy grip of the outside world penetrating into their homestead and wrapping Tamera and Edele in its icy embrace.

Soon, they were in almost complete darkness, only the palest illumination shining down on them from the smoke-hole. Tamera shivered, unable to stop her body reacting to the lowering temperature. But it wasn't just the cold which caused her flesh to tremble. Out there - just inside the walls of their home - where the darkness pooled like oil, came the subtle shuffling and whispering. Even though neither the front nor back door had opened, it seemed that the shadow people had somehow gained access. Tamera wondered what they were waiting for. Surely nothing was stopping them from falling on her and her daughter.

As if that thought had roused the child, Edele spoke in a weak, plaintive voice. "Mama, please. You're hurting me. You're holding me too tight. I can't breathe."

Forgetting, for a moment, where they were and what was happening, Tamera held her daughter out and looked at her.

And nearly choked on the scream which lodged in her throat.

Even in the faint light, she could see the girl's unhealthy pallor, the blue-tinged shade of her dry skin, skin which was too tight over the bones beneath. As the girl's head flopped back, her half-opened eyelids showed milky cataracts covering the pupils. It was the appearance of someone long dead.

Tamera felt her heart squeeze in pain, felt the blood slow to a sluggish crawl in her veins, and as the light finally began to leech from the cabin - and from the world - the unseen shadow-people crowded in and took Tamera as one of their own.

Cold Blooded

James Jobling

As soon as I step off the double-decker bus into the drenching deluge, I instinctively know something is wrong. The rain is warm. Tropical-like. A tangy, strange smell smothers each fat raindrop like an overbearing mother cuddling her offspring. Irregular lumps of ice are also falling from the sulking heavens - hailstones - beating my head and making my ears sting. Even with my briefcase held above my head as an improvised umbrella, I am already soaked to the skin by the sudden, heavy rainfall. Despite only being in the downpour for a few seconds, my clothes are already wringing wet and my leather shoes are squelching. As the bus belches and pulls away from the stop, an idiot in a Mercedes whooshes past, driving far too fast for such appalling weather conditions, splashing through a huge puddle and saturating me in a gigantic tidal wave of muddy rainwater.

Cursing in frustration, I run up the wet concrete steps leading into the Court two at a time; spinning around in the revolving door so quickly that I almost rotate for a second time before spilling out onto the black-and-white chequered marble floor of the foyer.

There's an old, posh bloke with a mop of white hair wearing a navy-blue suit sitting behind the reception desk. Wire-framed spectacles perched on a purplish nose. As he looks away from the screen of his buzzing PC, he squints at me as though the thick-rimmed glasses are of no benefit whatsoever. A hearing-aid is nestled in the hairy canal of each ear, and he mustn't be a day under eighty. Smiling toothlessly, he clears his throat and asks if he can help me. I return the gesture and introduce myself.

"And how may I help you, Mr Frost?" The receptionist's tongue slithers from between his thin lips, moistening the furry, white moustache nesting just beneath his nose. A spicy scent of Old Spice, Brylcreem and mothballs emanates from the fossil. His battleship-grey eyes flutter across my soggy coat and he wrinkles his nose as though offended by a foul smell. With a shrug and a smirk, the old codger dismisses me before I even have a chance of explaining myself.

"I'm in Court... I mean, I was *due* in Court this morning. Frost; Jack Frost. I have an appointment at ten-forty-five." I glance at the large clock mounted to the wall above the receptionist's head. Each savage tick tock is drum-like; loud enough to make my ears wobble. No wonder this poor sod is partially deaf, having to listen to *that* all day.

The receptionist peels back the sleeve of his sweater and stares at the gold watch strapped around his scrawny wrist. He ricochets his tongue off the scaled roof of his mouth, shaking his head tauntingly. "It's ten-past now," he snorts. "Ten-past *eleven*."

I swallow hard. A pellet of hail slithers down the length of my nose and drips onto the sparkling surface of the reception desk with an audible *plop*. "Yeah, I know I'm late. I'm sorry about that. I had to get the bus. My car is... well, it's in the garage, you see, and I... I... Please, I need to go in."

"Afraid I can't help you there," the receptionist tells me. As though to back up his claim, he settles back in his swivel chair, hands clasped behind his head. "You're in Court B2, right? Appeal against domesticated injunction?"

"Well, yes, that's *kind* of true, but I'm here to–"

"You're too late," the receptionist states dismissively. "Judge Tomkins adjourned the case fifteen minutes ago. Injunction remains."

"What?" I spit acidly. "What do you mean?"

"The injunction remains."

"What the hell are you talking about?"

"The injunction," the receptionist sighs, "that your wife imposed against you to keep you away from her and your two boys. I'm sorry, were you referring to something else?"

"Look, don't be bloody smart. You don't know my ex-wife. Angie can be..." I trail off to find the correct word to describe her. "Quite *sensitive* at times."

"Mr Frost, I tend not to get involved in private affairs, but I believe domestic abuse can make even the most hardboiled of people sensitive."

"Domestic abuse? What the hell are you talking about? I'm not an *abuser*!" A flower of rage blossoms in the pit of my stomach, stretching up my trachea with twisted branches of gnarl, plucking at the back of my gullet with thorny fingers, making me want to retch. Teeth clamp together in anger and I sink the fingernails of my rolled-up fists into the soft flesh of my palms. "I'm sorry, but, please, the judge can't have adjourned. I wasn't even here."

"Which is *exactly* why Judge Tomkins sided with your wife to keep the injunction in place."

As soon as I hear that weaselly voice, the tendons in my neck react with anger and I know who is standing behind me. I close my eyes tightly and count to ten. This is what Marion used to suggest at our AA meetings, trying to coax the good out of the Devil I had become. I count to no more than six when the shitbag speaks again, electrifying my heart with hatred.

"I tried, Jack," Eugene Edwards mocks, stepping up beside me, placing his DKNY briefcase on top of the reception desk next to my tatty cache. "I told Judge Tomkins what you told me last week - boys need a man in their life. Didn't work, though, I'm afraid.

The charge of battery made against Angela - as well as a long list of previous violent and drunken offences - were stacked against you. I tried, Jack, I *really* tried..." Eugene Edwards - Angie's lawyer - shakes his head slowly, displaying fake sympathy. "Of course, the fact you could not even bother showing up on time to protest the injunction of seeing Philip and Alfie on a regular basis speaks volumes about just what kind of a *father* you are."

"I *was* on time," I growl throatily, forcing each syllable through a wall of clamped teeth. "There was a storm. It came out of nowhere. Flooded the road. The bus had to detour. It wasn't my fault."

Eugene cackles artificially, cocking his head back, the fingers on one finely-manicured hand resting on his protruding gut as it wobbles. Even the receptionist is sniggering. "Ah, how many times have we heard that one, Fred?"

"Too bloody many," the receptionist wheezes, red-faced and on the verge of a heart attack. Chuckling. Chortling. He slaps a feeble palm against the desktop, using a handkerchief to wipe condensation from the lenses of his glasses. "If I had a pound for every time I heard that..."

"Look!" I slam both fists down on the reception counter. "I don't have time for your fucking games!"

Eugene Edwards - black hair slicked back and held in place with enough lacquer to put a capital O in the ozone layer - stares at me slack-jawed, perhaps regretting the ribbing now. His face is pale. Dour. The flesh around his eyes making him look albino. His mouth hangs agape, showing off a bloated tongue which looks far too crimson in contrast to his milk-white skin; making him look like a satiated vampire. Long fingers encircle the handle of his briefcase and he uses his other hand to sign out of the visitors' book with a gold fountain pen. With every squiggle he joins together, I envisage stabbing the nib of the pen into his eyeball.

"Should I call security, Mr Edwards?" Fred, the receptionist, asks, bottom lip dithering.

"I don't think that's necessary, Fred," Eugene replies, eyes fixed on mine. "I'm sure we can come to an arrangement here, right, Jack?"

I inhale shakily. "I want to see my boys."

"Then speak to Judge Tomkins next month," Eugene suggests, placing one hand in the middle of my back, ushering me towards the revolving doors. "Explain your situation to him. See if he-"

Something inside snaps like an autumnal branch and I grab Eugene by the scruff of his pristine shirt, spinning him around, shoving him backwards so the backs of his legs slam painfully into the sharp edge of the reception desk. Something - I don't know *what* - happens. I can't explain it. It's fucking impossible to even attempt to describe. A current of some description - electrical or spiritual, I don't know - is sucked from my very soul, exiting through my fingertips and, breathless, my knees lock. The oxygen in my lungs crystalizes and freezes. It feels like I have been *thwacked* by a speeding freight train and am spiralling through the air in slow motion. I can't breathe. I can't swallow. I can't even blink.

I have pulled the weasel to within a nose hair of my face, both hands clutching Eugene just above his beating heart. I can hear - not *feel* - each throbbing pulsation of his heartbeat inside my skull, reverberating around it.

Investigating Eugene's mortified face, I realise just how grey and horrified his sullen features have become.

Mottled flesh around bloodshot eyes and, as I continue to suffocate, lungs refusing to inhale, I notice the blood vessels in his pink scleras rupturing. Bursting.

Blackish goo oozing from the poor bastard's eyes.

Plump veins protrude from his forehead like bloated tapeworms, and blood trickles freely from his nostrils.

His mouth hangs open, like a ventriloquist doll, and his tongue juts from between stumpy teeth. A cloud of mist hisses from his mouth.

Eugene Edwards is freezing to death.

I try to remove my hand from Eugene's chest, but it will not budge. It is fastened there - *frozen* - welded to his sternum, slowing the clonking rhythm of his heart.

Bum-bum-bum-bum... bum-bum... bum... bum...

What the fuck is going on? I'm killing him! I'm killing the man! I want to speak - *apologise* - but my jaws have clenched together as though I am being electrocuted and my tongue feels as though it is made of granite. I need to–

CRACK!

And then I am on my back on the floor, arms and legs sticking up in the air, looking like an upturned table, gulping in much-needed oxygen and feeling my shrivelled lungs swelling like two helium balloons. Coughing. Retching. I swipe the back of my hand across my top lip, matting follicles with blood. Closing my left nostril with the pad of my finger, I snort a bloody clot onto the floor, evicting another jellified glob from the right in the same manner. Staring at the ceiling, I hear a commotion on the looming balcony. Footsteps - many pairs - racing down the staircase.

Security.

Cops.

Fred steps into my line of view. Eyes wide. Frightened. Globes of vision having laid testament to many harrowing events over his lifetime - none more harrowing than the last two minutes. Frail hands grip the keyboard from his computer which he has just walloped around the back of my head. Fred says something about an ambulance at the front desk into his radio, but nothing is coherent. My heart is pounding against my ribcage and I can feel the rush of blood thawing in my arteries and gushing around my system again.

Sitting up, holding the bridge of my nose as though suffering a gruesome migraine, I realize Eugene is spread-eagled on the ground next to me. I must have dragged him down when I toppled to the ground. I am no longer holding him, and I cannot tell if he's alive or dead. His eyes are open - staring straight at, but not seeing me - and black goo still leaks from his eyes. Fingers twitch spasmodically, but that might just be the throes of death. Instinctively, I go to probe his neck for a pulse, but the thought of touching him - and the possible ramifications - makes my skin crawl and my scrotum rise.

Climbing drunkenly to my wobbly feet, I mutter something apologetic to Fred (who backs away with his hands in the air as though I have just pulled an invisible gun on him) and run towards the revolving door, barging back out into the pouring hailstorm, heading towards home.

What the fuck is wrong with me?

Who am I?

What have I become?

I've killed him! I've frozen him to death. His heart has stopped beating because of me. The air in his lungs has glaciated because of me. I glance at the blackened fingertips on both hands, grimacing when I see just how charred and blotchy the digits are.

Burnt?

Frostbitten.

I study my pale complexion in the toothpaste-flecked mirror. Sitting on the edge of the bathtub, head resting against the porcelain brim of the sink, I have no other choice but to listen to the nonsensical jabbering of the police negotiator outside.

He has been hollering into a megaphone for the best part of an hour now.

He is safe and dry under a gazebo, taking no risks.

That phenomenal electrical storm has passed, leaving behind a flurry of falling snow. However, I stopped listening to him a long time ago - after I impaled Angie's father, Dennis, to the porch wall with a four-foot long icicle shot from my palm.

There's nothing the police can do for me. I am - quite literally - a cold-blooded murdering freak. Eugene Edwards. Dennis. The two police constables guarding Angie's house.

And now Philip...

The cops have already gone through the usual charade of telling me how none of this is my fault and that there was an abnormality in that sudden cloudburst earlier which soaked me to the bone. It has supposedly affected many people caught out in it. London, Manchester, Liverpool and Birmingham are all in chaos. People like me are running rampant. A team of analysts, biologists and lab technicians are awaiting my surrender to help control my supernatural urges.

Harsh strobe lights resonate from the flashbars of the many police and emergency vehicles parked outside of Angie's home - my *former* home - engulfing the tiny bathroom in rotating hues of electric blue. Every now and then, I catch small red dots dancing across the tiled walls, beaming straight through the frosted glass window, courtesy of the sights mounted to the rifles of the armed police crouching on the rooftops of the neighbouring houses. Initially, they were ordered to stand by and observe... but then I bayonetted Dennis to the porch wall and killed two of their own and now their instructions have changed.

They want to kill me. They want an eye for an eye. If this was a standard hostage situation, I would have been capped by now, but the police have been given their orders from higher up the chain of command. I am a freak. A mutation. A fucking X-Man. The government will want to run all types of tests and procedures on me. There's no way the order to kill will be given just yet...

I didn't mean to kill anybody. I certainly never *wanted* to. Eugene... well, Eugene just got my temper boiling, but Dennis and those two constables - one male, one female - placed *their* hands on *me* first. I merely reacted. I think that must be some type of trigger. Dennis was just being an overprotective father, trying to defend his daughter and grandsons from a maniac, and the police... well, they foolishly tried arresting me. This is not a weapon I choose to use, it just *happens*...

Although I did not intend to end their lives, I am not remorseful. Why should I be? They brought this on themselves. All four would still be breathing if they just allowed me to see my sons. Boys need a man in their life.

Angie is standing in the doorway of the bathroom, breaking her heart into the crook of her elbow, repeatedly asking "why?", "why?", "WHY?" and Alfie is stood behind her, petrified, trembling, protected by his mother's body. A human shield.

Why can't she see this is all *her* fault? How can she not take accountability for my actions? Boys need a man in their life! I told her this on the phone last night and I am sick of repeating myself. I didn't want things to corkscrew out of control and need to be settled in a Court of Law. I tried being reasonable. I know I pushed her beyond her limits with the drinking and gambling, but all I ever wanted to be was a good father - even if that meant having joint custody of *my* boys. Selfish bitch!

She keeps reaching for Philip. Trying to drag him to her. There's nothing she can do for him now, though. His heart froze to a block of solid ice as soon as we touched.

"Why did you come here?" Angie sobs, voice frail. Croaky. "Why did you do *that*?" She points accusingly at my dead son sprawled in a puddle of water on the floor. The water is defrosted ice seeping from Philip's every orifice. "He was *your* son!"

"I didn't mean to hurt him," I whisper, avoiding the searching red dot once again. The window pane is frosted glass, so the marksmen cannot see through. They are probably using thermographic scopes, but no body heat vents from my pores anymore. "I didn't mean to hurt Phil."

"He's not *hurt*!" Angie screams. "He's fucking *dead*! You *killed* him!"

"I didn't mean to!"

"Bring him back then."

Her abrupt command shocks me from my hazy stupor. "What?"

"You heard. You're a mutant, aren't you?" Angie asks, voice hoarse. "Well, use your fucking superhero powers, Captain Marvel and bring our dead son back to life."

"I can't." Tears well up in my eyes. One pushes itself free of the restraining lashes and rolls down my cheek. By the time it hits the porcelain basin of the sink, it is a pearl of solid ice which rolls marble-like down the drain. "I wish I could."

Angie nods slowly. "Pathetic."

"I know."

"Why'd you kill him?"

"*I* didn't," I snap bitterly. "*You* did."

"I did?" Angie furrows her eyebrows, quivering her top lip. "I killed Phil? Care to elaborate on that?"

"I've not seen Alfie or Phil for two whole fucking months because of that restraining order!" I stand up, pacing back and forth, blood crystalising. "I didn't deserve that. Okay, I admit, the boozing and poker were getting beyond a joke, but that doesn't mean you stop me seeing my sons. Boys need a man in their life. I came here this afternoon to say goodbye to them. I wanted to see them one last time, but you wouldn't grant me that. You called Dennis and the Old Bill."

"Can you blame me?"

"Yes, I blame you!" I bellow, running frostbitten hands - which are like two frozen clumps of Topside - through tangled hair which rustles when disturbed. "The police tried arresting me, Angie. The boys witnessed it. Dennis was giving it the big I am, trying to square off. The boys were frightened. They haven't seen me since August bank holiday! Philip ran to me, Angie. I reached for him on instinct."

"You killed him,"

"I didn't mean–"

The bathroom window explodes with an almighty *crash* as two hollow-point cartridges blast from the chamber of a high-precision rifle from across the cul-de-sac and drill into the back of my head. I do not have time to react. Tissue tears. Bone pulverizes. The bullets penetrate my skull from the back, racing straight through the meaty - frozen - goodness before smashing through the front, showering Angie in gobbets of blood and splodges of rigid grey matter.

The speeding bullets make easy shrapnel of my calcium, phosphorous, sodium and collagen cases; crumpling bone, abrading flesh. I think (ha-ha) that I manage to take two stumbling steps towards Angie and Alfie before my legs give up the fight and I plummet like human Kerplunk. My left eye is not capable of vision anymore and the right eyeball is no longer in its socket but, just before everything fades to black, I do hear one last thing; one little miracle that I will happily take to the icy cold depths…

Alfie.

Alfie's sweet, angelic voice.

"Mummy why has the snow turned red? It looks like blood?"

The Wind Warriors

Christopher Law

"Get away from the window."

"Why?"

"Because I told you to. It's dangerous."

There was nothing dangerous about it. They were so high up, the windows were extra thick and only opened a few inches, but Niall did as he was told. His room looked smaller and gloomier than ever; even after his mother turned on the light. She was carrying a small pile of clean clothes.

"Put those away. Now. Then come through for tea."

The pile of clothes wasn't large, and he stuffed them all in one drawer before returning to his window. It was going to get dark soon, autumn rapidly turning to winter, and he wanted to see as much of the storm as he could. They lived on the tenth floor, high above the surrounding buildings, and he could spend hours watching the trees sway or the clouds pass, even when there was only a light breeze. Sometimes, he was happy just to watch. Other times his imagination had an endless cast of characters and scenarios. The most complicated involved his action figures, but his favourites were the ones entirely in his own mind.

Today, the trees looked alive and tortured, thrashing and bending with the howling wind. The last leaves had been stripped and added to the gathering drifts, too damp after days of rain to be carried far or lifted once they stuck to others. Overhead, the sky was a blanket of grey, getting darker as the first spots of rain began to fall. It scared him looking at it, imagining the power it was holding back, waiting for night to fall. The fear was imaginary, the monsters in the sky part of a game he'd been playing for as long as he could remember, but he was young enough to feel his heart in his throat.

They ate dinner, economy burgers and oven chips, in the living room around the television. His parents, shifts aligning so they were both home for the evenings this week, and older brothers played along with the quiz show before the news. The atmosphere was tense, his parents bickering over the answers and his brothers laughing at their own stupid answers. There was nothing unusual about it, his parents often argued, and his brothers *were* idiots. Niall's attention wandered to the window and the clouds outside. The rain was getting heavier, blown into almost horizontal streaks, and the last light had faded - perfect conditions for the bad guys to attack.

There was no dessert and Niall slipped away to his room as the news came on, Mum finally drawing the curtains. The headlines were mostly about the storm, predicted to be the strongest to ever hit the country. The increasingly powerful hurricanes on the other side of the Atlantic were carrying more strength as they ricocheted East, although there was no truth to the tabloid claim a Category One was about to strike Britain. It sounded like there were demons in the wind as he closed his bedroom door, shutting out the sound of his parents arguing in full force. Dad was heading out despite the weather and Mum was mad.

At some point during the meal, probably after she went to the toilet before sitting down with the boys, his mother had slipped into his room and drawn the curtains. They had pictures of dinosaurs on them, matching the frieze on the walls. He wasn't that into dinosaurs. He preferred spaceships and stars, but the room hadn't been redecorated since he was a baby. Other than that, he liked it, the cramped conditions better than sharing with his brothers. He had a cabin bed, the small desk a jumble of pictures and felt-tip pens, and a small bookcase, plus a few shelves for his Lego models. He preferred books to toys. There were only a few figures in the crates stored inside the bed's miniature wardrobe.

For a moment, he thought about turning the light off, but there was a small window above his door and his mother would come in if it wasn't lit this early, particularly on a Friday. She hated him going near the windows, paranoid that the glass would break, or the hinges fail, and he'd go tumbling out. When Niall was young, she'd had nightmares about it and other horrible things. The nightmares were over, but she still had to take pills every day, arguing with Dad about if she had or hadn't remembered to take them. Making do, he ducked under the curtains and pressed his face against the cold glass, cupping his hands around his eyes.

Rivulets of rain ran sideways across the window, from right to left, pooling in the corners. Looking down, he could just about see the trees near the entrance to the tower block. Surrounded by the diffuse orange glow of the street lighting, they were blurred and black, whipping from side-to-side. Empty plastic bags and other litter swirled around them. Someone he instinctively knew was his father left the building and stalked across the road, bent double against the wind. His drinking hole was a five-minute walk away. There was no-one else out, not even any cars.

His brothers turned their console on, forced to play against each other by another unpaid Internet bill. They were in their teens and would be up until late happily shooting each other. Only eight, Niall had learned to tune out the racket they made, occasionally using the gunfire and explosions from their games as sound-effects for his own imagination.

The wind and rain got heavier until he couldn't really see anything except the drops running across the cold glass, but he kept his post all the same.

It was enough to hear the wind, feel the glass beneath his fingers vibrate with the strongest gusts, to know that The

Wind Warriors were out there, fighting for the survival of the entire world.

They were cheesy superheroes, dressed in blocks of primary colour when he tried to draw them, but in his imagination, they were ancient, made grim by centuries of fighting for a lost cause. They had names like Vortex and Maelstrom; other words he had found in the family computer's thesaurus when he didn't know enough words for wind. He knew maelstroms happened in water, he just liked the sound of it.

Like all heroes in books and superhero films everyone in the family liked - even Mum - The Wind Warriors had some very powerful enemies; monsters in the sky. It was a classic battle between good and evil; a war stretching back to the dawn of time. The monsters were demons or aliens from another dimension - Niall was never sure which he liked better - and the Warriors were a band of elite heroes, granted immortality so they could defend the world. If anyone had ever asked, he would have told them that there had once been thousands of Warriors, but they could still die and there were no new heroes to take the places of the fallen. No-one ever asked, and Niall never felt much like sharing, not even with the handful of friends he had at school.

Despite their name, the Warriors and monsters didn't fight with the actual wind. They weren't even made from it - like they would have been if they were elementals. They fought with psionic weapons and when the demon explanation was in play, magic. To normal eyes, ones that couldn't see, the clash of the weapons manifested as moving air. Every gust, no matter how big or small, was caused by a skirmish or battle. Even blowing dust from an old book was enough for a spat to be fought and won. He would have loved going to the library and old bookshops just to blow the dust and imagine, but they cleaned the library well and there were no bookshops close enough for him to go alone.

Dad came back a few hours later, earlier than usual. He slammed the front door and Mum erupted from the living room, her temper nursed with alcohol and social media - the Wi-Fi was suspended but she always had data on her phone. Niall left the window and darted to his bed, slipping under the duvet and grabbing his book to make it look like he'd fallen asleep reading. He didn't dare turn the light off and risk his parents noticing. Next-door, his brothers had turned the volume down and switched to a quieter game a half-hour ago, after Mum screamed at them. Once she was mad, she stayed mad until she slept. There was no point provoking her when Dad was the cause.

Outside, the wind howled, thudding against the windows with enough force to make them shudder - his mother's fears seeming feasible for the first time. In between each attack, it howled and shrieked, drove the rain against the glass with a machine-gun rattle. The heating was on and he felt cosy under the covers. His closed eyes were all the defence he needed against the world - unless someone came into his room.

His parents drifted to the living room, trading insults and dragging up old grievances. He ran on tiptoes to turn off the light, lit on his way back by the hall light coming through over the door. Back under the covers, he curled up on his side and focused on the sound of the storm outside, tuning out the shouts and screams echoing down the hall. It was late; he fell asleep before too long.

He woke with a start, half-rising from his pillow to fight something from his dream. The memory of it faded quickly as he lay his head down again, thinking for a second or two that he might get to drift back into sleep. The air was too cold, and although the monster he'd been fighting was forgotten, he could hear the echo of the sound that had woken him. He couldn't tell what it had been - not even if it had been in his dream or the real world - the echo simply ringing.

It was late, well past midnight, but still hours before dawn. He couldn't see the hands on his wall-clock (shaped like 1950's rockets, but not as luminous as the packaging had claimed), but the window over his door was dark and the sodium glow rising from the street was muted. To save money, the local council turned half the street lighting off between 2 A.M. and dawn. On a clear night, it was sometimes possible to see a scattering of the brightest stars.

Outside, the wind was still howling, less chaotically than before. The centre of the storm was passing over the city and a kind of rhythm had appeared in the gusts and lulls; a low throb that oscillated upwards every second or two towards a screech that died quickly. There was no rain, or what there was had been whipped away by the wind, and without the rattle against his window, he could hear the thick glass hum as it responded to the wind. There was no other sound, or none loud enough to hear over the wailing. Even the ageing fridge, with the hum he sometimes thought he would hear for the rest of his life, his memory playing it on a loop, seemed to have fallen silent.

He had been dreaming of the monsters and Warriors. He remembered that much as he felt the first tickle in his bladder, still lying on his side and hoping to stay where he was, safe and cosy except for the frozen air on his face.

Like always, they had been fighting in the sky and between the buildings, individual battles standing out amongst the semi-organised chaos all around. They had seemed more real than ever before, his dream even more vivid than the fever induced ones he'd had a year or two before. The heroes had been old and slow, no more than a half-dozen against a sky full of monsters. He'd been able to smell their sweat and fear, the staleness of resignation, and hear the pops and cracks of pensioner bones grinding together just to stand.

All the others were gone, the war done except for the final stand.

The monsters were hanging in the sky, belching ice and decay. It had seemed strange for them to wait until he realised that they were being restrained, kept on a leash until the greatest of them all arrived.

That was when he woke.

The itch in his bladder became a slight pressure and he rolled onto his other side, facing the wall, determined to fall asleep again if he could. It felt like Christmas Eve or the night before his birthday, except twisted and wrong. The certainty that something major was about to happen kept nipping at his thoughts, denying him peace and the pressure in his bladder continued to grow.

It wasn't long before he had to accept he would have to move, certain that if he did somehow fall asleep again he would wet himself. He hadn't done that in over a year, but still felt every stab of failure. Practising control, he stayed curled beneath the duvet for a few more minutes - listening to the wind and telling himself that the monsters were just his game, no matter what he thought he could hear in the shrieks and howls.

There was underfloor heating throughout the tower and, ten floors up, there was always heat rising from below, but the floor felt icier than the rungs of his ladder as he climbed down. A particularly strong gust hit the window with a deep thud, the air around him seeming to hum in response. There was a second, stronger blast, and his stomach lurched as the building swayed, if only ever so slightly. He ran to the light-switch, beside the door, and slammed it on as there came a flurry of equally strong blasts.

Under the electric glow, everything looked normal. Nothing had fallen from the shelves, and the patch of mould above the window was still there, waiting to be painted over again. The wind eased off, and for a moment, he was sure that he had imagined the swaying, disorientated by the dark and the noise

Wary of waking his parents - all the rooms had windows like his over the doors - he left his bedroom door open and scurried down the hall by that light. The bathroom was around the corner of the hall, enclosed by the other rooms, but he'd never lived anywhere else and found his way easily in the gloom. Everything still felt like it was swaying slightly, like the time they'd gone to France on the ferry, so he sat down to pee. He didn't want to make a mess and clean up in the dark. The fan connected to the light always woke his parents.

The swaying sensation grew worse as he returned to his room, bad enough that he had to lean against the wall for support and started worrying that he might throw-up. Part of him wanted to go to his parents. Their room was beside the bathroom, next to the living room, but they'd been drinking and arguing. It was better to wait for morning.

The blast that rocked the building was enough to make him stagger as he neared his bedroom door, the pool of light spilling out like a beacon. It sounded like Dad losing his temper, the times when he'd start rising slowly from the couch with a growl and finish with a roar and at least one fist flying. Then it hit, making the windows bark, muted and distorted, and he had to cling to the doorframe.

The moment of panic passed, bringing relief that he hadn't cried out like a baby and woken the others. Closing his bedroom door, he leant against it for a second, telling himself that it was okay for his legs to feel weak and that he wanted to puke. The storm was loud, but outside, kept at bay by the curtains and light. His bed looked like the safest haven possible. He started towards it carefully, wondering if he was falling ill. He could remember feeling as scared as he did now when he had the fever. It wasn't possible for the wind to blow hard enough to sway a building, not in Britain. Nausea and imbalance had to be signs of illness.

There was no warning howl or screech before the gust that shattered the windows. Niall had one hand on the ladder, one foot raised from the frozen floor when the tower lurched backwards with enough force to topple him and the shatter-proof panes exploded into the room. Screaming, already on the floor, he covered his face and hoped the onslaught wouldn't last too long. His bladder suddenly felt full again.

With his eyes screwed shut, all he could see were images from his dreams and stories - the ones from just before the heroes arrived to save the day. The monsters were ascendant, the wind a plaything. He had to open his eyes to escape the things in his imagination and saw his flimsy bedroom door torn from its hinges and toyed with before turning to splinters. The splinters were sucked into the hallway, joining the swirling debris cloud sucked from the other rooms.

"Mum!" he screamed, forgetting his nausea and running from his room. The wind sucked at his pyjamas, tried to pick him from the floor and fling him against a wall. "Mum!"

He reached his parents' door just as it was sucked from its hinges, his fingertips almost on the handle. Standing on the threshold, the debris cloud moulded itself around him, causing no damage. He watched the door spin over his parents' bed and catch in their window. It held for a moment before snapping in the middle and spiralling into the night with their duvet and pillows.

"Niall!" Mum shouted. She loved him really. "Run, baby... *run*! Get–"

She would have shouted more, clinging to the headboard with fresh bruises on her face, but the wind wrapped itself around her face and arms.

A thousand tiny splinters - wood from doors, metal from fittings, everything battered and torn by the wind - cut into her skin, and then her flesh.

She screamed as the grip was tightened, her last sight her own blood mixing with the wind, spiralling away. She died before her flesh was liquefied and her bones ground, but the wind held her up until everything was gone, stretching her skull into a scream.

Dad was still drunk, concussed from the fight that sent him home early. He fell from the bed as he woke, flailing on the floor before scuttling arse-backwards into a corner. Even in the dim light, it was easy to see the dark stain on the crotch of his pyjama trousers, the expensive ones he wore when he felt like he'd been the man or needed to demonstrate that he was. The cheap tattoos on his arms and chest were just smudges in the dark.

"Help me, boy!" Dad screamed, just before the wind wrapped around him and Niall fled. "Help me, you little fucker!"

His eldest brother was scrabbling into the hall as Niall came around the corner, not sure if he was running towards his bed or the front door. The wind already had his brother's foot, the leading edge of its fingers tipped with broken glass. Bone was already showing and, as Niall clung to the wall, the entire limb was torn away. Greedy for its prey, the wind whipped quickly around the other leg, shot an enthusiastic tendril into the mouth that tore off the lower jaw, droplets of blood spraying out. In the background, framed by the crumbling door, the middle brother was little more than a skeleton, hanging in the mist of his own body.

The building was definitely swaying as he ran to the front door, already imagining the fire-escape at the end of the hall. He could feel the wind clutching at his ankles, the residue it left so cold he could feel it burning the bone. The latch was wet and stiff, and he struggled to get it open, the wind pressing and pulling against him the whole time. In the distance, behind the shriek and howl, he could hear the monsters laughing.

The door opened and was sucked shut again. He wrenched it harder, setting his narrow shoulders as a brace, and found himself looking at the woman from next door. She was still almost young. Went jogging every day. Owned a cat. Niall didn't know her name and wished she hadn't looked aware as she clung to his hand, already stripped to the bone below the thigh and missing an eye. She held onto him longer than he held her and disappeared down the hall when the heavy front door gave out. It tore from its hinges and sent her careening down the corridor whilst he still protected somehow, dragged his way back to the bathroom and into the tub. He saw on TV once that bathtubs were good protection from tornadoes, and he couldn't think of anything else to do.

For a while, he felt safe in the tub - more so when he pulled the shower curtain from its rings and pretended it was a blanket, that this was all just a fever dream. Like the time before, he was only ill. This time he *knew* it. That was all.

The swaying became more pronounced, constant enough that the tower began to gyrate around its centre as it recovered and reacted to the attacks. Niall clung to the handrail, alternating having his eyes open and closed. With them open, all he could see was his knuckles and a patch of dirty enamel; closed, it was the monsters, toying with him. Either way, he heard the wind, words starting to form in the howling.

The monsters were taunting him. He knew that. But they were keeping him for later. He was young. Tired. He fell asleep, dreamed about heroes failing.

It was just past dawn when he woke again, the bathtub too hard and cramped to sleep for long.

Used to seeing the sky through his bedroom window, he didn't wonder, for a moment, how he could see it from the tub.

There was no window in the bathroom.

That was why there was a fan. He knew he was in the tub, could even remember fleeing there, but it still took a moment for him to understand what seeing the sky meant.

"Mum?" he called. "Dad?"

The tower had been eleven storeys tall, just one floor above Niall's. Each floor had ten flats. The eleventh floor and half the tenth had been torn away and, when he looked over the edge of the tub, he could see that the damage stretched down to the ground. Almost two sides of the building had been torn away, used as shrapnel to level the surrounding buildings. The two storey terraces, a simple maze connecting the towers, had been levelled, nothing left but rubble and smears of people. Two of the five towers in the neighbourhood had already collapsed. The other two were as badly damaged as the one Niall found himself in.

"Mum?" he called again, young enough not to care that he was about to cry. "Mum?"

The monsters were still at work, strong enough now that they could focus, didn't need the whole sky raging. Most of them had spread out across the world, but there was one left where it all started, a weakling picking for scraps amongst the rubble. Against a calm sky, almost a hundred feet tall and formed from debris and blood, it was enough to scare Niall - one monster much the same to a child. The fear was enough to attract the monster, little more than an infant itself, bringing the wind back to what was left of Niall's building.

It looked like a cartoon tornado as it approached. When it struck, slicing the ruin in half and toppling Niall from the tub in a shower of concrete and iron, it sounded like the noise that woke him, spared him a quick death in his bed. It was the sound - so deep and low it was felt more than heard - that should have roused the heroes, The Wind Warriors, to one final stand. If they had been stronger, braver, they would have. The monsters found a way, after all.

Falling from the tub, into the billowing cloud of dust, he was rewarded precious seconds to think before he hit the ground and was buried by his falling home. Niall hated his heroes for being weak. If they had been strong, at least a little stronger than they were, no-one would have needed to die. The storm would just have been a storm.

As he died, he was glad his heroes were already dead, suffering the same fate as the world they failed. It meant they had to suffer a little longer. That made him happy as he took his place in the sky.

Never Eat Yellow Snow

Kitty Kane

It had been one of those days. You know the type, right? Where you simply wish you'd stayed in bed. Ice all over the place. Damn car wouldn't start, so I had to brave the dreaded bus. Since when did buses start costing the price of a dinner for two for return journey two miles down the road? One of *those* days.

Got to the office late. How many bloody times does one bus need to stop in two miles anyway? Kasey, the bitch boss, must have been waiting for me. She jumped straight on my case, predicting dire things for my quarterly performance review. The Devil in a dress is a beautiful and sexy woman. I'd bang her any which way I could, but man, she is a *bitch*! Red bobbed hair. Emerald eyes that glitter with pure malice most of the time. Low-cut, expensive blouses which leave nothing to the imagination and skirts that I was pretty sure were belts. Stilettos that clip-clopped down the hallways, announcing her Ice Queen presence before you could lay eyes on her, finish off the regular ensemble. As sure as night turns to day, that is what she will generally have on.

She came and perched delicately on the corner of my desk and placed one perfectly manicured hand upon the stack of files that awaited my days' work. The nails were scarlet and looked as sharp as the talons on a raptor. Her eyes glittered like coals and her mouth curled into an evil grin. She wanted to see me after hours to talk about my performance. If she knew what kind of performance I was contemplating right then, those scarlet talons would probably have raked my eyes out. I just nodded sagely.

As she clip-clopped down the corridor, Arnold - the next desk over - grimaced at me. Well, it was for me, I *think*. He had found himself in her bad books more than once. I grimaced back and settled down to work. I'd not been there long when my attention began to waver. My attention span is rather shocking, but I'm a man, and that's my excuse. I looked out of the window and saw to my chagrin it was snowing heavily.

Great. Fantastic. Not only did I have a meeting with Atilla the Hun to look forward to, I now would have to walk home in a bloody blizzard. The stupid bus companies stopped services at the first hint of snow, and this was coming down heavy. Having only glanced out of the window periodically, I was surprised at how much the snow had drifted. A good foot and a half bedecked the courtyard, but I had to look again. The damn stuff was *yellow*.

Now, we are not used to having snow in this part of the country, but of the few times that we have had it, it's never been yellow. I'm not talking a slightly-off-white either. This stuff was fluorescent yellow! It glowed in the winter light. Eerie. Foreboding. I felt a shudder go down my spine. Something was not right here. Not right at all.

The sun was low in the winter sky, but the sky was not quite right either. A haze shimmered and the sun itself was a malevolent red. I'm not a religious man, but there was something apocalyptic about the sky. There were no birds either; not a one. Usually around the courtyard would be a good few crows, and on occasion, a seagull or two. Nothing - not a feather - was in sight.

I beckoned for Arnold to join me at the window. He looked as shocked as I. As we watched out of the window, we saw Jessie from accounts, headscarf trying to escape in the strange snowstorm as she trundled across the courtyard. Suddenly, thunder clapped overhead, and purple lightning forked down from the snow-laden sky.

The strange flakes swirled around her face, hitting her square on the exposed parts. As her usually smiling mouth was battered by the strange yellow stuff swirling around her like a whirling dervish, she began clawing at the gaily coloured headscarf. In one violent motion, she threw it to the ground, where it landed in a puddle of yellow. I could not see very well, but it looked as if she had pulled her face into a grimace. She began clawing at her shirt in a frantic manner, and before I could poke Arnold to check he was seeing what I was, she had torn not only her shirt but her coat, skirt and handbag off in one violent fluid motion.

I looked at Arnold and assumed his stunned face matched my own as she then quickly removed her underwear. Normally, this would be a great sight for us. Neither of us did particularly well with the ladies, but this was *shocking*. Jessie was naked, but it didn't look good, her skin was melting. Not just her skin - her flesh, too. It was dripping down her frame like a lit candle, molten flesh pooling in a sizzling puddle around her feet.

Her sensible, black pump shoes remained, but the legs stretching out of them were nothing but bone. Her entire body was now devoid of outer flesh; her skeleton gleaming bright white against the vile yellow snow and purple fork lightning. Terror gripped me. Surely, she was dead, right? I wanted to tear my eyes away, but I couldn't. Fascinated, I noticed that her interior organs still pulsated within her skeletal form and her eyes… oh God her eyes remained, but they had changed.

Glowing the same maleficent purply-red as the snow-laden sky, the exposed orbs turned upwards and saw us watching. Her exposed teeth stretched into a grimace of what I assume was terror, and she wobbled one bony leg in front of the other, staggering forwards. Suddenly, something red and white swooped from the air and dove straight at her. The thing used claws, talons, heaven only knows what, landing upon Jessie's exposed rib cage.

Turning to Arnold, I found his expression matching mine: repulsion. The newcomer was - or *had* been - a seagull, but was now a living skeletal monster, attempting to eat what I was beginning to suspect was a worse living skeletal monster.

Arnold and I seemed to silently agree that hiding would be a good idea, but as we were about to turn and bolt from our vantage point, we saw the downstairs doors open and staff from the lower floors pouring out; heading towards the stricken Jessie. Now, I'm a geek, and Arnold is a geek. Geeks know a thing or two about zombies, right? We just do. It's what we know. And we knew that Jessie was a bloody zombie. A snow zombie - born of the fucking weird snow. As geeks, we knew you just don't go out in it! But here were people - non-geeks, I suspect - rushing out to save what was now a denizen of Hell on Earth. This was not going to go well. Nope, not well at all.

God, they were all rushing around, shouting. Shouting requires open mouths, and into these open mouths went the putrid yellow snow concoction. The second the frozen flakes absorbed on the tongues of those poor saps, the clawing at the clothes began… followed by the hideous melting. Oh God, the melting flesh sizzled around the feet of those poor people. It didn't melt the snow, though. What the fuck was that stuff made from? There were now at least thirty skeletal forms with pulsating organs gleaming inside. Zombie seagulls and a few zombie crows swooped in to feed upon the changed.

The changed, however, were not keen on their precious, but now exposed organs, becoming bird food.

They were snatching the birds out of the air, ripping off their exposed skulls and raising them up to their toothy, grinning mouths. I was thankful I could not see exactly what was happening, but being the geek that I am, I presume they were sucking out the birds' brains and swallowing them like oysters.

They threw the discarded skulls on the ground, where they lay still, but the bodies didn't. Oh no, the bodies damn well kept on flapping along. Zombie people continued to swipe them out of the air, only for them to flap off again immediately.

Feeling decisively sick, but unable to tear myself from the grim spectacle, I motioned to Arnold that we really needed to move. I didn't know how long it would be before others in the building noticed, and would probably go outside because that's what people do when something is turning folk into zombies.

Then I heard a noise that made me shudder even more.

Clip-clap, clip-clap, clip-clap.

Oh fuck, I knew *that* sound. Atilla was on her way down the corridor and damn quickly, too.

"Alex? Arnold? Where has everyone gone? What are you two slackers doing staring out the window? Has everyone gone mad? It's just snow. Adults going out to play in the damn snow? I'll fire each of–"

I grabbed her by the scruff of her blouse and struggled to hold the little-redheaded ball of fury. I didn't like her much, but I was a gentleman at heart and the sights now splashed across the courtyard were getting grimmer by the second. She shrugged off my grip with an unholy strength, surprising me for such a wispy thing, but I made one last attempt at stopping her. However, I just ended up with a handful of her gorgeous red hair slipping through my fingers as if it were made of silk. I was disgusted when I felt my cock twitch in my pants in response to the contact. Damn woman was smoking hot… even in the event of a zombie outbreak, it seemed.

As she laid her eyes upon the carnage in the courtyard, I heard a strangled gasp. She turned around to look at me, and for the first time I saw something other than cruelty in her green eyes. I saw terror. Pale-skinned at the best of times, Kasey's skin went almost *translucent*. She was shaken, and I railed at myself internally for wanting to comfort her. She was a bitch, but at that moment, she looked like a lost and terrified child.

Stepping forward, I glanced once more out of the window. More people were changed now. There were at least fifty of the damn things out in the yard, and what was that scampering around the yellow ground? A squirrel! A fucking zombie squirrel holding fleshless paws on top of a discarded crow skull; daintily licking at remaining brain bits. Damn, I never knew squirrels had such long tongues.

Red polished nails dug into the back of my hand. I once more met the eyes of Kasey. I knew that look. Questions were coming my way.

"Alex, what is going on out there? What's happening? Why is the snow yellow? Is that Jessie's scarf on the ground? Oh, my God, Alex, tell me what's happening! What do we do?"

I've no idea as to why she thought I had any answers. Well, except maybe the question about Jessie's scarf. It was as though she seemed to think I could fix the damn problem. I think this needed slightly more than the universal problem-solving action of 'turning it off and on again' that seemed to work so very well for most things. I was hoping it was a dream and I would wake up, but it was taking far too long for consciousness to appear. No, it was no dream. People were STILL going out.

Arnold grabbed me and pulled me to his window, gesturing outside. A man walked into the courtyard from the outside entrance, holding the fluorescent yellow harness of a guide dog. My heart dropped as the weird snow whipped around him and he seemed to gasp. Snow went into his open mouth and once more the change began. However, we were not watching him. We were watching his guide dog.

Trained with military precision, guide dogs were some of the most well-behaved creatures on the planet. What interested us though, was that although the snow fell upon the dog, it didn't change.

"It hasn't eaten any," said Arnold.

He was right. Faithful all the way, the golden Labrador stood by its now skeletonised master, but it *wasn't* changing. My heart jumped. If we could somehow confirm this theory - that the snow had to be eaten to turn the living into these hellions - then maybe, just maybe, we could save some people. I had no idea how widespread this weird ass snow was, but if this was an apocalypse, then every apocalypse needed a hero, right? And I quite fancied being one. I voiced this idea, and the three of us stared at each other, none wanting to volunteer. I guess none of us were true heroes.

I was just about to sigh and indicate that I would do it when Arnold simply nodded once and stepped away from his window. He grabbed hold of a small wastepaper bin from inside the meeting room by which we stood. Emptying its contents upon the floor, his eyes bored into Kasey's, daring her to say something. Her pretty face looked for a moment as if she would, but for once, she stayed silent. I clapped him on the shoulder. I wasn't sure what to say, so I said nothing.

It seemed like forever that we heard him thundering down the stairs.

It echoed so much, it told me that there were not many people left in the building. All outside. All changed. We saw the door to the courtyard swing open and Arnold stepped out. He placed the bin on his head and stumbled and slid in the snow.

The merciless onslaught of yellow flakes landed quickly on the grey receptacle, illuminating his tweed shoulders, too, but he didn't change. My heart leapt as I realised that I was right. You MUST have to eat it to become changed. If only we could get the word out. Opening the window, I shouted for Arnold to come back, but he either didn't hear me or ignored me. Tilting his makeshift wastepaper helmet, he began to shuffle through the drifting, malevolent snow. Suddenly, I knew what he wanted. He wanted the guide dog.

Progress was hindered by his restricted vision, but I saw him take the bin off his head and my heart lurched. He turned so we could see him and indicated his tightly closed mouth. My heart pounded, but I could do little more than watch as he made his unsteady progress across the courtyard.

Seconds seemed like hours as he shuffled and slid, but finally he reached the dog. He tried to grab the harness, but the blind man's hand held it fast. Tugging, Arnold finally gave the fleshless arm a kick, his leg lifting high and fast. Damn, I never had him pegged as a martial arts fan. The arm snapped, and the hand and forearm skittered across the yellow courtyard. Grabbing the dog closer to its collar, Arnold pulled desperately, trying to coax the animal to follow him, but the poor dog was loyal to the end.

I could almost feel Arnold's desperation, and I saw him lift the creature in his arms. This shocked the dog and its muzzle opened, only slightly but enough, and I heard Kasey gasp and step closer to me as snowflakes whizzed into the open jaws. We both shouted a warning to Arnold, but it was too late. The dog in his arms changed, melting down his tweed jacket.

Skeletal crows swooped in, awaiting the brains that would surely reward them. The crows caused the other changelings to turn towards Arnold. My heartbeat palpitated. The gleaming orb eyes of the Hell creatures turned upon the unchanged Arnold. Suddenly, with strength unholy, several of the zombies leapt upon poor Arnold. Tearing and biting, renting and clawing, they set about him, making short work of him. The changed dog ran around in circles, snatching up one of Arnold's recently removed fingers, gobbling it down. The crows came for his organs, and the zombie people smashed open his skull.

Kasey screamed, an ear-splitting, high pitched sound which resonated through the now deserted corridors. I went to her and wrapped my arms around to comfort her. At first, she tried to shrug me off; tried to resist my embrace. However, with a sob of despair, she eventually buried her beautiful face into my chest. I held her for a few moments; feeling her sobs lessen. I would have loosened the embrace then, but something strange began to happen.

Her hands behind me began to move, stroking my back at first, sending tingling shivers of delight down my spine. Then I felt her nails gently tracing concentric circles on my back. Her face was still buried in my chest, but I felt the pace of her breathing increase. Hell, I felt the pace of my own breathing increase, too. Something else that was increasing rapidly to my horror was the size of my cock. I was getting hard! Damnit! Why had this beautiful but beastly woman that invoked so much desire in me chosen now to play this game?

Gently, I pulled her away and looked into her bloodshot, emerald eyes. I wanted so much to shake her, to stop her, to stop 'this', but as she looked up at me, suddenly she kissed me.

Hard. She kissed me so fucking hard that her tongue slipped into my mouth and her scarlet nails clawed at my shirt. A couple of the buttons popped off and skittered down the hallway, tearing my shirt off. I felt one of those red fingernails trace the outline of my now solid cock through the thin and material of my trousers.

Damn it, there was a fucking zombie apocalypse happening right outside and I wanted to fuck my boss? Well, so did Atilla, it seemed, and seeing as I may never get another chance to fuck anybody - let alone this fireball of a woman - ever again, I surrendered to the carnal desire.

Gently but firmly, I backed her into the meeting room, closing the door I inwardly chuckled. Who was I closing it against? The zombies? Doubt they would care much about what I was about to do to Kasey. Kissing her hard, I unbuttoned her expensive blouse to reveal an emerald green lacy bra; the exact colour of her eyes. Her skin was buttermilk pale. Freckled. She had a tiny tattoo of a butterfly on her ribcage, and I traced down to it with my tongue, kissing it.

Her gasps told me she was enjoying the attention, but she grabbed hold of my face and brought it up, my eyes meeting hers. I usually cannot read women very well, but at this moment, her eyes challenged me to satisfy her like no woman had challenged me before. Fuck, did I want this bitch of a woman that had caused me so many hours grief working for her? I backed her up further and further until we reached the whiteboard upon which she had drawn so many flow charts and pie charts and graphs over time in our meetings.

I couldn't push her any further back. *What now*, my mind and body screamed with the desire of sexual relief. Reaching behind her, I fumbled for her zipper on her skirt. Fuck! I couldn't find it! Damn, her skirt was short enough anyway. Grabbing the hem, I yanked it up around her waist and nearly came in my pants as I saw the matching green panties and a fucking suspender belt attached to her stockings.

"Are you sure?" I breathed into her mouth.

In reply, she turned around, pressed her front up against the board, opened her legs slightly and pulled those panties to the side. I was pleased to notice that she did not shave and that she was the same fiery red down there as she was on her head. She slid two fingers into her slit, taking them out, licking them, grabbing me by my jutting cock. I pulled my zipper down and freed myself through the hole in my boxers. I don't think I'd ever been this hard before.

Asking one last time if she was sure, as soon as her nod came, I pinned her wrists up against the board with one hand, yanking her very damp panties to one side with the other, positioning the head of my cock against her hot opening, pushing inside. Fuck, she was unexpectedly tight. As I thrust,

I felt my balls tightening, I would normally want to take my time, but she was too hot. I had to have her hard and fast. The deeper I went, the louder she cried out her own pleasure. The pressure built until finally I exploded inside of her. I cried out, and as our trembles finally subsided, we both slid down the board into a heap of an embrace upon the floor.

Her face was bright red, her eyes flashing but not with cruelty anymore. Now, they flashed with satisfaction. I wanted to stay in this moment forever, but I knew we couldn't. Wordlessly, we began to rearrange our clothing back to normal. I stared at her and she stared at me. There was so much I could have said in that moment, but the geek in me let me down. Instead of sweet things and endearment, my mouth opened, and I blurted out that we really ought to plan on how to get the fuck out of here alive.

Kasey stared at me, then threw her head back and laughed. "Yes, I suppose we ought. What is the plan, Mr Comic Geek Man?"

Thrown, I came back to Earth with a start. Yes, indeed, how were we going to get out of this alive? It doesn't change you if you don't consume it, but the zombies will simply consume you anyway. How many people out in the world had been changed? Were there other survivors? How could we tell them not to eat the yellow snow? Suddenly, I remembered that across the road were the offices and studios of a TV station. Not a big one, but not a tiny one either. Sharing this with Kasey, we resigned ourselves to the fact that we would have to attempt to get there. We had to try.

Grabbing her hand, we set off down the corridor, her shoes once more clip-clapping. Ducking into our offices, I grabbed my anorak I had worn this morning and scouting around, I grabbed other jackets and coats, thrusting them at Kasey.

"Cut that anorak into two triangles big enough to tie across our noses and mouths," I said to her.

She nodded straightaway.

Bundling ourselves up as much as we could, we grabbed our personal belongings and went downstairs. Not wanting to take the courtyard door because, well, you know… zombies, we hurried out of a fire exit. A shrill alarm sounded. Cursing, I grabbed her hand and we bolted outside. Glancing around at first, I couldn't see any of the changed. But the alarm must have alerted them because they soon appeared.

They didn't move fast, thankfully, but we did have to constantly duck the skeletal crows which seemed to be everywhere. We could see the TV studios, and we picked up our pace. Out of my peripheral vision, I was aware of another two figures barrelling towards us. They were not changed. They wore Hazmat suits with a nuclear symbol emblazoned on them. The four of us reached the doors of the studio together but found it locked.

Hammering desperately, we huddled in the doorway until a timid-looking girl came to the door. She motioned for us to show our faces, which we did, and she quickly slid the door open. The four of us bundled in and the girl locked the door again. I got my first good look at the two figures in the Hazmat suits then. Both were men, both around forty. All of us were breathing so heavily, we couldn't speak. Once we gathered our breath, it was one of the suited men who spoke first.

"I'm… sorry. My God… I'm so sorry. It was an… accident!"

Kasey and I and the girl stared at him, I beckoned him to continue.

"At 10 A.M. this morning, one of the reactors at the nuclear plant got stuffed up with snow.

We were ordered to begin clearing it, but we had some apprentices working with us. I admit we were being lazy and told them to do it.

Somehow, they increased the ejection pressure that usually ejects the smoke and blew out all this radioactive snow. It's all our fault, but we can't stop the pressure. It's building and building. Reactor number two is gonna blow at any moment. We've come here to try to warn any folk that haven't been affected."

Fighting the urge to hit them, I turned to the girl and asked if it was still possible to broadcast right now. She nodded and beckoned I follow her. We all moved into a large room, lit by a huge green screen. Huddled inside were approximately fifteen people, all shell-shocked. This was where they broadcast the weather from. How bloody ironic?

After sorting out with the TV people how to broadcast, myself and one of the power plant workers stood in front of the green screen with a camera pointed at us, preparing to attempt to save, if not the world, at least a small part of it. The camera began to roll.

"Please, do not adjust your TV sets. We realise we are not what you are expecting to see, but we beg you to listen to us. We are here to save your lives. Listen carefully. I'm handing over to Steve Harris of Fulcrum Nuclear Power Plant who will explain what has happened. Please, listen closely. This is not a joke. I repeat this is not a joke."

The guy in the Hazmat suit called Steve stepped forward. His face was fearful, and I knew how he felt. Heaven knows how I managed to get those few lines out. I didn't even know if there was anyone out there left to listen. Steve stepped forward and drew in a long breath.

"At ten o'clock this morning, a mistake was made by Fulcrum Nuclear Power Plant. We admit it, and we will take whatever is coming to us, but for now, I am trying to save survivors.

The heavy snowfall overnight blocked the chimneys of the reactors. Instead of clearing it correctly, some junior members of staff sought to save themselves a job and blow the snow out. Sadly, what they didn't realise was the snow had become radioactive. They increased the pressure in the reactor, which caused the radioactive yellow snow that has been falling. We now know that if consumed orally, this snow causes living beings flesh to melt. Their interior organs and bones remain, but basically, they become the living dead. They seem to be driven to kill the unchanged with a view to consuming their brains. I guess you could say it's a zombie apocalypse and we caused it."

Steve took a deep breath and continued.

"Further to this, the increased pressure in reactor number two has not returned to normal. It is, in fact, growing and growing and it is now not a case of if it explodes, but when. We forecast this to happen in approximately three hours. The results will be catastrophic.

Nothing in the blast zone will survive. Most will be vaporised. In the next ringed area outside the vaporisation zone, the radiation will be so strong that any living beings will succumb to radiation sickness immediately.

Those in the next area will survive but will suffer effects of radiation sickness. Further to this protocol, we normally would be trying to prevent this explosion. Sadly, we must allow it to happen. The changed must be destroyed.

I don't know how much of the country outside the disaster zone - if any - has been affected, but please if you live within these zones and you are not changed, gather what you can and leave.

Help the elderly and disabled.

Carry young.

Animals are not immune from the effects of the snow. If they consume it, they will become changed and they will kill you. Leave animals. Leave quickly. Do not eat the yellow snow. I repeat, do not eat the yellow snow. May your various Gods save you all."

With tears streaming down his weathered face, the other man from the power plant stepped forward and stumbled. Kasey caught him and helped him in front of the camera. With a shaking voice, he addressed the nation… if indeed there was still a nation out there.

"I wanted to say how very sorry we are. I realise that doesn't bring back your loved ones or change what will happen soon, but dammit, we are so very sorry"

Kasey tried once more to catch the man as he stumbled and fell, but his face turned puce. Shit! He was having a heart attack! I rushed forward and loosened his clothes. He wasn't breathing anymore. Pinching his nose, I began to breathe into his mouth. I gestured at Kasey to help, and for once, working in perfect harmony, no longer boss and staff, but equals, she began to pump his chest, no words needed between us.

It wasn't long when we realised that he had gone. Like so many others had on this day from Hell, he had slipped away, but for him, it had at least been swift and peaceful. I draped my suit jacket over him. Kasey muttered something that sounded like a prayer. Together, we walked off the set. The camera still rolled, but there was nothing left to be seen or said. Now, we had to prepare for our own Armageddon.

I'd like to say there was a happy ending, but there could never be a happy ending to this awful tale, could there? As my children - twins, flaming haired - sit to listen to their father telling the story of the worst day of his life (somewhat less graphically than the version I share with you), I once more silently thank the stars that that awful day did happen. For out of the radioactive fallout, for me and Kasey at least, a phoenix of hope rose.

We all got out of the studio alive, except John, the nuclear power plant worker. Steve insisted on staying with the plant until the end. We knew this meant his death, but I think he made peace with that. Kasey had a minor strop about leaving her gleaming BMW behind, but it had gone a grim shade of yellow anyway from the putrid snow that had begun the day from Hell. We piled into Arnold's old Mondeo estate car. I had found his keys on his desk next to the picture of his long-dead parents that he kept there.

I knew I had to get us far enough away, and I did.

There were many survivors outside the fallout zones. It hadn't been as apocalyptic as we thought, but we took a high vantage point silently with others and waited for the inevitable.

When it came, it lit up the night sky for hours; a mushroom cloud like you see on the films. Kasey snuggled into me, seeking comfort which I gladly gave.

That horrible night, in the wake of so much death and destruction, we fell in love.

That was five years ago now. The fallout zone is deserted and will stay that way for many years to come. Kasey and I have our own counselling service now for PTSD sufferers. Who knew that Ice Queen Kasey could become such a caring person… and indeed a doting mother.

The subjects of that dotage now stood before me, dressed in woolly hats, warm coats and matching gloves and scarves. My children. My life. I bet their peers were not receiving quite the same lecture as they prepared to go outside and enjoy the very first snowfall of their young lives, but I knew that somewhere out there, other loving parents would be warning the lights of their lives, their offspring and heirs, to never eat yellow snow.

Just Another Winter's Tale

Mark Woods

The first thing that Mike noticed as soon as he woke up was the snow.

Overnight, it was almost as if a blanket of white had descended and covered the whole of town, which, he supposed, it had. Everywhere he looked there was crisp, white snow; more flakes still falling from the sky as he looked out of his bedroom window.

For once, he thought, *the weathermen had been right. Suppose it had to happen someday…*

They had been predicting snow for the last week or so; a cold front coming over from Alaska, the like of which - or so meteorologists claimed - this country had not seen in about ten years. But up until last night, there had been no sign of the snow that had been promised. Bookies, who had closed their books on the odds of there being a white Christmas this year, suddenly reopened the betting, and it had begun to look like the whole thing had just been a false alarm… and now this.

Fucksocks, Mike thought, looking out, realising he'd spoken aloud.

"What is it, Mike?" his wife asked from the comfort of their bed, still snuggled beneath the warmth of the duvet. Mike wasn't even sure what had made him get up. He didn't *think* he needed the toilet. He looked back at his wife, feeling more than a bit envious that she was still comfortable while he stood by the window, freezing his bits off.

"I think you might need to de-ice the car this morning," Mike said, an understatement if ever he'd heard one. "We've had a bit of snow during the night."

"How much?" she asked, meaning was it enough for her to call off going to work.

"Not *that* much," Mike begrudgingly told her. "But it's still falling.

"What's the time?" she mumbled, rolling over, not only wrapping the duvet tighter around herself but also taking most of it with her; stealing what little was left on his side of the bed.

"About five in the morning," Mike answered. He looked back out the window and saw that, what had been a light flurry five seconds ago, was now falling thick and fast in fat, white flakes which blurred his vision and made it difficult to see through. "You've still got a while before you need to get up for work." Mike realised he was speaking to himself. He could hear his wife, Susannah, snoring that loud, raspy snore she always made when she fell back to sleep after waking.

"Come back to bed then," Susannah mumbled, proving him wrong by still being awake - even if it was only barely.

"I will in a minute," Mike said.

Now he was up, Mike suddenly realised that he *did* need the toilet, after all. He took one last look out of the window behind him, before heading out of the bedroom and down the hall to the bathroom.

Fucking Goddamn weather, he thought.

Three hours later, Mike was getting their son, Bobby, ready for school. Bobby was already dressed, had brushed his teeth, and was now sitting down to a bowl of cereal in front of *The Thundermans* on TV, while Mike enjoyed a breakfast of lightly buttered toast when Susannah rushed through the small kitchen/dining area like a mini hurricane.

"Are you sure you're going to be alright taking Bobby to school in this?" she asked, brushing past Mike, stealing a bite of his toast.

After briefly stirring earlier, Susannah had gone back to sleep and overslept.

Now, she was in danger of being late for work. Mike had none of these concerns.

As a freelance journalist and horror author, he worked from home. Apart from the school run, or when he was working on a particularly juicy story, he rarely left the house unless he had to, which was little and often. "I mean it," Susannah said. "I know I am running late, but I can still run him to school if you want." They only had the one car, meaning if Mike was going to take Bobby to school, they would have to walk the half mile journey in the snow, which was still falling to Mike's consternation. However, that wasn't why Susannah was asking him.

Mike suffered from Hominochionophobia, not a fear of snow - that was plain old Chionophobia - but a fear of snowmen. He also suffered, to a lesser extent, from Automatonophobia – a fear of humanoid figures, such as mannequins or waxworks. It was something he'd suffered from for as long as his wife had known him.

Mike's fear of snowmen, so he claimed, stemmed from a drunken night out back in his teens when he'd gotten lost and had woken up in a farmer's field the next morning, surrounded by snowmen that someone had bizarrely built around him in the night. Still a little drunk and hazy from the night before, Mike had woken up to all these figures around him and, for a minute or so, had started to freak out.

Ever since then, snowmen had continued to freak him the fuck out - to the extent that just seeing one was enough to bring on a panic attack.

Thankfully, for the last decade or so, this part of Norfolk hadn't experienced much snowfall and any they had did not last very long, meaning most of the kids in the last ten years had not had much of an opportunity to build snowmen.

For the most part, Mike's phobia had started to go into decline. But this recent snow threatened to open old wounds.

"I'll be fine," Mike reassured her. "I'll take my anti-anxiety medication with me. I'll even take a couple now. Besides, Bobby will be there - at least on the way - to make sure I don't get myself into any trouble. Right kid?"

Mike winked at his son, whose attention had briefly wandered away from the television during the ad break and smiled as the ten-year-old winked back.

"Right Dad," he said, finishing his last spoonful of cereal. "Nothing at all to worry about. I'll keep you safe."

"See?" Mike said. "Nothing to worry about. *I'm* more worried about *you* driving all the way to Norwich. You just take it slow on that old A47, you hear? I know the gritters will probably have been out but just take care. I mean it."

"I'll be fine," Susannah said, leaning in for a kiss. "And I'm touched by your concern, but you've seen how I drive on the bypass. That thing is like a death-trap at the best of times with people driving like idiots; I always take it slow when I'm on there."

"I know you do, hon," Mike said. "But just be careful anyway. I don't know what I'd do if I lost you."

Susannah glanced at her watch "Look, I really need to go."

"Then go," Mike told her. "Me and Bobby will just be fine. I promise."

"I just hate leaving you two in this weather, I feel bad."

"Just go already," Mike said. "You're going to be late.

Susannah gave him one last goodbye kiss. "Okay, okay, I'm gone," she said. "See you later, Bobby. Have a good time at school."

"Yeah, bye Mum," Bobby said, his attention once more drawn back onscreen to the adventures of the fictional superhero family known as *The Thundermans*.

Susannah left the house.

"Ten more minutes and it's our turn to go, too, kiddo," Mike told his son.

Bobby waved his hand at his dad in reply. "Yeah, yeah," he said.

Mike left to go grab his winter clothes. He wasn't looking forward to stepping outside. It looked colder than a witch's tit out there.

There's something different about this snow; something strange, Mike thought, as he and Bobby left the house ten minutes later. The snow was still falling, but not as thick and fast as it had earlier. There was something that felt a little *off* about it, though, that Mike couldn't quite put his finger on. He stuck out his tongue for a taste, just like he had when he had been a kid, and there *was* something odd about it; a slight chemical taste, like the snow, had been treated with something.

He wondered if had anything to do with the Greenacres Science Institute that was situated only twenty or thirty miles away? There was always rumours about what went on up there and, as they walked, Mike found himself questioning whether maybe something they might have been doing had some sort of effect on the snow?

He vaguely remembered reading about them having an Environmental Science Division, Maybe the slight chemical taste had something to do with pollution being produced by some of the nefarious experiments they allegedly got up to over there.,

Better probably not taste it again then in that case, Mike thought, quickly shutting his mouth to prevent any more of the potentially toxic snow going in. He looked down and saw Bobby sticking his tongue out, copying his dad, and Mike shook his head. "No, Bobby, don't," Mike said. "The snow could be dirty. We don't know where it's been… and I think there's something not quite *right* about it."

"*You* did it," Bobby insisted.

"What have *I* told you?" Mike said. "Do as I say, not as I do."

They continued walking towards the front gate and out onto the path that ran right by their house which, when followed, lead to Bobby's school. There was a big patch of snow by the hedge as they reached the front gate, Mike noticed that it must have been blown into a heap by the wind. But that seemed odd to him.

The hedge acted as a wind-breaker normally and, by rights, there should have been no way the wind could have gotten into their garden and blown snow up into a heap. It was quite a big mound as well. Not a small one.

"Come on, Dad," Bobby said, pulling at his hand. Mike suddenly realised he'd ground to a halt. "We'll be late for school if we don't get a move on." He pulled at his dad's hand, and this time Mike started moving again.

He took one last glance back at the mound as they passed through the front gate and then the strange heap of snow was gone, completely out of sight.

Out of sight, out of mind, Mike thought. But that was not strictly true. All the way on the walk to school, his mind kept going back to that strange mound in the garden. *There's something about it,* he thought. *Something unsettling.*

On the walk to Bobby's school, Mike was distracted, so bid little attention to the few snowmen that had already been built by other children making their way to school and paid them little mind. But on the way back home, alone, that was when he first started noticing them.

He had always thought there was something creepy about snowmen. The way they just stood there, watching you with cold, dead, black, glass eyes that seemed to be all-seeing, but not-seeing, if that made sense. Whereas other kids would always delight at snow and the chance to build snowmen,

Mike had been one to shrink away and do his best to avoid it as much as possible.

Oh, he had liked playing in it and throwing snowballs, just like any other kid, but he had always had this feeling like there was something *unnatural* about it… and there was nothing more unnatural than *snowmen.*

Though he did not follow any faith, his adopted parents had both been Jewish and had regaled him as a child with scary stories, not of monsters that lived in the closet or under the bed, but of the Go-lem; a creature who resembled a human, fashioned not of flesh and blood, but of stone and clay, and who was supposed to have been used in generations past to seek revenge on all who opposed or betrayed those of Jewish faith.

Mike had grown up seeing snowmen as a kind of wintery version of the Go-lem from his adopted parents' tales. This had certainly not helped him sleep at night or helped him with the anxiety and phobia that had gone on to follow him into adulthood.

As Mike walked back to his house, he did his best to try and ignore the snowmen that had been built around his neighbourhood. He felt his anxiety starting to rise and, for a moment, thought about taking another couple of pills, but his psychotherapist had told him to take them sparingly; only two every three/four hours because the side-effects could serve to counteract the very purpose for them being prescribed in the first place.

As he walked, Mike tried to put into the practice the breathing exercises his therapist had suggested - *recommended* - for him to do whenever he started feeling anxious and was between pills.

Breathe in, two, three, four, Mike thought, *breathe out, two, three, four, five…*

The idea was to slow down his breathing and regulate his heart-rate; try to slow down some of the thoughts running through his head. Like the pills, sometimes this worked, sometimes it didn't... Mike was pretty sure the pills were just placebos anyway.

He had written an article last year on big pharmaceutical companies and had discovered - because in recent years anxiety and depression had become a billion-pound industry - that many big, supposedly reputable companies, were deliberately obfuscating some of the ingredients and chemicals used in their medication to help disguise the fact that most of them was just sugar-water, with a little flavouring and some other stuff thrown in for good measure.

Depression and anxiety, so it was believed, were entirely psychosomatic and bore no physical correlation. If you could convince people that the medication was doing some good...well, the results seemed to speak for themselves.

Mike didn't believe this to be true - he had read too many articles that showed or indicated that depression and anxiety were both triggered by fluctuating levels in endorphin and dopamine levels, but he had to admit that if people *thought* they were taking something to make them feel better - even when they were not - then that created positive results.

Mike was home before he knew it.

He had been so distracted by the thoughts running around his head that he had not even realised how far he had come - in fact, he had almost missed his house completely and carried on walking.

The mound of snow he had passed on his way out was still there, Mike noticed, but it looked like it was *bigger* somehow. It also looked as though it had *moved*. Only a few feet, but still... it looked closer to the house than when he'd left.

What the fuck, Mike thought, then dismissed it as his imagination. *Must just be mistaken, that's all,* Mike told himself. He went inside the house and tried to give the mysterious mound no more thought.

For a while, he almost succeeded.

Mike spent the day finishing off an article on cloning for a big science magazine he had been commissioned to write. To be fair, most of it was already done - he just needed to give it a quick read-through, an edit, and iron out some of the finer details, then it was done. However, it still took him most of the day. By the time he had sent it off to his editor, it was time to leave and go pick Bobby up from school.

As he left the house, Mike glanced over to where that strange mound of snow had been earlier, and suddenly stopped with a start. He was sure the mound had moved again. It was even closer to the house than it was before. It had also *changed.*

While Mike had been inside, writing his article, someone must have snuck into his front garden because it now resembled a snowman. A half-finished snowman to be fair, but still a snowman. Mike looked around, wondering if perhaps he might have disturbed someone mid-construction, but there was nothing. Not even any footprints, other than his own, that might indicate someone had been here. The newly-constructed snowman was not just closer to the house, but also closer to the path that led to the front gate and, as Mike went by, he lashed out with his arm and knocked the snowman's crude head from its body.

Fuck you. Frosty, he thought as he passed through the gate and walked to pick Bobby up from school.

On the way back from school, there were even *more* snowmen than that morning. They now lined the gardens of all the houses they passed, and seemed, more than ever, to be watching them as they went. Mike reached into his pocket and pulled out his pills, popping a couple more, despite having only taken a couple an hour ago, just before he had been due to pick up his son.

Bobby must have sensed his dad was starting to become anxious because he took his dad's hand and told him it was okay. He was with him. No harm would come to him because Bobby was protecting him.

Isn't that the wrong way around? Mike asked himself. *Surely, I should be the one protecting him?*

But Bobby wasn't the one feeling anxious.

As they reached their house and passed through the gate, Mike noticed someone had returned and replaced the head on the snowman that he had knocked off just under an hour ago – the journey to and from school taking about twenty minutes each way.

At first, Mike thought whoever had done it must have simply scooped up the head he had decapitated and put it back on the snowman's body but, as he looked closer, Mike could still see the smashed mound that had once been a head on the floor in front of the snowman. No, this on its shoulders now was a *new* head that someone had made. It almost looked like it had grown out of the neck of the snowman to replace the one that had been lost. But that was just a silly notion, he told himself.

"Are you okay, Dad?" Bobby asked, realising they had stopped. "Hey, did you build that? Is your phobia better now?"

Mike reluctantly shook his head. He couldn't seem to take his eyes off the snowman that, at the same time, also seemed to be staring back at him; almost as though it was trying to devour his soul.

"Let me get rid of it for you then," Bobby said, proceeding to kick and lash out at the snowman until all that remained was a thick pile of snow, like the one that had sat there earlier. "C'mon," Bobby said. "Let's get inside, Dad. It's cold out here, and my hands are freezing.

Mike allowed himself to be led inside. But he couldn't stop looking back at that big pile of snow.

It's moved closer to the house, was Mike's last thought before him and Bobby closed the front door, cutting them off from the outside world and, more importantly, that big pile of snow that he knew still waited for him.

Later that evening, Mike got a phone call from his wife.

Susannah was stuck in the city and wouldn't be home tonight. Her company had arranged to put her up in a hotel overnight as they agreed that it was too dangerous for her to try and drive home in such terrible conditions

Mike had been watching the news. He had seen stories on one of the local broadcasts about people being attacked by looters taking advantage of the current blizzard; had heard about people getting stuck in their cars whilst attempting to get home

He had seen something earlier about a car being discovered first thing that morning with its driver still inside, frozen to death. Not far from the car, the body of a farmer had also been found - likewise frozen to death and turned into a popsicle - who must have collapsed and died in the early hours, or succumbed to hypothermia whilst trying to rescue the driver; no doubt unaware he was already too late

No, Susannah staying in the city until the snow clears is for the best, Mike thought. The story about people being attacked disturbed him, though. *How short a time it took,* he thought, *for society to break down and people to stop obeying the rules. No, better she stays in a hotel where she's safe*

After he'd hung up the phone, Mike washed the dinner dishes. Bobby was upstairs in his room, playing with his tablet no doubt. Though not autistic (according to the doctors they'd taken him to) he *did* have learning difficulties and Mike had downloaded a load of educational programmes designed at helping his son progress with his learning through a series of puzzle-solving exercises. Bobby loved solving puzzles. He was a wonder at Sudoku and would sit up in his room playing with his tablet for hours.

Mike had downloaded some software, so he could track his son's progress, and there *had* been some visual improvement with his learning since he had started playing his games. Now, as Mike stared out of the kitchen window, finishing off the dishes, he thought he could make out something in the dark, out there in the back garden. Turning, he moved the dial on the dimmer switch in the kitchen, increasing the intensity of the overhead lights, and looked back out of the window again.

There were snowmen out there! Three of them! Three snowmen sitting in his back garden!

They hadn't been there earlier, he thought. *I'd have seen them! I know I would!*

When he and Bobby had sat down for dinner, he was pretty sure he would have noticed three snowmen in his garden, despite it having been dark when they had eaten. They were there now, though. Someone must have snuck into his back garden and built them while he was busy dealing with Bobby.

As he moved closer to the kitchen glass, Mike thought he detected movement out of the corner of his eye and saw *another* snowman standing in the shadows, watching him from off to the right.

Four of them! There are four of them out there!

When he looked again at the original three, Mike bit back a gasp. The snowmen had *moved*. He was *sure* of it.

They now seemed much closer to the house than before, and he was sure it wasn't just his imagination this time. Nor a trick of the light.

No, he thought, *the fuckers had moved!*

Grabbing a broom from the cupboard in the kitchen, Mike unlocked the back door and stepped into the back garden.

Thick, fat flakes were still falling from the sky, as they had been all day, and Mike could barely make out his hand in front of his face, despite having been able to see clearly through the kitchen window moments before.

Biting back his fear, Mike charged at the snowmen and, one-by-one, smashed them all to pieces - his phobia evolving into near-hysterical anger as his fight or flight response engaged itself, manifesting itself as rage.

Without realising it, he growled and yelled as he smashed each of the snowmen into smithereens, and it was only when he looked up that he realised his son, Bobby, was standing at the back door watching him.

"Dad?" his son asked, confused as to what was going on. "Dad, whatcha doing?"

"Nothing, son," Mike said. "It's fine, it's all fine. Everything's fine. I promise you." He was out of breath, exhausted, obviously more out of condition than he had thought. He picked up the broom that he had dropped in his blind rage and started walking back towards the light of the open back door.

"Dad?" Bobby asked. "Where did all those snowmen come from?" He pointed back the way Mike had come.

"What snowmen?" Mike asked. "There aren't any more. I just destroyed them all."

"No, I'm talking about *those* snowmen," Bobby said, still pointing.

Mike looked back.

There were four snowmen emerging out of the shadows over by the hedgerow that marked the perimeter of their back garden. Mike could have sworn they hadn't been there a minute ago. It almost looked as though they were *smiling* at him, *grinning* at him.

A faint breeze started blowing, sending flurries of snow into his face and, as Mike wiped his eyes, he saw several small mounds of snow being formed by the wind in the very place where he had just smashed the earlier snowmen - almost as though they were slowly trying to reform themselves.

"Get inside. It's time for bed in a minute anyway," Mike said, ushering his son back indoors. He had no idea what was going on, he just knew he no longer wanted to be out there.

After putting Bobby to bed, Mike went downstairs and stared out the kitchen window again. There were six of them out there now. Six snowmen! And they were closer to the house than they had been earlier. He was *sure* of it now.

Moving back to the living room, Mike stared out the front window. There was another out there; no doubt the same one he and Bobby had both destroyed earlier. Though he couldn't see it without going outside to check - something he *wasn't* about to do, phobia or no phobia - he *knew* it was out there, facing the house, slowly moving forwards closer, and closer, and closer, and closer…

Mike pulled the curtains together, poured himself a stiff drink, then went upstairs to bed. What he couldn't see, couldn't hurt him - but he still checked both doors, front *and* back, to make sure they were both locked before he went up.

Outside, the snowmen continued to move closer…

Mike dreamed.

He dreamt snowmen were trying to get into the house.

He dreamt he and Susannah had already barricaded the windows and doors - *and when did she get home?* Mike wondered in his sleep - and Bobby was safe upstairs, but he could hear them outside, beating on the front and back doors, trying desperately to break in so they could make him, Susannah, and Bobby just like them.

They wanted to turn them all into snowmen. If Mike and Susannah could stop them from getting in, they would be safe. He had no idea how he knew this, but as this was a dream, he just did.

The doors were starting to break; not being sturdy enough to withstand the assault by the raging elements for much longer. While Susannah rushed to the back of the house to block up the back door with whatever she could, Mike hurried into the living room, trying to manoeuvre the sofa into the hall to block the entrance through the front door. They had told Bobby to hide. Right now, if he was doing what they had told him to, he should be safe.

As Mike turned towards the back of the house to help Susannah, he passed the door to the cellar. That was strange. He couldn't recall them ever having a cellar before. There was a sound coming from inside - a sound like something slowly slithering up the cellar stairs, towards the door he was currently standing outside. Seemingly unable to stop himself, Mike unlocked the bolts that secured the door and opened it to see what was making all the noise and what, if anything, was currently moving up the stairs.

There was a snowman there, Mike realised as he opened the door, a man made entirely of snow, with legs and, as Mike watched, it continued ascending the stairs towards him.

I should shut the door, he thought. *Shut the door and trap it in the cellar; turn around and flee; go, grab Susannah and Bobby and just run.*

But for some reason, he couldn't.

It was like all his limbs had suddenly stopped responding to him.

It's too late, he realised. *Too late for all of us.*

The snowmen were already in the house. And there was nothing any of them could do. The snowman coming up the stairs finally arrived at the top and reached for him with both arms; wrapping its hands around his head.

Mike could feel the icy cold numbness of the creature's fingers seeping into his skull as the snowman began slowly crushing his head to make it burst, even as he heard Susannah screaming from somewhere behind him as another snowman broke through the back door and attacked her. The last thing Bobby would hear, Mike realised, before the monsters eventually came for him too, would be the sound of his own parents being slaughtered. He only hoped his son's death was swifter than either of theirs.

Mike screamed and, and as he did, the snowman attacking him burst completely apart, drowning him in thick, white snow. The last thing Mike thought before he woke up was, *so, they can be beaten…*

And then, he was awake.

Bobby was there, in front of him, shaking him awake.

They were *his* cold hands on his face, Mike realised, coming out of the deep sleep. *Not* the snowman's.

That had just been a dream.

Bobby's hands were bitterly cold, frozen in fact.

By the side of Bobby's bed, a baseball bat rested. It had been a Christmas present from an American uncle on his mother's side a few years ago, Mike remembered, though he didn't think Bobby had ever used it up until now.

"Dad, wake up!" Bobby said, urgently. "I've been outside, and I killed the snowmen. I had this dream they were trying to get inside, and they were, but I stopped them. I stopped them good, Dad."

"That's nice, Bobby," Mike murmured, still not really awake. Then he suddenly registered what Bobby was saying. "Wait a minute - *what*?" He shook himself fully awake and climbed out of bed.

"They're all gone. All dead, Dad. I promise. I pulverised them; smashed them until there was nothing left. They were trying to get in! They were right by the front and back door when I woke up, but I stopped them, Dad. I stopped them good."

Mike followed his son downstairs. There were clumps of snow that Bobby had trodden into the house, piles and piles of it in the kitchen and hall.

But no snowmen, thankfully.

"Did I do good, Dad?" Bobby asked, seeking approval. "Did I do well?"

"You did, son," Mike said, ruffling his son's hair. "You did very good." The boy was growing taller, Mike noticed; almost as tall as his father. It wouldn't be much longer before he'd be too big for Mike to ruffle his hair anymore. He wasn't sure how his son had managed it, but Mike had a relaxed feeling like the danger was now over. For some unknown reason, Mike didn't think the snow posed a threat anymore.

"Come on," Mike said. He looked at his watch and saw it was six in the morning; only just getting light outside. "It's still early yet. Let's go back inside. With any luck, they might even cancel school in the morning if you're really lucky."

"Yay," Bobby replied. "I can go out and play in it then."

A good few years ago now, Mike had bought Bobby a sledge but, up until this year, he had only had a chance to go on it once.

"Come on," Mike said again. "You never know, Mummy might even make it back home today."

The snow that had been constantly falling since last night, had finally stopped. The sun was out, and it looked like being a nice day. With any luck, the snow might even have melted by lunchtime…

The two of them went back upstairs.

Later, as Mike and Bobby ate breakfast, there was a sound at the front door. Mike got up, and Susannah was waiting for him in the hall.

"It stopped snowing," she explained, "so I got in my car and left at first light. A half hour journey took me two hours. I was, like, doing 30 down the A47 the whole way."

Bobby came flying down the hallway with a "Mummy! Mummy! Mummy!" and launched himself at her for a hug.

"So, what have you two been up to then?" she asked, looking at Mike. "I see someone finally got their phobia." She raised an eyebrow at her husband. "Did someone have fun last night?"

"What do you mean?" Mike asked, confused.

"I'm talking about all the snowmen out in the front garden..." Susannah said, feeling more than just a little confused herself now.

Mike moved into the living room, towards the big picture window which overlooked their front garden. Where there had been one big snowman last night, now there were lots of little ones; all spread across what little you could see of their lawn under the snow.

"*Fuck*!" Mike exclaimed, ignoring his wife's cry of "Language! Not in front of Bobby!" as he rushed towards the back of the house. Looking out the kitchen window, he saw there were literally hundreds of small snowmen out there, surrounding the house, reaching for the back door with their stick limbs.

"Fuck! Fuck! Fuck" Fuck! Fuck! Fuck!" Mike shouted.

Susannah rushed into the kitchen behind him. "What is it? What is it, Mike?" she asked, worried now.

As she approached him, there was the sound of the back door opening; the creak of the hinges that Mike had been meaning to oil for months were all too apparent. She turned as a flurry of snow blew directly into her face, momentarily blocking her vision as something from *outside* slowly forced itself *inside*.

Mike tried to yell at her to shut the door and lock it, but it was already too late - the snowmen were in the house and coming for them all. The last thing Mike heard as more snow blew in from outside, blinding him, was the sound of Bobby screaming from the hallway as the front door came open and the snowmen around the front slowly forced their way inside, away from the warmth of the early morning sun.

As chaos descended inside of Mike and Susannah's house, slowly the rest of the snowmen crept forwards... ever forwards... headed for inside the house...

Mike and Susannah's neighbours didn't fare much better.

The snow was coming.

And it would not be stopped.

Smite Thee Down

Dale Robertson

ANNAN, SCOTLAND

"That's the one," Kenny mumbled to himself, as he watched the woman across the street.

He stood at the edge of the alleyway, the peak of his baseball cap and toes of his trainers the only visible items to people passing by until they were close enough to view him, then a look of disgust crossed their face as they either walked a little faster or crossed the pavement to avoid him. He was so used to this reaction. It barely registered anymore. People avoided him based on the negative stereotype of how he looked. Fortunately, he *liked* it and fell right into what the stereotype perceived. He was a junkie; always looking for his next fix, always on the lookout for his next victim.

It hadn't always been that way. He had vague recollections of happy times with his parents and friends. Uni. Parties. Girls. That was the start of his downfall. One hit at a Freshers party was all it took for him to slip cheerfully into the dark abyss of drug use. His friends stuck around for a while, seeing what was happening, trying to help but, eventually, they left him well alone after countless rebuttals. His parents stuck by him, until he robbed their life savings. That was the last straw. They kicked him out and disowned him.

So, here he was, scouring the streets for potential people to rob. He had perfected the art over the years and could sometimes grab a purse or mobile without the person realising.

Often, there was some sort of violence, whether it be a shove or a smack to the face. Sometimes even *he* took a kicking.

He also knew how to evade people who gave chase, especially men who had seen women being robbed of their valuables and wanted to play superhero.

All the side streets, lanes, nooks and crevices about town were his warren, where he could get people lost and disappear without a trace. The numerous abandoned houses and shops helped his situation immensely.

The way he was dressed, thanks to the judgement of society, singled him out as a "no-gooder", and he would change if he could just be arsed, but the truth was, he couldn't. By the time his fix was satisfied, there was very little to no money left for nice clothes. Life would be a lot easier if he could just rob people by getting them to lower their guard thanks to him looking smarter.

Bringing himself back to reality, Kenny ogled the high-heeled, leggy, power-dressed blonde across the street. Watching her hips sway gently from side to side as she left the cash machine with a wad of notes, slipping them into her purse for all to see, her mobile pressed to her ear. Jesus, people just *asked* for trouble these days. Did everyone think they were untouchable? A smile graced his face and he shook his head. An old woman walking her Westie looked at him as if he'd sprouted another head, and she pulled the dog along as she trotted quicker along the pavement. The poor dog looked as though its head might pop off.

He slinked out from his not-so-secret viewing place and matched her stride-for-stride. Luckily for him (unluckily for her), the street was relatively quiet and, well, would you look at that - she has even turned down an alley! God was certainly on his side today. He could maybe even try and get a quick grope whilst getting his loot. He turned his head skyward and said, "Thank you."

Quickening his pace, Kenny dodged oncoming cars as he crossed the road. Honks of the horn filled the air.

He flipped the driver a finger without even turning around.

He got to the corner of the alley and glanced down it.

There she was - nobody else around - and plenty of bins and litter would mask his approach. He made a last check for anyone walking nearby and, seeing the coast was clear, followed his prey.

"So, I said to him, 'No, I'm not into *that*!'" The woman said into the mouthpiece of her mobile. "That's the trouble with these dating sites; I just seem to attract weirdos."

She giggled at whatever the caller had said and carried on chastising men and dating.

Clink!

"Hold on a sec," she said, removing the phone from her ear. She stopped and spun around to see the backstreet clear behind her. She took stock of where she was and frowned. Her heartbeat quickened as she zoned out and took in her surroundings. Litter-strewn alleyway. Wheelie bins stacked side-by-side. General gloominess.

This wasn't her usual route. *Shit, I must have taken a wrong turn*, she thought. *Must. Stay. Off. The. Phone.* Facing front again, she saw the alley continued until it hit a wall and turned right.

A tinny voice brought her back to the here and now, and she looked at her phone as if it was an alien device. She lifted it to her ear. "Yes, yes, I'm still here. No, nothing's wrong." She turned around to make her way back to the street to rectify her mistake.

As she walked past bins stacked waist high with rubbish, a blurred movement caught her eye, but it was too late.

A force hit her side on, barrelling her into the wall, bouncing her off it.

As she stumbled to the ground, the thin material of her tights and the flesh of her knees was scraped away.

One of the heels snapped from her shoes. Her phone slid across the ground. She was grabbed and slung into the wall again, hands moving over her body, grabbing whatever they could; her bag, her jacket, her *breasts.* She curled into a ball as her bag was wrenched from her, the straps snapping in the process.

Then it stopped.

All she could hear were the birds squawking high above, and the sound of fading footsteps. She curled up in the foetal position and cried.

Success! That was so easy, Kenny thought, disappearing around a few corners and slipping into another street. He tucked the stolen bag into his tracksuit jacket, which was suitably hidden thanks to his skinny frame and baggy top and put the phone in his pocket. The phone had a few scratches on the screen but would still bring in some decent cash.

People and their fucking Smartphones, eh?

He found a shortcut back to his den, which ran adjacent to the local butcher's shop. He stopped, crouching next to a wall which went behind the butchers to survey his pickings. He pulled out the bag and scrambled past lipstick and feminine products, before finding the purse. The bag was chucked to the ground. Lipstick rolled to a stop under a sack of garbage. He popped the purse open and a wad of notes made his eyes widen. Kenny flicked through the roll. Twenty. Forty. Sixty. One hundred! Two hundred! Fuck, he was going to have some fun tonight. This was the jackpot. Nothing could remove the smile from his stubbly face.

Submerged in his fantasy world of upcoming debauchery, Kenny failed to recognise the skies darkening above him.

It was as if a time-lapse video was being played, turning day to night in seconds.

As darkness fell, shadows crossed the notes he held. His head turned skyward. "What the hell?" he muttered, "Surely it isn't night time already."

He checked his watch - 15:35. He peered around the corner, straining his eyes to see the street at the entrance of the lane. It looked light. Normal daytime. No blackness or shadows. He looked above again to see the clouds gathering.

He stood up, tucking the money into his pockets, and started to walk back the way he had come. As he was about to turn the corner, thunder rumbled above him. It wasn't even distant - he ducked, it was that close. His heart jumped, and he looked up, gazing into the collection of clouds that had grouped together. There were blue electrical snakes streaking through them. Sensing a storm brewing, he decided to run to his den, before he got caught in the rain. Three steps into the run, a flash of lightning struck the ground, inches from his feet. He skidded to a halt, heart thumping faster in his chest. He leant over to catch his breath, resting his hands on his knees, and saw smoky tendrils rising from the impact on the ground in front of him. He turned to go the other way instead. Thunder rumbled again and, a second later, lightning flashed before him, striking a nearby metal bin. The noisy *crack* echoed in the tight alley space, spinning it around, knocking it over. Sparks shot out close to him. Kenny yelped and rapidly began to pat his hands over this tracksuit, convinced he was about to catch fire.

He let out a nervous laugh at the strange weather behaviour, looking back and forth to see if anyone else was around to witness it. He looked up again. He was stuck for his next move. Before his brain had chance to formulate something, a crash of thunder rocked him, shaking the ground where he stood. A beat later, lightning snaked its way down from the heavens and bolted Kenny right between his eyes.

His body jerked as the high voltage energy coursed through him, his skin blistering.

Smouldering. Vapour rose from his crackling skin.

His legs were planted to the ground, and his head was fixed aloft.

The sight would have been quite the spectacle had anyone been nearby to see it - this man, lodged to the ground by a bolt of lightning. What were the odds?

Two minutes later, it stopped, just like that. He stood upright for a few seconds, but his legs eventually gave way, and his body crumpled to the concrete, a bubbling mess of flesh. His eyeballs had popped, and his skin had melted from his face.

The clouds dissipated as quickly as they had arrived. The world carried on as normal in the ocean blue sky and crisp air.

BLACKPOOL, ENGLAND

As the school bell rang, Michael gathered his books, slid them into his bag, and was out of the door before it had ended. He scanned the hall, left to right, before making his way to the exit, his feet trying to walk faster than his body would allow. He gained suspicious glances from his fellow students who lingered in the hall, chatting away. He stopped by the double doors and stared out, searching the surrounding area. He let out a sigh of relief, his breath misting the glass, and pushed the doors open.

Stepping into the cool fresh air, he buttoned his jacket up to his neck, ducked his head down, and headed for home.

"Oh, Mickey!" a voice seductively called from behind him. "You forgot something." Erratic giggling followed.

His head spun around instantly at the sound of the shrill voice, and he spotted the two girls standing on the top step, glaring his way. They blew him a kiss and waved excitedly. A spattering of kids on the grass looked around to see what the commotion was, their eyes ping-ponging between Michael and the girls. They would have had the same thought as any other random onlooker: Michael had gained a couple of admirers. Michael knew better though, and he wished the rest of them did as well. Maybe then, instead of laughing at the scenario, they might have helped.

At twelve-years-old, being the new kid in town was always going to be tough. Settling into a new school and trying to break in to the already made up cliques was nigh on impossible. Thanks to his dad's new job, they had to relocate to this seaside town. He had to leave behind the friends and places he was familiar with. He had tried to protest, but it fell on deaf ears - they were moving and "that was final". His parents had eventually softened, sitting down with him, reassuring him that making friends would be easy and that he just had to be himself. Unfortunately, he wasn't exactly the social type, to begin with. His previous friendships had taken time to solidify. His new school seemed fine and, when he wasn't in classes, he spent most of his time in the library, hiding away and keeping himself to himself. Some kids were friendly enough and tried to engage him in minimal conversations, which he returned, whilst others looked at him as if he was the Devil himself and avoided him. Some would even nudge into him, knocking books out of his hand, turning to leer at him.

And then came Gemma and Deborah - two girls who, at fourteen, seemed to home in on his insecurities right from the start. They would make a beeline for him whenever they saw him enter a room. His lunch would be spat in. They would punch him on the way by. Push him into doors, walls, even a drinks fountain (which sprayed water over his trousers, making it look like he had pissed himself - something that everyone found highly amusing). The behaviour seemed to go unnoticed by others (bar the bogus trouser pissing) and, even worse, by teachers, as the girls switched their behaviour to super-sweet whenever one approached. He felt he couldn't tell his parents, especially his dad, as he imagined them laughing at the thought of girls bullying their son. Whenever he thought he had some freedom, even at weekends, they would magically appear, as if the Devil himself had zapped them to his location to torment him.

He stared at his oppressors, as they eyed him with mock excitement. Time seemed to freeze. His surroundings slowed down. People moved in slow motion. His brain raced to find a plan of action. It came up blank. He decided just to run.

He ran awkwardly, his satchel bouncing on his back, the corner of the books digging into his spine. He got to the pedestrian crossing and risked a glance around, as the busy road flowed with traffic. He saw the girls had disappeared; they weren't on the step, and they weren't following. He allowed himself time to slowly examine the route he had run. It wasn't far from the school, and there weren't many hiding spots. No trees. No bins. No nothing! Maybe they just wanted to put the shits up him. It certainly worked.

His heart slowed to its regular pace and the little green man signalled that it was safe to cross. He turned and carried on, walking to the newsagents that sat further up the road. It was always busy with kids once school had finished, so much so, that the owner had put up a sign letting them know that only two teenagers were allowed in at the same time after a spate of shoplifting incidents. There was currently a handful standing outside the shop, which meant maximum capacity had been reached.

He contemplated bypassing his sugar rush and heading straight home but, after his recent scare, he decided that being around people would be a good thing; would provide a haven, especially since one of those people would be an adult. So, he stood at the end of the line, his eyes on constant alert to everything around him, convinced that Gemma and Deborah were still nearby, even though he couldn't see them. His spider senses were tingling.

The queue disappeared quickly, and he was soon in and out with his goodies, his haven not lasting long at all. The walk would give him plenty of time to eat the evidence before he arrived home. His parents hated him gorging on sweets before dinner time.

Michael hurried along, stuffing sweets into his mouth when hands reached out from nowhere and pulled him into a passage that ran between two derelict buildings. Before he had a chance to see who his attackers were (although he guessed), he was on his arse, being dragged by his shoulders further into the rundown path. He spat sweets from his mouth and, as they dribbled down his jacket, he tried to catch his breath.

"Oh Mickey, you're so fine, you're so fine, you blow my mind, hey Mickey!" one of the voices sang.

"Quit it, slut."

"Fuck you, Debs."

They both giggled as they dropped Michael to the ground.

"What's up, Mickey?"

Michael looked at them both, his eyes darting between them, his mouth wide open, his heart trying to escape through his chest. He tried to crab walk backwards, but Gemma moved quickly, kicking his arms out from beneath him. He slumped to the floor, his head bouncing off the concrete. He winced and rubbed it with his hand, pleased to see there was no blood. It still hurt like Hell, and his eyes glazed over with tears.

"Oh no, did that hurt, Michael?" Deborah said, the question dripping with sarcasm. "Are you going to *cwy* now?"

He looked up and saw she had her phone out, pointing it straight at him.

"Smile for the camera."

He looked down, dreading what would happen next, and doing his best to restrain the waterworks that were threatening to burst. Gemma hauled the bag off his back, unzipping it, tipping out books and school equipment, kicking it all over the ground. She picked up the books and began to tear the pages.

"Please don't," Michael whimpered.

"Did I say speak?" Gemma asked. "Shut your trap, new kid. You don't belong here. You should fuck off back to whatever hole you came from."

Deborah and Gemma closed in on him, Deborah with her phone focused on him. Gemma kicked him hard in the arm. His face screwed up in pain. Deborah slapped him across the face, the noise reverberating along the narrow path like a gunshot. "You like that, huh? Let it loose. Let the tears out," Gemma said, sensing their prisoner was about to break. She stamped on his ankle for good measure.

The dam broke; tears began to flow freely from Michael's eyes as he succumbed to the pain. He held his face in his hands, sobbing as the girls ran off, their laughter echoing all around him.

Deborah and Gemma walked along the promenade, viewing their latest act on Deborah's phone, openly guffawing at Michael's humiliation. "Stupid prick. Serves him right," Deborah said. "I can't wait to get this uploaded to Facebook and Twitter. People *love* this shit. Think about how many likes and shares it's going to get."

Gemma giggled.

They stopped beside a lamp post and turned to face the sea, both leaning over the barrier to view the drop to the water below. The murky water was gently lapping against the wall. Deborah checked her phone signal to see if she could upload the video there and then, instead of waiting until she got home. Two bars and 'E' were displayed. "Shit."

She held her phone out and swung around to see if it would change. Still the same. She stood on the highest rung of the barrier and jumped backwards, as high as she could - her signal briefly changing to 'H+'. "Bingo!" She held onto the lamppost and climbed up to the top rung again, which sat a few feet off the ground.

"Jesus Christ! Just wait until you get home, you pleb," Gemma said.

"No chance. Not when I can do it here." Deborah hugged the post, precariously balanced on the metal rung. She was so engrossed in her phone that she failed to notice the wind picking up. It seemed to come without warning, the water below flowing back and forth aggressively.

Gemma looked around at the nearby trees, noticing them bend in the gust. Bins started to blow over. Rubbish fluttered across the street. "Debs… I think you had better get down… the wind is picking up."

"Yeah, yeah. Nearly done," Debs replied, eyes still glued to the phone.

Gemma was far too distracted by rubbish being blown around the street and bins clattering off walls to think about what was happening *below* them. The churning waves were in full flow - smashing high up the wall, flowing back out, then repeating their attack. Water seeped over the edge of the wall, soaking her trainers. The wind had increased, and Gemma instinctively put her hand behind her, grabbing the barricade to steady her swaying body.

Deborah reacted the same way, wrapping her arms tightly around the post, digging her feet into the rung on instinct.

"Debs!" Gemma yelled. "Get down! I don't know what the fuck is going on, but this is crazy. Let's go!"

She couldn't be sure if Deborah heard her or not. However, she never answered. A smile graced Deborah's face and she held the phone aloft in triumph. "Done!"

At that moment, a colossal wave erupted from the sea and crashed over the wall, hitting the girls with all its force, slamming them to the ground, swirling them around, banging them against the barrier, cracking bones, dragging them out to sea.

The wind died down immediately, and the sea settled. It was as if nothing had ever happened… until passers-by saw the bins scattered amongst a fine layer of water lying on the pavement. No sign of the girls existed apart from Deborah's mobile phone. It sat beside the lamppost, the text **UPLOAD FAILED** on its shattered screen.

DORSET, ENGLAND

Doris had just settled down with a cup of tea and a nice biscuit when the doorbell rang. She sighed, placing the tea on the table, and rose to answer it. She muttered to herself as she shuffled along the hall, viewing the dark shadow through the front door window with trepidation.

Upon reaching the door, she gazed through the side window at the man standing before her, bag on the ground. She frowned. She didn't recognise him.

The man caught a glimpse of her face through the window and smiled, lifting an ID badge that hung around his neck, showing her it.

She screwed her eyes up but couldn't make out what the badge said. A vague picture appeared alongside fuzzy text, rather than the perfect image her eyes would have viewed twenty years earlier. She looked past the man towards the road, where a white van with unclear graphics sat at the end of her drive. She observed the man again. He stood looking at her with a pleasant smile on his face. She returned the gesture and eased the door open.

"Mrs Taylor?" The man asked.

"Yes. Can I help you?" Doris replied.

"My name is Mark. I'm from SouthStar plumbing company. We are doing a routine check of the neighbourhood boilers. My colleague is doing the houses on the other road."

He pointed behind the house. "I've been assigned your street."

Doris automatically looked over her shoulder, then back to Mark. "Oh. Oh right. Can I see your ID again?"

"Sure," he said, holding up the badge. This wasn't his first rodeo, and he knew his badge held up to reasonable scrutiny.

Doris pretended to examine it. "Ok. I suppose you better come in. Will you be long?"

"No, ma'am. Just a quick check of the boiler, and I'll be out of your hair."

Doris swung the door open enough to allow the man in. He picked up his bag and entered.

"I can show you where the boiler is, then I'll leave you to it. Would that be okay?" Doris asked.

"Perfect."

They headed down the hall, past the living room and dining room, and into the kitchen. Doris led him to a large storeroom door that sat in the corner.

"It's quite old. I can't remember the last time it was checked, so it might be quite dusty," Doris said.

Mark chuckled. "That's fine. I'm used to it."

"I'll just be through there." She pointed back down the hall. "Second door on the left, if you need anything."

"Thank you. Oh, could I possibly use your bathroom before I start?"

"Yes, of course. If you go back down the hall, up the stairs, it's the door straight ahead of you."

"Thank you so much," Mark said. He sat his work bag down beside the door and headed back to the stairs. Doris followed and took the turning to the living room, settling back down to her tea and biscuit. She picked the cup up and winced at the cooling slop.

Mark got to the top of the stairs and quickly glanced around at the other rooms. He wouldn't have much time.

Thankfully, there was only one room either side of the bathroom, so it shouldn't take him long.

He guessed one would be the bedroom and the other a storage room, maybe even a spare room. He took a gamble and opened the door to his left. He eased the door open discreetly in case the hinges squeaked, but he got lucky. The door swung open to reveal a bedroom. A double bed against the far wall with drawers' bookending it. A wardrobe against the side wall. Wide vanity unit below the window.

He walked over to the unit first and grappled with the drawers. There were six altogether, and it didn't take long before he found what he was looking for - jewellery. And plenty of it. He stuffed as much as he could into his pockets, leaving nothing behind. He knew from experience that it didn't matter what it looked like, it could still be very valuable. Especially the older looking stuff. He slid the drawers closed and left the room, gently closing the door behind him.

Mark opened the bathroom door and stepped in, flushing the toilet, giving him cherished seconds to look in the other room. He swiftly paced to the other room and opened the door. The room was bare, not a scratch of furniture in it. The walls had dark patches in the corners, indicating the beginning of mould, and the blinds were stained an off-yellow colour. He closed it and went back into the bathroom, turning the taps on, going through the fakery of washing his hands. He put his hands in his pockets to stop the jewellery from jingling as he headed down the stairs.

"Thanks, Mrs Taylor," he called, as he passed the old woman in the living room.

"You're welcome, dear."

He went back to the storage cupboard and opened it, viewing the old boiler on the wall.

The whole contraption confused him; they always did. It was just as well none of the old biddies stood over his shoulder while he 'worked'. He hooked the bag with his foot and dragged it into the room with him, closing the door a little to block his next move. As quietly as he could, he emptied the contents of his pockets into the bag. Once he was finished, he covered them with a towel and some tools that he used to beef up the disguise, should anyone think to challenge him. He zipped the bag closed and opened the door, banging the boiler cover to signal some sort of completion on his part.

He walked to the living room and said, "That's me done Mrs Taylor. Nice and easy. Didn't take long at all."

Doris struggled to stand up and Mark raised his hand, "No, no, please, there's no need to stand. I'll see myself out. Have a pleasant day."

Doris smiled. "Thank you, young man. My legs aren't what they used to be. Enjoy the rest of your day.

Mark left the house with a huge smile on his face. Oh, he would enjoy the rest of his day.

Doris sat back down. "What a charming man," she muttered to herself.

Mark chucked his bag into the passenger seat and started the van. The old motor grumbled to life and he let it settle before taking off along the road. He looked back at Mrs Taylor's house, but she wasn't at the window. Thank God! Otherwise he'd have to stop at the next house. Instead, he carried on. He made his way out of town and pulled into a layby to survey his earnings. He could never resist stopping to examine what he had taken. Even though it was a huge risk, it was one he just couldn't stop.

The sun was high in the cloud-spattered sky, blazing down an uncomfortable heat through the windscreen. Mark rubbed the back of his neck and wiped his brow with the back of his hand. He reached for the bag and opened it to view the contents. *Pretty good job,* he thought. Worn-looking rings. Necklaces. Bracelets encrusted with diamonds and other gems. He scooped them up in both hands and let them slip through his fingers, relishing the snaky feel of the chains as they slithered back into the bag.

His eyes squinted as the daze from the sun caught his peripheral vision, light glinting off his treasure. He pulled the visor down to block it out, but it seemed to get brighter. He raised his hand to shield his face. The warmth spread across his hand like a forest fire.

What the Hell?

He brought his hand back down to study it. A faint red mark was present. He gave it a rub and looked out of the window.

"Jesus Christ!" he exclaimed. The sun looked as though it was right outside of his van; as if it had fallen from the sky to hover outside his windscreen. It gazed straight in, spreading its immense heat. He shook his head and rubbed his eyes to shatter the illusion. No luck. He couldn't look directly at it. His eyes felt like they would burst… which is exactly what happened a few moments later.

He screamed in pain and shock, his whole body feeling like it was on fire. He scrambled about in blindness, searching for the door handle, burnt fingers pawing at the door but, as he pulled the lever, the door stood fast and wouldn't budge. As the temperature rose, he tried to duck in the footwell to take cover, but it felt like the sun had moved position to attack him even more.

"What the fuck is going on!" he screamed, running his smoking hands over his body, clawing at melting clothes to alleviate the heat, feeling them disintegrate beneath the blackening flesh of his hands. He hammered on the windows and kicked the doors, but they held. His hands and feet stung with pain from the outburst. The exertion of energy drained him. He couldn't take it any longer. Mark lay down across the footwell, his back arched awkwardly over the bulge where the gearbox sat, and his legs bent under the steering wheel.

The sun continued to burn in through the driver's side window, refusing to give him any respite, aiming its intense beams straight at him, focusing on nothing else. It didn't take long for Mark to burst into flames, his body jerking and twitching in the compact space. His burning figure quickly ignited the petrol tank.

The sun rose to the sky, leaving the van burning by the roadside, and went into hiding behind a screen of fluffy clouds.

CHANNEL 5 NEWS

"There have been several reports of bizarre weather phenomena up and down the country over the past few days, resulting in numerous deaths. The government is not sure what has caused such inexplicable occurrences, and scientists are baffled at this precise moment. We will keep you posted, but advise you keep vigilant if venturing outside."

TEXT EXCHANGE.

LOCATION UNKNOWN

UNKNOWN: Having fun?

UNKNOWN 2: Who dis?

UNKNOWN: I might have guessed you would have forgotten me.

UNKNOWN 2: Moses? Noah?

UNKNOWN: Fuck, Dad, really?

UNKNOWN 2: Holy shit. It's you. How did you get this number?

LUCIFER: Bingo! JC passed it on. I told him I wanted to make up.

GOD: That was obviously bullshit. How could he do that?

LUCIFER: Well, you know what he's like, always trying to see the good in people. Even an outcast like me.

GOD: What did you mean, 'having fun?'

LUCIFER: You seem to be sending a lot of people my way. It brings me joy to see my army growing.

GOD: Bloody sinners need to be cast from Earth.

LUCIFER: There will be nobody left on Earth at this rate.

GOD: I still have my devoted followers and there are plenty of other good people, too. Don't you worry about that.

LUCIFER: I'm not worried. The more you strike down, the merrier I become.

GOD: Don't get too comfy.

LUCIFER: That a threat?

GOD: No, just a fact. Now, fuck off and leave me in peace.

LUCIFER: Love you too, Pops. TTFN x

LUCIFER: #WINNING

The Snow

Peter Germany

Paul Fagg always found it unsatisfying travelling along the A2 at thirty miles per hour. Although it wasn't technically a motorway, but a dual carriageway, everyone treated it like a motorway and sped along it at speeds more than seventy miles per hour. Normally driving this slowly meant there were four lanes of cars backed up because some prat had caused an accident. Tonight, it wasn't like that. Tonight, there was a blizzard leaving visibility down to a couple of car lengths and only one lane in use. Although some vehicles were trying to shoot past the single-file traffic, Paul wasn't stupid enough to try that. He'd done an Arctic snow driving weekend a few years ago in Norway.

He was in his 2014 Land Rover Defender, a short wheel-base model that was top of the range, which was normally only for when he went Green Laning - off-roading through woodland. He was pretty good at it, and it explained the various dents to the jet-black vehicle. It had a snorkel, upgraded suspension, off-road tyres and a winch, which he was fully expecting to use to pull the odd car free at some point during the night. He'd made sure his GoPro was running as well. Might be some decent footage for his Green Lane group's YouTube channel…

The gritters hadn't been able to get out until gone 5 P.M. due to it having rained all day, but also because no-one had predicted this snowfall.

The forecaster who'd just been speaking on 5-Live had said this storm had come from nowhere.

The temperature drop was unprecedented, and they were recommending people not to leave their homes unless it was necessary.

He'd seen complaints on social media as to why the roads hadn't been gritted earlier in the day, and the gritting team had to point out a few times they couldn't come out until it had stopped raining as it would just wash away, but they also needed to know it was going to snow for them to be ready with the gritters. When Paul thought about it, the gritters had done a damn good job getting out as quickly as they had done. When they had finally got out, most of the main routes had been done quickly, but no amount of grit was going to stop the country from being snowed in come morning.

Paul hadn't seen snow this heavy for a very long time. There was already a good six inches on the ground, and the forecasters were now threatening a couple of days of this. Paul wasn't bothered. Once he'd picked Lizzy up from work, they both had the next ten days off. They weren't going anywhere. A staycation as one of their friends had called it. He didn't care what term it had, all he was concerned with was spending some much-needed time together. Six years together, four of those married, and it would be the first time they'd had off at the same time in the last three. If it meant being snowed in, he could live with that. Even if they got a power cut, he wouldn't be too gutted; they had a gas fire and cooker. There was plenty of food in the cupboards. Due to Lizzy's need to have candles lit whenever they were at home during the darker months for 'atmosphere' they had enough to see them through.

Yeah, it was going to be good. Okay a power cut might suck, but they lived in Cliffe Woods and hadn't had a power cut in a fair few years. They'd be okay.

In his daydreaming, he almost forgot to pull into the Bluewater feeder lane. No other vehicles were ahead of him, and none pulled off behind him either. Judging by the faint tyre tracks, no-one had come off here in a while.

The roads around Bluewater didn't look like they'd been gritted, and as he rolled along, a prat in a Mercedes went flying past him in the outer lane, lost control and slid towards the roundabout sideways.

"Lucky pillock," Paul said as the Mercedes came to a gentle stop without hitting anything aside from a small bank of snow that stopped it.

"When it snows hard, it's always in February," he said to himself as he eased off and braked by changing down a gear. A tap on the brakes at the wrong moment could be lethal.

The roads into Bluewater hadn't been gritted but had seen a lot of use and the snow was compacted, but the fresh snow was falling so quickly he didn't think the compacted snow would freeze over.

Paul directed the Defender around to the mid-level car park by the cinema and exhibition centre. Normally, he'd park on the upper level, but he didn't want to park where the vehicle could get snowed in if they got held up here longer than usual. He had a spade and a snow shovel in the back but didn't want to have to dig it out if he didn't have to. He parked as close as he could to the entrance and went in. Lizzy worked at Boots, so this was the closest of the car parks to her and there was also a Costa Coffee where he could sit and wait. On his way in, he'd seen a few cars that were covered in snow, but would likely still be able to get out okay. He was sure the Bluewater management were looking at the problem.

He turned the engine off and pocketed his phone, then pulled his hood over his head, got out and jogged for the entrance. Yes, there was now snow magically falling in the covered car park, but the wind still had a bitter edge to it.

Inside, he pushed the hood back and subconsciously ruffled his hair. As he walked up the slope to Costa, a couple were just going up to the open level of the carpark.

"Watch yourselves out there. It's getting nasty."

"I'm sure I can handle that. I've got a Scooby. It'll be nice to give her a bloody good go out there," the woman said, smiling wide.

"Still, I'd be tempted to take it easy. It's getting deep and even if you know what you're doing, others don't. Some fart in a Merc spun it out approaching the roundabout up there."

"I'll make sure she behaves herself," the man said.

"That'll be a first," the woman said with a wink as they both went out the glass doors.

Paul smiled at their youthful exuberances as he made his way to Costa to wait for Lizzy.

He didn't hear the couples' scream from outside.

With a hot chocolate to go, Paul sat watching no-one. Even on the quietest of evenings, there were normally a few more people about than this. He liked to sit and watch the world go by, especially during the festive period. He always found it amusing the stress that time of year created. Currently, the January sales were all but over and the centre was returning to its normal amount of traffic.

Most of the shops were already closed and Paul had barely had a quarter of his hot chocolate before he saw Lizzy and a couple of her work colleagues walking over to him.

"You all set?" Lizzy said.

"Yeah, lets rock and roll." He got up and the four of them headed for the exit.

"Oh wow, I hadn't realised it had got that bad out there," Christine Pine said.

"It's the worst I've seen it in a long time," Paul said. "Do you two want a lift?"

The two women looked at each other. They both lived in Gravesend, which wasn't far out of his way.

"Do you mind?" Janet said.

"No, of course not."

"Thanks," said Christine.

"Let's roll out." Paul led them towards the ramp down to the middle car park. They stopped to look up to the upper car park as a man jogged past them and out the exit.

"Is it safe to drive in that?" Janet said.

"Yeah, piece of piss. It's actually lighter out there now than it was when I got here." As Paul spoke they heard a scream from the top car park and saw the man who had passed them being waved around in the air by something white. The white creature tore the man's leg off and slammed him into the concrete pillar by the entrance. Christine screamed as blood splattered across the glass entrance. The body dropped to the ground, sinking into the snow as it came to rest. Blood seeped from the body, turning the crisp white snow a bright red. Then the white object grabbed the body and ran into the blizzard.

"What the fuck was that?" Paul said. The staff from Costa had come to see what the commotion was, as had a couple of people who'd been nearby.

"What's going on?"

Paul turned and almost jumped out of his skin as he saw two armed police officers. "That's not good."

"It's not an unusual sight around here, to be honest," Lizzy said.

Paul couldn't take his eyes off the weapons.

"A man just got torn to pieces out there," Janet said.

"What do you mean?" one of the officers asked.

"Just that. It looked like the snow literally tore an arm off the man and whacked him against that column. Just look; you can't miss the blood on the window."

The two officers shared a glance and one of them walked up to the exit. The glass automatic doors slid open.

"We've got a lot of blood here, David."

His colleague ran up and joined him.

"Holy shit," David said, both edging out as the first officer called it in.

"I don't think that's a good idea," Paul said, but neither officer responded as they stepped out into the blizzard. Paul ran up to the sliding doors as they began to shut, stopping halfway and opening fully as the sensor picked him up. He stood in the doorway to prevent them from shutting.

"What do you think you're doing? Get back here!" Lizzy called.

"I'm not going out there, but if they need to run, then the door being open will help."

Paul was surprised to see the two officers were a good twenty feet from the entrance and the blood. He squinted and saw more blood where they were. Paul watched as they trod carefully around the red stained snow. They both turned and one of them yelled out a warning. Then both began firing.

Paul's mouth dropped open as a solid white shape the size of a Range Rover charged at them. It moved across the car park at an alarming pace.

"Get back in here!" Paul yelled. The officers were a good thirty feet from the door now and were hard to see.

"Fuck it! Go!"

Paul heard, and saw the figures running his way. The thing out there changed direction to follow its prey. The officers did their best at running, but the snow hindered them. They slipped through the open door and skidded to a stop. Paul watched in stunned silence as the snow monster stopped outside the canopy of the entrance, where only a little snow had drifted in.

The two officers untangled themselves and quickly trained their guns on the now shut glass doors. Paul backed away as the creature disappeared into the falling snow.

"What in God's name was *that*?" one of the officers asked, crossing himself.

There was a scream from another part of the centre.

"Go check it out, David. I'll stay here and call it in."

David, the officer who'd made the sign of the cross, got up and ran in the direction the scream came from. The first officer radioed the incident in.

"What is it?" Lizzy said.

"I don't know," Paul answered. "It's hard to see anything more than twenty-five feet or so. Whatever it is, it's the same white as the snow."

"I think somethings happening over by Marks. That's where the scream came from," Janet said. She turned a cigarette around in her hands.

"Let's hope it's just the one," Paul said, then watched what colour remained in Janet's face drain out of it.

"What was that?" The officer said.

"Well, there might be more than the one, whatever it is out there."

Officer David jogged back to them. "Two more people over on the top level of Marks car park, Greg. Five people reported seeing the same thing, which was what we saw."

"What *did* we see?" Officer Greg wanted to know.

"Snow that came alive and killed people," Paul said. "It tore that fella apart."

" Are we safe in here?" a barista asked.

"Whatever it is, hasn't come in here yet. So, until it does, let's assume it can't," Officer Greg said. His radio squawked, and he walked off a little to answer it.

"That doesn't mean we're safe. It just hasn't come in yet," Paul said quietly to Lizzy.

"You think it will?"

"God, I hope not."

With his second hot chocolate of the night, Paul watched the glass doors, but only saw snow.

It had started to fall heavier again, and even if there wasn't something murdering people out there, he didn't think any of them were getting out tonight.

Even in his Defender, and having done some snow driving, he didn't think they'd easily get out of the quarry the shopping centre was built in.

The police had got the centre's staff to go through and gather all the people together. Many were at this Costa, despite what had happened just outside.

There were, Paul guessed, twenty or thirty people here, but none of those were staff members from the shops, aside from a handful from Boots.

"It looks like we're the only ones who this is affecting." Lizzy had her focused face on as she scrolled through one of her social media accounts. "And people think we're bullshitting."

"And if you post any pictures, they'd say it was photoshopped."

"For fucksake, how long are we waiting here?" A lad in his early twenties asked.

"Until we know it's safe out there," Officer Greg said.

"There ain't nothing out there. If there was, why ain't it come in?"

"Dude, just look. Blood. A shit ton of blood," Paul said.

"You're all fucking pussies."

"One more word, then you're under arrest." Officer Greg got nose-to-nose with the lad. Well, not nose-to-nose exactly because the police officer was a good six inches taller and noticeably broader. The lad, seeming to shrink before the eyes of the onlookers, sat back down. "We've got support on the way. Once they're here, we'll be able to get a better idea of what's going on out there and think about getting everyone out."

Officer David Marsh smiled as three BMW X5s pulled up to the entrance to the food court. The armed officers got out with weapons at the ready and searched for threats. David had warned about what had struck at them. Dispatch seemed to take it seriously, and the way they were moving told him they were. He knew they would - he and Greg had good track records, but even so, saying a snow monster had killed people wouldn't have rung much truth with him if he was on the other end of the call.

They started to move towards the entranceway. The lead X5 shot into the air, flying towards the twelve officers. It hit four of them before landing in one of the ponds in front of the entrance. Another snow monster swept across the other officers, knocking them off their feet. For a moment, David couldn't see any of them. Then three climbed out of the snow and stumbled around.

David stepped forward and out the sliding doors; "Run! Come on!" They did, and the snow began to move around them. David shot at the shapes, but like his first encounter with these things, bullets didn't have any effect.

The snow slowed the officers, allowing the monster to catch them. One of his colleagues was torn in half. Another disappeared under a blanket of snow, arms and legs flailing to an abrupt stop. The third officer almost made it, but white snow turned red as it burst through his stomach. He was close enough that the blood splattered David, who backed up a few feet.

The man stood there, looking down at the alien object that had impaled him, then his head had dropped backwards, and blood dribbled out of his mouth.

The snow tentacle (David had no idea what else to call it) stayed where it was and seemed to stare at him. The animal it came from was the size of a small car, pure white. He couldn't make out any of its features.

The bloody limb moved up to David's eye-level and held there. He felt like it was assessing him, weighing up whether he was a threat. David backed up a few more feet. The tentacle followed him, moving the corpse it had javelined through as it did. It got as far as the downward heater that was just inside the door. It reared back like it had been struck. The body slumped to the ground as the creature fled from the entrance. The doors slid shut

David watched the creatures tear the corpses apart. The one that had impaled the officer stood on the small bridge over the pond. The blood made it easy for him to follow its movements as it went back to the others, one of which was investigating the X5s. It gave one of them a nudge, and then it picked it up and hurled it at him. It crashed through the entranceway just as David dived out of its way. He scrambled to his feet and pointed his weapon at the destroyed entrance, and snow swirled inside.

"Oh shit!" He backed further away as footsteps raced to him. He risked a glance over his shoulder to see two of the security guards sprinting his way.

"What the hell was *that*?" one asked, stopping dead as he saw the snow coming in behind the totalled BMW.

"How did that happen?" the second guard said.

"They threw it in." Something red dropped down from David's eyebrow. He touched his hand to his head and it came away bloody. "Crap, am I bleeding badly?"

The second guard tentatively stepped forward and had a look. "I don't think so. Looks like a cut, but it's not deep."

"How did they do that?" The first guard hadn't taken his eyes off the BMW that was resting on its side. The grill lights were still flashing blue, but the roof lights were crushed.

Greg sprinted over, "David, you okay?"

"I think so. Just a graze. One of those things lobbed that, though."

"Here comes another!" the second guard said, and they all ran as another X5 crashed through the glass front of the food court.

"Everybody back upstairs!" Greg said.

The third X5 flew through the glass front. Now, the entire food court was open to the snow, which was already sweeping in on the wind, along with the bitter cold.

"They can get in now!" David felt the other three looking at him.

"What do you mean?" one of the security guards said.

"They've broken the windows! They can get in now!"

"I think they're sensitive to heat. One got close to me, and when it got to the heater in that entrance, it reared back like it had been stung."

"And the heat's all getting out now."

"We need to find everyone in here," the security guard said.

"Yeah, let's get everyone together, find the best shop to secure ourselves in."

Paul and Lizzy were halfway along the lower concourse when they saw the two police officers and two security guards running their way.

"What's happened?" Paul called out.

"Upstairs! Now!" Officer David yelled.

They didn't need telling twice and both were up the escalator by the time the four others had reached the bottom of it. They waited at the top for them.

"What was that crash?" Paul asked.

"Whatever they are, they threw three X5s through the windows of the food court. It's totally open down there now," David said.

"Can you see anything moving out there?" Greg asked with a nod to the car park entrance by Costa.

"No, nothing for a while now. Wait, you're saying they've *thrown* four-wheel drive vehicles. Like decent sized ones?" Lizzy asked.

"Yeah, from the car park, by the main entrance into the food court. They had some force to them as well," David said.

Paul looked at the glass doors that lead out into the car park. "I wasn't exactly feeling safe before... now not at all."

"What's this mean? Can they get in now?" Lizzy asked.

"I think so. I think they're sensitive to heat."

"Just heat? I mean, they seem to be made of snow, so doesn't that mean they need snow to be where they want to go?"

The two officers looked at each other.

"I really don't know," Greg said.

"Does anyone else feel how cold it's getting in here?" Lizzy said. "You're talking about them not liking the heat and it's getting colder."

"Okay, let's get deeper into the centre," David said. "We'll go downstairs and–"

They all jumped as a car crashed through the upper entrance. It stopped as it hit a railing. Then they heard something smashing its way through the centre's ground floor from the direction of the food court.

"They're in," David said

THUD!

They all looked up at the roof.

The centre of the roof was glass and covered in snow.

THUD! THUD! THUD!

One of the windows shattered, dropping snow and glass into the shopping centre. A solid white shape dropped through it, hitting the railing before landing on Lower Thames Walk. There was more noise as the thing crashed its way to them from the food court. Then the vehicle that had just been hurled into the entrance was pulled out and something so white it was almost blue filled the entrance.

Paul grabbed Lizzy and backed away from the monster. Its build reminded Paul of a gorilla, but with a couple extra limbs and the size of a Range Rover. He couldn't make out any features beyond its basic shape.

The one that had fallen onto the lower walkway leapt up and grabbed one of the security guards, who had backed against the railing. He screamed for a moment before a stomach-churning crack silenced him. Lizzy gasped, and Paul jumped in front of her.

Chaos erupted as those in the centre scattered everywhere as the armed police opened fire at the beast that lumbered in from the car park. Another dropped from above them, landing on the upper walkway, grabbing an older woman as it landed. Paul watched as it held her by her head in one hand and slammed her face-first into the floor. A third fell through the window and grabbed fleeing humans as it landed.

Paul and Lizzy had kept backing up until they hit a shopfront window. Lizzy went to run, but Paul grabbed her.

"Wait! The car is just through that door." He pointed to the exit to the mid-level of the car park, which was being obstructed by the animal the police officers were shooting at.

Their weapons clicked empty. Then it charged at them, gaining an unbelievable amount of speed in such a short distance. It hit Greg with such force that when he hit the ground he was dead. David turned to run, but it grabbed him by the leg and slammed him repeatedly into the floor until his body separated from the leg the thing was holding onto. It then turned to the others who'd now been cornered by one that had come from the other end of the shopping centre.

Paul grabbed Lizzy's hand. "Run!"

Guilt racked Paul as they sprinted towards the car park because screams filled the air and he wasn't doing anything to help them.

He didn't look back, he just squeezed Lizzy's hand harder as he slowed to let the sensor pick them up and open the door.

It was slow, though, and they had to wait for it to open. They both looked back and saw Christine running towards them.

"Come on!" Paul moved to help her, but one of the smaller ones pounced on her and began beating her.

Lizzy let out a cry and the animal looked their way.

"Run!" Paul grabbed Lizzy's hand again and they got out the sliding door as it was shutting.

His Land Rover was only a few strides from the entrance and they were in it as the snow ape crashed through the glass door. Paul quickly locked the doors and slid the key in the ignition but didn't crank it over. Having seen the strength that the bigger ones possessed, he didn't want to risk finding out how strong this one was.

"Don't move or do anything," Paul said as the animal searched for them. He couldn't ignore the amount of red that was staining the animal's white body. As it got to the Land Rover, Lizzy took his hand. He put a finger to his lips and she nodded. This one wasn't as big as a Range Rover like the other one, but this one resembled a Smart Car.

They flinched as a limb tapped the front of the vehicle. Then it walked around the passenger's side and nudged the Defender. Paul figured the animal thought this was a gentle touch, but it was enough to move the vehicle a few inches to the side. It went out of sight as it went around the back of the vehicle and then was by Paul's window. Even this close, there was nothing to define the animal. It looked like it had the rough build of a gorilla, but with tentacles. It was almost like he was watching a blurry video of an old 8-bit game.

Abominable Snowman sprung to his mind, as it moved on all fours away from them.

"Fucking hell!" Lizzy breathed.

"I thought I was gonna shit myself."

Lizzy rested her head on his shoulder. "What do we do now?"

"We drive out. It's a chance, but I really don't want to wait for that fucker to come back and have a better look," Paul said as the creature went back into the shopping centre.

"It looks like it's stopping out there."

Paul looked out and saw the blizzard had eased off noticeably. The flakes were still large, but they were falling much slower. Visibility looked better.

"We can make it. This'll cut through the sitting snow easy. I don't know how those things see, but that one didn't see us in here, so maybe they don't use sight. That'll help us."

It's still a big chance to take." Lizzy looked worried.

"I know, but we'll have a head start. They're inside and might not hear us."

"And if there's more outside?"

"That's a chance we'll have to take."

"That Arctic snow driving course I got you had better prove its worth now."

"Alright, put your seatbelt on."

Paul clipped his in, and then slid the gearstick into first. He turned the key to the first click and waited for the glow-light to go out. Once it had, he started it up, pulled forward and headed to the nearest exit, looking in his mirrors as much as he could. As an afterthought he flicked on his GoPro.

He felt good, fired up to be doing something. Maybe if he'd done something earlier, people wouldn't have died, but what they had done had been right. There'd been no way to prepare for these things.

They reached the end of the covered part of the car park and he slowed down, not wanting to hit the snow that had drifted in too hard. As the wheels dug in they found some traction and he was able to pick up speed. Lizzy looked over her shoulder as the vehicle wound its way along the roads around Bluewater.

"You see anything?"

"Nothing,"

"I can see blue flashing lights up there."

Lizzy looked up to the flyover which was one of the routes in and out of Bluewater. "Which way are we going?"

"We'll go out the main way, towards the roundabout. There's bound to be more police up there. That slope will be easier as well."

"Okay." She turned back to look out the back window.

As they passed the food court, Paul had a look but couldn't see much down there. He caught something out of the corner of his eye, just before it struck them. The impact had been on the rear passenger's side and sent the arse-end of the vehicle sliding. Paul cursed as he tried to stop the car from spinning out, but he couldn't, and the Defender ended up pointing the way they had come. He'd managed to dip the clutch in time to stop it from stalling, though.

"Motherfucker," Paul cursed as he tried to get the vehicle rolling and in the right direction again. "Can you see it?"

"It's behind us, but it's on its side. Go! It's getting up."

"Fucking prick must've dented my car," Paul said as he got the Land Rover back in the direction that took them out. On the wrong side of the road, he took the vehicle towards the exit of Bluewater as the animals chased it. They began to pick up speed, which he knew wasn't the best idea, but he thought he had more chance controlling the Defender at speed if they were getting rammed. He saw another small one up ahead on an intercept course.

"Let's see how tough these fuckers are. Hold on."

Lizzy looked forward and saw what he was going to do. "Are you fucking mad? You can't play chicken with one of those things."

"Who said anything about playing chicken?"

Paul steered into the charging animal, the Defender's wheels tearing through the perfectly flat snow, but not losing traction. There was a *thud* as the creature and the Land Rover collided. Paul pushed his foot down and the Defender pushed forward quicker. He was sure he'd seen the thing bounce off to the side, but he didn't want to take any chances with it. He pushed the vehicle harder as it went under the flyover and felt his spirits lift as he saw more blue flashing lights than he had ever seen.

"Shit! Big one right behind us!" Lizzy yelled.

Paul glanced in his mirrors and saw the beast behind them. Fear of losing control of the vehicle flew and he dropped it down a gear and floored the accelerator. A line of police vehicles was at the top of the slope and within spitting distance, but the damn monster was almost on top of them. Then there were muzzle flashes from the police line and that seemed to slow the beast down.

The police moved one of the vans with its riot bars over its front screen out of the way as they shot through. Paul brought the vehicle to a stop and him and Lizzy both let out a collective sigh of relief as police ran up to them.

Sat in the back of an ambulance, the two officers looked at them in shock. They'd just recounted what had happened for the second time and the police officer who seemed in charge looked like he wished he wasn't.

"Did you hurt the big one just now? Bullets didn't seem to bother them down there."

"I don't think so. It seems to have chosen not to chase you down."

"Is it just happening here?" Lizzy asked.

"Yeah. We've not had one other reports of anything like this country or countywide. This storm has covered the country."

"What are you going to do about it? There might be survivors down there," Paul said.

"We've been ordered to wait until the army gets here."

"At least it's just here," Lizzy said. Safe now, they had to go to the police station to give their full statements.

Then maybe they'd be able to get some rest.

"You twat. I told you we wouldn't get through that," Gabby said.

"It didn't look that deep," Tony said.

"It's been snowing all day and all night, and just because you've got a big four-wheel drive doesn't mean it'll go through anything, you doughnut."

"Yeah, but you still love me, don't yah?"

"That depends on whether you can get us out of this?"

"I reckon I can."

"Good, because there's another mile and a half of this little country lane that way, a mile behind us, and I don't think you're dressed to be going for help," Gabby said, tugging on his shorts leg. "All those pockets and you still didn't put your phone in one."

"Speaks the woman whose phone battery is dead," Tony said looking over his shoulder and sliding the gearbox into reverse.

"It wasn't my idea to come out and play in the snow at silly o'clock in the morning."

Tony smiled and revved the balls out of the engine as he pushed his foot down on the accelerator pedal. The ML budged back a little, then he shifted into Drive and the vehicle jerked forward.

"We would have got through it if I'd been going slower," Tony said as he repeated the reverse/forward exercise.

"Yep, this isn't Mario Kart where brakes are ignored," Gabby said, "Is it me or is that getting really heavy out there again?"

Tony looked out and saw that the snow had doubled in strength. "Shit, those flakes are huge."

"I've never seen snow this bad before. Not even a few hours ago."

"Me neither, but don't worry. We're not far from home, and I've got a full tank of petrol. So even if we are stuck, we'll have plenty of fuel to keep the old girl ticking over and the heaters on. I put a shovel in the boot."

"Well, you best get digging then."

Tony got out, went to the back of the Mercedes and took the shovel out of the boot. Gabby watched him as he went to the passenger side front wheel and began digging. She couldn't see him that well, but she heard him scream.

She screamed, too, when she saw his blood streak across the windshield and his limp body landed on the bonnet.

Duplicity at Dugway

C H Baum

Most people don't realize that the Salt Flats in western Utah are a direct result of the slumbering parasites in a small pool at the Dugway Proving Grounds. Everything around that pool is dead and barren for miles and miles. Now, the government will tell you that they test all sorts of biological weaponry, chemical sniffers, and environmental hazards at the Proving Grounds and that they put Dugway out in the middle of nowhere because it was uninhabited and less of a danger to the general public. While that is true to an extent, the real reason for the military installation is to contain a brilliant piece of genetic engineering created by none other than Mother Nature. Man can think up all sorts of nastiness but is limited by time and mortality. Many a secret has died out with the passing of a single generation. Mother Nature, with her infinite aeons and infallible patience, facilitates death on a grand scale that mankind could never match. And Mother Nature never forgets.

The static was an annoying side effect of the untraceable, encrypted phone call from Dispatch. "This is Alchemist...... sscrtsssh ....I repeat, Alchemist. There was a tornado at Dugway .... sssschssss ..... It touched down right over the pool .... sssstch ....We lost contact with the base. You are closest ...... schwlssssh ......Get there NOW! .... swchsss .... Use breach containment protocol."

Sarah just stared at the "unknown" number on her phone in disbelief. "What? There are no tornados in Utah! This isn't funny Alchemist."

"They happen. They are rare ….. sshshktsssh ….. But I'm telling you we lost contact with the base ……. shdhssh ….. The pool was ground zero."

Sarah rubbed the sleep from her eyes and shot back, "I'm on it," while trying to keep her voice measured and calm. She didn't want Alchemist to hear the terror she felt creeping into her response. "I'll clean it up."

Sarah was an elite employee of the Environmental Protection Agency. She was unknown to military Black Ops, the NSA, and even the President. The only way to keep a secret from getting divulged was to not tell anyone else, so they kept a very small team of containment officers near five specific sites in the United States that contain volatile environmental hazards. Dugway was by far the most dangerous; the parasite in that pool was the most insidious creation she had ever come across. All five officers would react to a containment breach, and she knew the others were on their way, but it would take hours to get their private jets to the airport in Salt Lake City. They were too far away to triage or even help, so it fell to her to act.

Blood rushed to her head as she bent down to crawl under the bed, feeling around until she connected with the rough handle of the dusty tactical bag that held her containment kit. She referred to it as her "bug out bag" because it contained a hazmat suit and duct tape, along with heavy rubber gloves and sturdy galoshes. Buried under the hazmat suit, she kept a flashlight and a Glock. She also had personal touches in the bag like an iPod with a couple thousand songs, some peppermint gum, and a pair of custom socks that were branded with the letters, "EPA" above a skull and crossbones.

She didn't know what she would find at Dugway after the freak tornado, but she would be as prepared as she could be. She dressed in heavy khaki pants and a soft flannel shirt, taking time to carefully slide the Glock into her Kydex holster.

Last but not least, she pulled on the EPA socks, slipped her feet into her Birkenstocks, and threw her bug out bag into the passenger side seat of her Prius. She put the car in drive but kept her foot on the brake as she rummaged in the side pocket of her tactical bag. Once the iPod and gum were procured, she connected through her USB port and let it charge while playing through her speakers on the drive over. She always hit shuffle so she was surprised by the song that played next, although she loved them all. James Brown grunted, "Hit meh," as she rolled down her driveway and popped a piece of ancient peppermint gum into her mouth. It started gritty and crumbled rather than chewed, but eventually warmed up to its natural state in her saliva and under the press of her molars.

The government had known about the pool since prior to World War One. They tested it on animals, cadavers donated to science, and during World War Two, some of the Nazi death camp facilitators. Sarah still remembered the horrifying still photos, and then the black and white reels of horrendous experiments. Several of the team members had thrown up the first time they viewed the films. The government had considered using it as a weapon in several instances but were afraid that it would break through their containment, and destroy with unintended consequences. So the EPA took control of the knowledge of its existence in the early Seventies and spent years systematically removing all information of the pool and its contents from any records.

Sarah's iPod shuffled to Black Sabbath's, War Pigs, and blasted out, "Gen'rals gathered in their masses, just like witches in black masses….." as she recalled one story of the pool hidden away in the archives of the Mormon Church that had to be delicately erased. A heretic patriarch resisted the dissolution of polygamy and he and his seven wives marched into the pool to be devoured by the parasites while screaming something about the Garden of Eden.

Lights from her Prius raked the front gate of the Proving Grounds as she turned into the base. She expected the usual military MPs at the gate with their heightened suspicion of EPA employees and extra scrutiny of her security clearance that was higher than their own. But it was dark and silent. Nothing moved, nothing made a sound, and it felt as if the very Earth held its breath. She backed up several yards from the gate and donned her hazmat suit in the darkness. It would look funny walking down the road to the gate, but better safe than sorry. Sarah used the duct tape to seal the suit to the boots, and to the rubber gloves. She carefully tightened her belt so that it wouldn't pinch the suit, but still supported the weight of the handgun. Finally, the hood went on over the iPod earbuds and she flicked on the battery-powered breathing filter before taking uncertain strides towards certain doom. The facemask of the suit blurred the lights around the gate but was more of an irritant than any real obstacle to her vision. She hit the button on the EPA issued garage door opener and the backup generator whirred to life, pulling the gate open on squeaky, galvanized tracks.

She could see from the gate, that the tornado had ripped the roofs off all the buildings, leaving splintered wood and galvanized sheeting strewn about the compound. She was pretty certain that several of Dugway's inhabitants had been either crushed or speared by flying debris if they hadn't made it to shelter in time. She ignored the outbuildings and headed towards the main laboratory. If they had a tornado warning, they would have sheltered there. The silence was eerie and oppressive, and an ominous mist swirled around her ankles, her flesh protected by a thin layer of plastic. There should have been people bustling around, attempting to search for survivors, and reclaim the security of the base, but it was dark and lifeless.

Sarah took at deep, filtered breath at the threshold of the lab. All the windows were blown out, and nothing moved inside the structure, but the mist spun away from her steps. She flicked on her LED flashlight and stepped into the lab. The concrete walls had held under the onslaught of the tornado's winds, but the windows blew out and glass was thrown around like flying razors. She expected to find lacerated bodies but encountered the work of the parasite instead. It was clear to her that the parasite had been blown into the building; it had eaten everyone on the base. She was witnessing, first hand, why the parasite was so dangerous; it ate flesh with a voracious appetite. They would burrow under your skin, consuming meat, ligaments and cartilage. Within a matter of minutes, nothing would be left, except the skeleton and the digestive tract. There must be some unsavoury bacteria in the digestive tract, so the parasites don't eat it. The bones are too hard to penetrate, but the parasites eat them so clean they look waxed and buffed. The entire staff of Dugway had been reduced to polished skeletons and gut piles. Sarah was grateful for the hazmat suit, not just because it was protecting her from the parasites, but because the stench would probably overwhelm her. She knew it would smell like a cross between rotten compost and hot faeces.

Sarah made her way to the vault where they kept all the other deadly chemicals and punched in her override code. The seal on the door gave way with a loud hiss, and the ventilation system sucked the mist slowly into the vault. A surprised, shaven head soldier stepped out from behind one of the stacks, his shoulder flashing three yellow chevrons to identify him as a Sergeant in the Army. The mist swirled towards him, and he pointed directly at Sarah, "You idiot, you've just killed us all."

Several personnel stepped from behind the rows of shelving containing deadly viruses, aggressive bacteria, and torturous chemicals. Sarah had just long enough to say, "I….I'm so sorry. I didn't think anyone was in here." The iPod shuffled to a very inconvenient Modern English, "I'll stop the world and melt with you. I've seen the difference and it's getting better all the time."

It started in their eyes of all places. Each eye melted under the aggressive parasites, drooling down the face of the survivors. The skin started to perforate next, becoming Swiss cheese while their screams turned to gargling bubbles. Their bodies contorted, squirming like toddlers throwing a temper tantrum until there were only shiny bones and unattached intestines. The whole process had taken less than one minute.

It dawned on her, she was the only living human in Dugway. As a secret warrior for the planet, this was her chance. She had waited years for exactly the right moment, and Mother Nature had just given her a perfect opportunity. It was time to give Nature a helping hand in her battle against humankind. These same humans that had been damaging, burning, polluting and pillaging natural resources of the Earth for generations. Sarah was in a perfect position to help the Earth get her revenge. She grabbed a tempered glass beaker with a hearty seal and headed down to the parasitic pool. One litre in a water supply and anyone that took a shower, brushed their teeth, or splashed around in the toilet would be dissolved down to guts and bones.

She used the same garage door opener to get access to the spring and waited patiently for the massive iron door to squeal open. As she crouched next to the pool, she submerged the beaker and the iPod shuffled to the next song. It couldn't have been more fitting. The sweet, melodic lead singer of Kansas blared through the earbuds and Sarah sang along, changing the lyrics to, "GUTS in the wind. All they are is GUTS in the wind!"

Red Sky At Night

David Court

Anytime you'd ever speak to Old Ma Waldron, no matter whether she was behind the counter at the Stop n Shop or just sittin' out on her front porch looking cranky, she'd remind you how she was dying. Every Summer would see her red as a beet complaining about how she was fixin' to die of heatstroke, and every Winter would see her as white as a Klan hood and the fella inside it, meaning that she'd be dead by Spring.

For someone who'd been nigh-on-dead for so long, she was doing a terrible job at meeting her maker. Mind you, if the Grim Reaper ever did visit the Stop n Shop, he'd have found himself standing outside with an empty wallet and a handful of stale candy afore he knew what was happening.

That said, she was deader than most. Ma Waldron was one of those women who was *born* old. Even those of us who'd been living here for goin' on thirty years can't remember her being anything *but* old. "She's got one of the faces," Father Wakeford had always insisted, "that naturally falls to frownin'". She'd always spoke about how in her youth, she was pretty as a picture, but truth be told, that must have been an oil paintin' left out to blister and warp in the sun. Her eyes were too close together, and she had a big old bulbous nose that was as red as her moods. Each ear looked like it had been pinned on by a kid in a blindfold at a party like the tail on a donkey. A cleverer man would say she looked like a Picasso picture brought to life, but as far as we were all concerned, she was the spittin' image of the Potato Head figure from the yellowin' sun-faded box that was a permanent fixture in the Stop n Shop window and had a nickname to match.

She didn't walk much these days, seemingly just appearin' in precisely the place she could cause the most aggravation, or get the biggest audience for her complaining. Woe betides anybody younger than her (which was pretty much everybody south of Methuselah) who got within the range of Ma Waldron and that damnable stick of hers. She'd shuffle slowly up and down the street with her tiny feet kicking up plumes of sand and dust bigger than she was, constantly chattering away to herself or cursing at others. Where most of us had a heart, Old Ma Waldron had an over-developed bile duct.

Up until about a week ago, that is. The rumours started when the weather started to turn fine, with Father Wakeford sayin' that he'd sworn he'd seen Old Ma Waldron smilin' away to herself. That seemed about as unlikely as Dan Abrams puttin' up a Black Lives Matter flag in his backyard, but then a few others said they'd seen the same.

Me? I guessed something was up when I was browsin' through the Stop n Shop looking for some new rolls of twine when I heard a noise that no human being has heard since Neil Armstrong took his giant leap – it was an alien noise, like nothing I'd never heard. "Beyond the realms of mortal ken", whoever *he* is.

Old Ma Waldron was wishin' me a good morning.

There was a shelf to support me against, which was lucky because it got stranger still. She started engaging me in what I can only define as *conversation.* There was an excitement to her tone I hadn't heard since she was caught bragging about poisoning Dan Abram's Rottweilers, Sturm and Drang. Not about her comin' death for once, but the weather.

"It'll be glorious in a week or so. You mark my words, Tom Bastow," she chuckled, rocking in that old chair so hard it was squeakin' like a horny mouse. News travelled fast, and Old Ma Waldron's personality shifting from grumpy old curmudgeon to optimist was all anybody in the town could talk about.

That was until the evenin' of the red sky just six days later, anyroads.

In a farming community like ours, there's an excitement in the air when there's a red sky in the evening. Goes back to Bible times, that one. Matthew wrote about it. "When it is evening, ye say, fair weather: for the heaven is red.". What it means in fancy science terms is pressure movin' in from the west, making it more than likely the next day will be perfect for us out in the fields.

And golly, were those heavens red that night. It was a July evening, with the sweet perfumed smell of the alfalfa drifting over the hills. Usually, there'd be a tad of variety to the shade - gorgeous oranges, reds, and purples - but this evening there was none of that. Just a thick blood-red scarlet, horizon to horizon, pierced by a flesh pink moon.

I was puttin' the world to rights in O'Malley's with a cold beer when Hickox came bargin' in, as ruddy faced as one of Doc Quince's underfed pigs. He was agitated, spluttering over the words as he tried to spit them out. Took a beer to calm him down, which I suspect was his plan all along.

"It's Mrs Potato Head," he coughed out through his beer-foam moustache, "you need to see this for yourself". And instead of insisting the damn fool tell us all rather than waste our time, that evening saw half a dozen of us traipsing up the hill towards Hickox's farm and across his potato field.

We heard her before we saw her, that raspy voice of hers singin' "Johnny Appleseed" as loud as her tiny lungs would allow. Then Hickox stopped and pointed down.

There was Old Ma Waldron, in a shallow hole she'd dug herself, just lying there amongst the roots and the tubers. We looked down at her, and she looked back at us with a huge cracked yellow-toothed smile, as though lyin' with the potatoes in the dry dirt was the most natural thing in the world.

Hickox stepped in to try and lift her out, but she whipped out with that stick of hers like an ornery rattlesnake. He fell backwards on his ass, and we couldn't help but laugh. But as we're laughing, Waldron just starts singing louder to drown us out.

It'd repeat for anybody who went near. Anybody went to pull her foolish hide out of that hole got a crack of the stick, and anybody who leaned in trying to convince her to come out was drowned out by verses of that damnable folk song.

I knew exactly what Hickox was going to suggest when he sidled over to me with that sneaky look in those monobrowed eyes of his and damned if I was right.

"You keep her distracted, Bastow," he said shiftily, "and me 'n the boys will grab her."

There was quite a gathering of us now, a good dozen or so standing around the hole. I waved my arms in the air until they were all looking at me.

"Now, fellas," I implored, trying to bring some sense back into this crazy evenin' in which we'd found ourselves, "if Old Ma Waldron wants to lie with the potatoes singin', I don't see why any of us should stop her."

Hickox looked dejected, but the other boys just looked relieved. That stick *hurt*, and nobody looked that desperate to be its next victim. Only advantage of the blood red glow that filled the heavens was that it hid their bruises.

"Anyways," I proclaimed, already beginning to slowly stroll back, "there's time at the bar for another two or three drinks yet this evening. Who's with me?"

And so, it was that we left Old Ma Waldron in the hole, bellowing as loudly as she could. She was still singing when we got back to the bar and even though it was a damned warm evening, we closed the doors and windows to drown her out.

I will swear on my grave that when I emerged out into that blood red night, staggering out of that bar back to my bed with four glasses of cold beer swillin' inside of me, she was *still* singin'.

It weren't just my eyes that were bloodshot next morning. When I woke up, I was worried I hadn't slept at all - even now, the sky was still that persistent brilliant scarlet. Looking at my bedside clock though, it was morning. Just that the sky hadn't changed, is all.

Red skies in morning? They ain't so good. Especially when there ain't even no sun.

Waldron had stopped singin' though; that was some small blessing. I was convinced I'd heard her in my sleep, half-tempted to storm out to Hickox's potato field and bury the damned witch.

Despite the fact the skies looked like something from a child's drawing of Hell, life carried on as normal. The rain clouds suggested by the dawn's red glow never appeared, and the whole day passed by in a weird, balmy haze.

Nobody saw Mrs. Potato Head that whole day, but nobody was daring to bring it up. The Stop n Shop had been left open all night, so it was clear she hadn't gone back to her bed. It would have taken any of us just a few minutes to walk back to that hole right now to check up on her - hell, Hickox must have taken a damned detour on his farm to get into town and *not* walk past her. Old dear like that, left alone for the evening lying in a damned ditch? Truth was, nobody wanted to be the one to find her in her ready-made *grave*.

We sat there in that bar that evening, still under that damned red sky, nobody wanting to make eye contact with anybody. All of us sat in silence, staring into our beers. In the end, I couldn't stand the guilty quiet any more.

"I'll go," I said, slamming my empty glass onto the table and standing up. A few eyes looked at me. "I know what you're all thinking," I shouted, pointing my finger at every one of them. "It was Tom Bastow said to leave her, so it's Tom Bastow's fault."

I went to leave.

"Old witch was nearly dead anyway. Ain't a man here who wouldn't wish it, neither," I muttered, slamming the door behind me.

As an aside, there ain't no point in slamming a saloon door shut. Truth be told, it just swings in and out without a noise, which damn sure diminished the dramatic impact of the exit I attempted.

As I drew closer to Hickox's farm, I could hear the whispering behind me. They'd followed me out of the bar, but at enough of a distance that when I snapped around, they all made out they was just loiterin' and not trailing behind me at all. It was only when I reached the field and was walking to that hole that I felt I had to say something.

"Goddamnit," I shouted, spinning on my heels to turn to face them. They all started concentrating on each other or paying attention to the dirt beneath their feet, but I damn knew they were listenin'. "Anybody who wants to see what's in that accursed hole, come join me. Tarnation, Bill Hickox, this is *your* blasted farm so quite why you're being so sheepish back there, I don't know."

If I'd embarrassed him, this red hue we were all immersed in hid it damn well.

With hindsight, I don't know why I was quite so nervous and what I expected to see down there in the dirt. Waldron had looked like a decayin' corpse at the very best of times, so there wouldn't be any surprises.

Through squinted eyes and with a beating heart, I stood on that crimson soaked soil and stared into that similarly crimson soaked hole.

Empty. Nothing but a whole tangled bunch of roots, potatoes, and tubers.

I climbed in, looking for any sign of her, anything she might have dropped or left. The soil was damp, and everything down there was covered in a layer of moisture and a sweet sap that stuck to my arms and hands. A thick metallic smell filled the air, even noticeable over the earthy scent of the alfalfa.

Two dozen anxious real eyes and one glass eye stared down at me.

Like the Lord above flicking a light switch, the redness faded, and the evening sky was restored to its rightful pin-pricked inky blackness. The moon suddenly shone into life like a bulb, lighting up the field and all who occupied it.

And like a searchlight, it shone into the hole in which I was kneeling. Like you'd see at a fancy theatre, marking me as the centre of attention. Only now could I see the ground around me was specked with clots of a thick coat of bright glistening scarlet, the same deep crimson that coated the skin on my hands and arms. The same blood which coated those thirsty potato roots clung to me, dotted in parts with thicker congealed lumps of gunk; gristle, clumps of matted hair, tiny chunks of wizened stripped flesh, and strips of flayed skin that was once wrapped loosely around a haggard and grisly old potato-faced coot.

"You ask me, we're wastin' our damn time," said Dan Abrams for the fifth time that hour, as he half-heartedly prodded the long grass in which we were walking.

"We don't need to ask you, Dan, you just keep on tellin' us, regardless," I snapped, tired of his incessant complaining. Damn my luck for being paired with that old bigot. He looked ready to whine again, so I said something I knew would shut him up.

"What are we keeping you from anyway, Dan? You got some choir practice planned at home, maybe some singin' of those Fatherland songs with your boys? Deutschland, DEUTSCHLAND ÜBER ALLES..."

"Tom Bastow, you've been riling me for too damn long now," he stopped, waving that gnarled old stick in my direction, "I ain't no Nazi. I just like the memorabilia is all. I *inherited* that coat and medals."

"And you just wear 'em around your house for fun, right?"

"Ain't no point in medals if you can't wear 'em every now and again. Much as how you're wearin' most of that Waldron hag on your hands and arms. Ain't no chance we're finding anything else of her tonight."

Truth be told, it pained me to say, he was probably right. If we did find her, there wasn't much of her that she hadn't left in that potato hole.

Bears, it was decided. That, or coyotes. People seemed to forget we'd seen neither round these parts in the best part of twenty years, but people will often look for a simple explanation rather than struggle to think of an alternative.

So, in his infinite ursine wisdom, some bear (or pack of bears) had wandered to Hickox's farm - possibly in league with some conspiratorial coyotes - and had snatched up Old Ma Waldron from her hole. The more optimistic amongst us liked to think she'd tried to fight 'em up, maybe cracked a few of 'em with her stick, before being dragged away to their lair.

Any relatives she had either openly despised her, had been disowned by her, or both, so her funeral was a quiet ceremony. I'd washed off as much of her as they'd found in that hole, so her coffin ended up as empty as those cheap knock-off, stale fortune cookies she used to try to sell.

We buried it facing Father Wakeford's chapel.

She'd have *hated* that.

You know when you have a toothache - one that's just a nagging pain, not yet agony, so you tolerate it? And then one day, ages later, you get it sorted by the dentist or it just vanishes by itself? That was what life without Old Ma Waldron was like. You didn't like her grumpiness, but you'd gotten *used* to it.

It didn't seem right going into the Stop n Shop without being stared at by somebody convinced you were going to rob her blind, same as it didn't seem right when you weren't screamed at when you got to the counter for not having the exact change.

But time goes on. We were all extra cautious about looking out for bears and coyotes for a while, but that passed. Old Ma Waldron was forgotten about, same as we stopped talkin' about the day of the red sky.

The extraordinary gets explained away, or simply passes on. The sheer volume of the mundanity of small-town life drowns everything else out, eventually.

Until Hickox and his damn potatoes.

"Are you sure this is a potato?" I asked, holding the withered, gnarled thing up to the light. It was weird and malformed, with a thick red skin that resembled bark. Stems protruded from it, looking more like matted, dried hair than vegetation. The twisted little thing I held between my thumb and forefinger looked more like discoloured root ginger than it did a potato.

"Yup. Whole damn field came out just like this 'un," said Hickox. "They taste fine. They just look a little odd, is all."

I looked from him to the potato, and then back to him. I had to ask.

"Hickox, you didn't use any of the potatoes that grew in the..."

He screwed up his face, offended by my line of questioning.

"What do you take me for, Tom Bastow? I fenced off that part of my field. I ain't using any part of it that went anywhere near that damned hole."

"And they taste okay, you say?"

"As good as any I've ever grown. Only reason they cost less is because they don't look all that appetizin'."

"I'll take a bag then. And you still owe me four beers from the weekend, so we'll call it quits."

You could almost see the cogs whirring and grinding behind his eyes as he tried to do the calculations, an effort his brain decided was just too much. He smiled and handed me one of the bumpy burlap sacks.

These things weren't only ugly, they were *heavy*. I was out of breath by the time I'd hauled that misshapen bag into my pantry, resting it against the wall. Hickox certainly had packed 'em in - the sack was full to overflowing and a few of them had fallen out. They didn't roll though like a potato should - being so knobbly and warped, they just stopped where they landed.

I picked one of them up and took it into the kitchen, studying it on the way. Now I was lumbered with a bag of them, I was wonderin' what the hell to do with 'em. You couldn't peel 'em - they were so awkwardly shaped, it'll be like trying to bathe a cat, as in you'd end up bleeding with the skin scraped from your fingers. Like the other one, it was shaped like a stumpy and hairy five-pointed star. Had a stink to it too, that I hadn't noticed before - a whiff of staleness to 'em, like they'd gone bad already.

Hickox had better not have sold me a bag of rotten potatoes.

The thing was dry to the touch, not even a hint of moisture to it. I placed it on my kitchen counter and took the penknife from my keyring, hoping to cut open the thing to find out what state it was in. Admittedly, the blade was dull and hadn't been sharpened for some time, but it barely made a mark on the thing. Skin of it was so thick, it was like trying to slice into the gnarled bark of a tree.

I spent a few minutes sharpenin' one of my kitchen knives, determined that little bugger wouldn't the better of me. I held the potato in place and, the tip of the blade already on the table, sliced down with the quickest motion I could.

Damn thing shot across the room, bouncing off my kitchen window and landing in the sink. Ordinarily, that wouldn't have been too bad, but there was three days of washing in there and I had to reach into the stagnant gravy, oil, and coffee soup to fish it out. As I held the soaked thing to the light, I could see I'd carved a shallow neat line across it, little more.

Next time, it wasn't so lucky. I sliced across the same line against, holding it stronger this time and sheared it neatly in two. A pungent liquid trickled from the heart of it, released from a hollow of that yellowy-white flesh. It made me gag, bringing back memories of the coppery scent in that potato pit. Only now I'd cut the thing in half, did its skin strike me as a mite odd - it was as thick as the shell of a coconut and nearly as coarse.

The smell was vile. Even just this tiny thumb-sized quantity of liquid had a pungency that filled the room, forcing me to open the windows to get some damned air in. The paint on the kitchen surface had already faded to a bleached pale stain from where it had pooled. Ain't no way I was cooking with these malodorous little starchy fuckers.

I hoisted the sack, which I could have sworn was heavier still, out into the garden and poured the contents into the compost tumbler. They mightn't be good for cooking, but they'd decay into adequate fertiliser. Seeing them all lying there in that deep metal drum, it struck me how alike they all were. I'd imagined them all to be random little collections of lumps, but no, they were all very similar - only slight variations amongst 'em in size or shape. All were bloated, five-pointed stars, one tip of each bristling with wiry stems. My thoughts went to the little pool of bilious toxic shit brewin' in the heart of every single one of the little buggers.

Hickox needed to be told before he went and damn poisoned somebody. I set off later that evenin'. Being public-spirited is one thing, but nothing says you can't have a nap first.

The walk to Hickox's place takes you past O'Malley's, so I took the opportunity of peering through the windows to see if he was there. Unusually for this time of the evening, he wasn't. The bar looked quieter than usual but still provided an awful temptation, yet my urge to do the right thing presently outweighed my need for a cold beer. The fact that Hickox owed me a few free beers to compensate me had nothin' to do with the bearin' on that decision.

There was a dull red hue settling across the sky as I walked up the path to Hickox, and the cold was creepin' in. I briefly glimpsed over to the fenced-off patch of field where Waldron had been taken from us, remembering that fateful night those few months back.

Bill Hickox looked after his house and farm alone after his good lady Annie had passed on two winters back. Time was, you'd find every kind of vegetable in his fields, but now it was just taters. It was easier, and people would always need 'em.

His front door was ajar when I got there, a thin smattering of soil leading from the path into his house. Annie Hickox would have had his guts for garters in the old days, insistin' he take off his filthy work boots before coming in to their humble abode. In her absence, standards had long slipped. Still, I ain't one to speak - times have been where'd I'd be drinkin' coffee from a bowl rather than make the effort of washin' a cup.

"You about, Bill?" I yelled. The man had a shotgun, so it was best to make my presence known. No answer. This wasn't unusual; many a time I'd come in here to find him passed out drunk on some under-fermented Poteen. I'd have to carry the fella to his bed, with him breathing whisky fumes over me and callin' me Annie.

Truth be told? I'd rather have found him like that.

As I walked towards the door to his living room, I heard a weird sound - like the scurrying of rats with a whole mess of tiny footsteps followed by silence. I called out Bill's name one more time before pushing the door open.

Whether the things working on Bill's face hadn't heard me approach and scampered away with the others, or were simply too engrossed or brave to care, I'll never know. He was lying back on his fully reclined La-Z-Boy chair, one of those things perched on his shoulders and another one balancin' on his chin.

The protuberances on the two little blasphemies weren't the tips of stars - they were limbs. Two little potatoes, neither more than four inches or so in height, balancing on two little stumpy legs while busily working away with their squat little arms. They were both doing something with Hickox's face, and I stood there for a few moments in horrified silence watching the frenzy of movement from the pair of them.

I'd often wondered how I'd cope with being exposed to something so out of the ordinary that it'd make me question my very existence in this fragile plane I laughably call reality. Turns out my first reaction'd be to piss my pants and cuss.

"Shit," I found myself sayin', rather louder than I'd intended.

Almost comically, the two little potatoes slowly turned to face me, their little stem buds winkin' where their eyes would have ordinarily been. Figures. As one, they both hopped down, each onto an arm of the reclining chair.

I could now see Hickox's face.

His skin, ordinarily wrinkled like one of those tortoises from National Geographic, was smooth, but bunched in all the wrong places, like it was modelling clay that had been worked on. Despite the two little taters staring at me accusingly, I couldn't stop staring at that face.

I'm not ashamed to say, I pissed myself again.

The pink clay was stained dark red in places wherever there were features. His two eyes were set at different heights on that lop-sided face, each possessing different sized dark pupils. The nose that sat beneath them wasn't his - it was dainty and feminine and hanging at an awkward angle. The mouth was the worst - two lips attached to a patch of flesh of a different shade pressed into the soft pliable skin and drooping at both sides.

I could see Hickox trembling, a muffled moan coming from behind those closed alien lips.

It was then I saw the scattered bodies on the floor, all with similarly crudely assembled faces. Eyes, noses, ears, and lips had been forcibly pulled from each and transplanted on another body. Some of those bodies were still, and some writhed like they's partially paralysed but still conscious. A few of them had even been scalped, the tops of their heads glistening domes of bleeding crimson flesh. There was Father Wakeford, his bald pate topped off with Widow Davis's blood-streaked, blonde curls. Abrams was wearing Old Man Stockley's glass eye like a cyclops, the glass orb crudely pressed into malleable flesh.

Like the Potato Head in Waldron's window.

They emerged from the shadowy recesses and the darkness in the room like a flood, a thundering of tiny feet as hundreds of the tiny little taters charged towards me. A chorus of cackling shrieks came from each, the familiar bilious tones of Ma Waldron reverberatin' around the room.

That noise alone is enough to rouse me from my piss-stained torpor and my thick work-boots get to stampin' on the first wave. My own defiant screams drown out that incessant noise as I make short work of that first batch.

The thick skin on 'em counts for little as I'm stamping down on the little fuckers. I've hammered nails in with these boots. With each of the little shits I tread to a lumpy paste, the smell in the room gets worse, that acid at the heart of each of 'em filling the air with an acrid burning odour. I can feel myself start to go faint, but seemingly shocked by my frenzied retaliation, the next wave backs off. They stand there watching me as I stare down at my handiwork.

A few dozen of the things litter the ground beneath me, pulped potato skin and flesh coating both the carpet and the soles of my boots.

A monster mash.

I turn to run, and am out that door quicker than you could holler "sentient potato". Turns out though, these spuds are *smart*. It would only take a clumsy or panicking man not looking where he's goin' with a few of those taters underfoot and lyin' in wait, and such a soul could find himself plummeting face first onto the path, leaving himself a mite vulnerable.

They're on me like a plague, tearing and gouging. Before I realise what's happening, a few of 'em are holding my mouth open and another is clamberin' right on in. I bite down as hard as I can and then realise that's exactly what they wanted - that damned acid fills my throat, hurtin' all the way down. I can smell it too - they're leaking it from their skins and rubbing it into mine, and all I can smell, or taste is burnt flesh. I can hear Old Ma Waldron cacklin' from a hundred tiny mouths and I find I ain't even capable of fightin' back no more. All I can do is stare up at that damnable red sky, and now I can't tell the sky apart from the blood in my eyes, and then even they're gone.

Author Biographies

C.H Baum

By day, CH Baum is an unassuming mortgage underwriter. By night, he dons his superhero outfit and goes to bed early, ensuring that he gets eight hours of sleep, so that he can awake refreshed and ready to take on your loan application. He lives with his two boys and his stunningly beautiful wife in Las Vegas, Nevada. What happens in Vegas, usually happens without him.

He loves to write, ride his bicycle, make furniture, and read.

He does all that while avoiding pickles, eggplant, and hummus; because everyone knows those things are just gross.

Other published works by CH Baum:

Gods of Color (Fantasy novel)

The Augment (Fantasy short)

The Conversion of Andrew Currant (Horror Short)

And many, many more to come.

Matthew Cash

Matthew Cash, or Matty-Bob Cash as he is known to most, was born and raised in Suffolk; which is the setting for his debut novel Pinprick. He is compiler and editor of Death By Chocolate, a chocoholic horror Anthology, Sparks, the 12Days: STOCKING FILLERS Anthology, and its subsequent yearly annuals and has numerous releases on Kindle and several collections in paperback.

In 2016 he started his own label Burdizzo Books, with the intention of compiling and releasing charity anthologies a few times a year. He is currently working on numerous projects; his second novel FUR will hopefully be launched 2018.

He has always written stories since he first learnt to write and most, although not all, tend to slip into the many-layered murky depths of the Horror genre.

His influences ranged from when he first started reading to Present day are, to name but a small select few; Roald Dahl, James Herbert, Clive Barker, Stephen King, Stephen Laws, and more recently he enjoys Adam Nevill, F.R Tallis, Michael Bray, Gary Fry, William Meikle and Iain Rob Wright (who featured Matty-Bob in his famous A-Z of Horror title M is For Matty-Bob, plus Matthew wrote his own version of events which was included as a bonus).

He is a father of two, a husband of one and a zookeeper of numerous fur babies.

You can find him here:

www.facebook.com/pinprickbymatthewcash

https://www.amazon.co.uk/-/e/B010MQTWKK

David Court

David Court was born and resides in Coventry in the heart of England with his patient wife Tara and three less patient cats. When not reading, blogging angrily on www.davidjcourt.co.uk, drinking real ale, being immune to explosions, writing software for a living, or practising his poorly developed telekinetic skills, he can be found writing fiction. David has had several short stories printed in various anthologies, including Fear's Accomplice, The Voices Within, Sparks, Visions from the Void, Weird Ales and Hydrophobia. He has three published collections of short stories - The Shadow Cast by the World, Forever and Ever, Armageddon and Scenes of Mild Peril.

David's wife once asked him if he'd write about how great she was. David replied that he would because he specialized in short fiction. Despite that, they are still married.

Paul M Feeney

Paul M. Feeney has been writing seriously since 2011, with his first published short – *The Weight of the Ocean* – appearing in 2014 as a Kindle-only release. Since then, he has had various stories in various anthologies and publications, and two novellas; *The Last Bus* (2015), a pulpy alien invasion story from Crowded Quarantine Publications (now sadly out of print), and *Kids* (2016), through Dark Minds Press. His writing tends towards a dark, *Twilight Zone* aesthetic, with the occasional foray into more emotive territory. He has a number of projects due throughout 2018 and beyond and is currently (still) working on his first novel. Along with various shorts and novellas. He also contributes reviews to horror website, This is Horror, under the name Paul Michaels. Find him on Amazon.

Peter Germany

Peter Germany is a writer of Science Fiction and Horror from Gravesend in Kent, England.

He is influenced by writers like Dan Abnett, Scott Sigler, CL Raven and Joe Haldeman.

When not pretending to be normal at a day job, he is writing or dealing with a supreme being (a cat), an energetic puppy, and trying to wrangle a small flock of chickens. He also spends an unhealthy amount of time watching good and bad TV and movies.

He has had stories published the anthologies Sparks: An Electric Anthology and 12 Days of Christmas 2017.

You can find him at his blog: petergermany.com

Paul Hiscock

Paul is an author of crime, fantasy and science fiction tales. His short stories have appeared in several anthologies and include a seventeenth-century whodunnit and a science fiction western.

Paul lives with his family in Kent (England) and spends his days chasing a toddler with more energy than the Duracell Bunny. He mainly does his writing in coffee shops with members of the local NaNoWriMo group or in the middle of the night when his son has finally gone to sleep. Consequently, his stories tend to be fuelled by large amounts of black coffee.

You can find out more about his writing at www.detectivesanddragons.uk

Dave Jefferey

Dave Jeffery is the author of 12 novels, two collections and numerous short stories. His Necropolis Rising series and yeti adventure Frostbite have both featured on the Amazon #1 bestseller list. His YA work features critically acclaimed Beatrice Beecham series and Finding Jericho, a contemporary mental health novel which has featured on the BBC Health and the Independent Schools Entrance Examination Board's recommended reading lists.

Jeffery is a member of the Society of Authors, British Fantasy Society (where he is a regular book reviewer), and the Horror Writers Association. He is also a registered mental health professional with a BSc (Hons) in Mental Health Studies and a Masters Degree in Health Studies. Jeffery is married with two children and lives in Worcestershire, UK.

www.davejeffery.webs.com

James Jobling

James Jobling has been a rabid fan of anything horror for most of his life, blaming his older brother for leaving a copy of James Herbert's fantastic novel The Rats lounging around the living room when he was only a child for starting his obsession. A huge fan of the horror book genre, James regards Herbert and David Moody as being his writing heroes.

James lives in Manchester, England, with his world - his beautiful wife, three adorable, sleep-avoiding children, and Nanook, his pet beagle. He can be contacted through Facebook and would be honoured to hear from anybody who might wish to get in touch.

Lex H. Jones

Lex H Jones is a British cross-genre author, horror fan and rock music enthusiast who lives in Sheffield, North England.

He has written articles for websites the Gingernuts of Horror and the Horrifically Horrifying Horror Blog on various subjects covering books, films, video games and music. Lex's first published novel is titled "Nick and Abe", and he also has several short horror stories published in anthologies alongside such authors as Graham Masterton, Clive Barker and Adam Neville. When not working on his own writing Lex also contributes to the proofing and editing process for other authors.

His official Facebook page is:

www.facebook.com/LexHJones

Amazon author page :

https://www.amazon.co.uk/Lex-H-Jones/e/B008HSH9BA

Twitter: @LexHJones

Kitty Kane

Kitty R Kane is a horror and dark fantasy writer from the south of England. Mainly appearing in extreme and bizzaro horror anthologies at the beginning of her writing career, she now concentrates more on dark fantasy and supernatural folk horror and has had more than twenty stories published by a variety of independent presses.

Her first solo collection is due to drop late 2018, as is her debut novel. In addition to her own writing, she is editor in chief at Plague Doctor Publications and makes macabre things to sell to unsuspecting bystanders. Richard Laymon is her God, her hair is subject to change without notice and when not writing horrible things she can be found surrounded by all things wild.

Christopher Law

Christopher Law is the author of Chaos Tales and Chaos Tales II: Hell TV. He has also appeared in a number of anthologies with more on the way. After taking the majority of 2018 to deal with some personal he is planning to return with Chaos Tales III: Infodump, expanding on the vision of Hell first shown in Hell TV, in October.

You can find him at facebook.com/evilscribbles and evilscribbles.wordpress.com, where there are some free stories and general musings.

Adam Millard

Adam Millard is the author of twenty-two novels, twelve novellas, and more than two hundred short stories, which can be found in various collections and anthologies. Probably best known for his post-apocalyptic fiction, Adam also writes fantasy/horror for YA/MG, as well as bizarre fiction for several publishers. His work has recently been translated for the German market.

Dale Robertson

Hailing from the South West of Scotland, Dale Robertson is a writer who lives with his partner, two children, and pet dog. Growing up, his first taste of horror came from shows such as *Eerie Indiana*, *Goosebumps*, and *Are You Afraid of the Dark?* The first movies he remembers are *Child's Play* and *Aliens*, which only enhanced his fascination with all thing scary. Reading wise, he was (and still is) a huge fan of Stephen King, Dean Koontz, James Herbert, and Richard Laymon (in no order), as well as being a movie, book, and video game enthusiast. He started writing at the grand age of thirty-five, and self-published his debut short story, *Dobson Drive*, on Amazon. Currently, he has two short stories and a novella available, although some of his other tales have appeared in anthologies and the work of other authors. He is continuing to write and working towards getting more stories out there.

You can find him here:

https://www.amazon.co.uk/DaleRobertson/e/B01PKT868/ref-dp_byline_cont_ebooks_1

www.dalerobertson.co.uk

Nathan Robinson

Horror author Nathan Robinson lives in Scunthorpe and is the father to darling eight-year-old twin boys.

So far he's had numerous short stories published bywww.spinetinglers.co.uk, Rainstorm Press, Knight Watch Press, Pseudopod, The Horror Zine, The Sinister Horror Company, Static Movement, Splatterpunk Zine and many more.

He writes best in the dead of night or travelling at 77mph.

He is a regular reviewer for www.snakebitehorror.co.uk and Splatterpunk Zine, which he loves because he gets free books.

He likes free books.

His first novel "Starers" was released by Severed Press to rave reviews. This was followed by his short story collection "Devil Let Me Go", and the novellas "Ketchup with Everything" and "Midway" and the novel, "Caldera."

He is currently working on his next novels, "Death-Con 4" and a sequel to "Starers" as well as his next short story collection, "The Tell of Strangers"

Follow news, reviews and the author blues at www.facebook.com/NathanRobinsonWrites or twitter @natthewriter

Phil Sloman

Phil Sloman is a writer of dark fiction. He was shortlisted for a British Fantasy Society Best Newcomer award in 2017.

Phil likes to look at the darker side of life and sometimes writes down what he sees. His short stories which can be found throughout various anthologies.

In the humdrum of everyday life, Phil lives with an understanding wife and a trio of vagrant cats who tolerate their human slaves. There are no bodies buried beneath the patio as far as he is aware.

Occasionally Phil can be found lurking here: http://insearchofperdition.blogspot.co.uk/ or wasting time on social media - come say hi.

Mark Woods

Mark Woods is a successful Head Chef, a doting dad to a beautiful daughter, and one of the UK's leading up and coming horror authors. His short fiction has appeared in numerous anthologies, and his novels include *Time of Tides Collector's Edition*; the short story collection, *Fear of the Dark; The Go-lem; Arachnattack – Attack of the False Widows*, and the forthcoming novel, *Killer Cruise* set just after the Second World War. He is also one of six authors responsible for the Vampire novel, *Feral Hearts*, and writes erotica under the pen-name, Naomi Matthews.

Other Charity Anthologies From Burdizzo Books

These tales will put the fear of God into you

Become a Burdizzo Book Beastie and give something back

Burdizzo Book Beasties is our campaign to give books, whether they be unwanted or well-loved. We want to encourage people to read. We leave our books, as well as other author's books, mostly in the horror genre, in public places: parks, trains, planes, buses and trams, anywhere as long as they are protected and found. For just £2 you can be part of our little campaign, contact us on our Facebook page and we will send you your Beastie Pack and you too can feel great about giving something back too.

Printed in Great Britain
by Amazon

58596457R00148